THE NEBULA CHRONICLES

VOLUME 2

sb white

sb white

authorHOUSE®

AuthorHouse™
1663 Liberty Drive
Bloomington, IN 47403
www.authorhouse.com
Phone: 833-262-8899

Published by AuthorHouse 02/06/2023

ISBN: 979-8-8230-0046-8 (sc)
ISBN: 979-8-8230-0045-1 (e)

Library of Congress Control Number: 2018900523

Print information available on the last page.

BOOK 4

THE VOLAN WARS

THE REUNION

The Alpha and Beta team protectors finished their late lunch and were the last to leave the huge dining hall. Phoenix, Vega, and Arris, who made up Alpha team, and Ursa, Minor and Sirus, who made up Beta team, had spent most of the time catching up and not eating. The others had not seen Arris for almost a year, and it felt good to be together again. Ursa had voiced that feeling for the others when she'd said that the protectors were now complete.

That morning, Arris had returned to Nebula Headquarters from the planet Daedro. She had been helping her Aunt Celeste rebuild the capital, which had been destroyed by an evil general, and establish her rule as queen. Arris had worked for months beside Queen Celeste and had never once wanted the title for herself. But she had still almost been killed a number of times because the general thought she was the last of the line of rulers. Before Arris had returned, she had watched as the queen married Major Flaine, who had subsequently been promoted to

General Flaine and now served as leader of Daedro's newly established army.

Arris had talked through much of the meal, but before she'd begun, she'd questioned Vega on his recovery. He had been badly injured from a rocket blast when fighting the evil general's army. After Vega had assured Arris that he was back at 100 percent and maybe even better, she'd brought everyone up to date on the happenings on Daedro.

While Arris had been away, Beta team had completed two assignments, and they were now waiting for their next one. Phoenix had been assisting Kent in communications, working with the various teams living at NAHQ on their assignments, and Vega had been recovering from his injuries and working to rebuild his strength.

Vega had admitted that waiting for broken bones and stitches to heal was frustrating. And then there was having to start over at the most basic level of physical exercises to regain his once perfect physic. At the mention of his perfect physic, Vega had received a number of comments from the other protectors. The comradery between the two teams had not changed, and there was a unity that they all felt. They were all willing to risk their lives for each other.

As they left the dining hall, Arris walked between Sirus and Vega; Minor lagged behind, looking at something or someone; and Ursa and Phoenix walked in the front of the group. They passed the common area and came to the escalator that led to their living quarters. The plan was to return to their rooms, change into their workout gear, and spend the afternoon in the gym.

Vega challenged Arris to beat his time on one of the games, and she accepted. He had commented that Arris was out of shape from being treated like royalty on Daedro. She'd wanted to respond that one day of trying to keep up with everything and meeting everyone that was in charge was as challenging as one of Sirus's workouts, but she'd held back. She would show Vega just how wrong he was.

But before the group ascended the escalator, Ursa suddenly stopped, and Arris almost bumped into her. Ursa was frozen in place, and the look on her face was not happy.

"What is she doing here?" she said in a threatening tone.

The other protectors looked in the direction Ursa was staring and saw Spider entering the transport with someone. It was hard to tell from the distance, but the person seemed to be slightly taller than Spider and extremely fit from the way she carried herself. The uniform she wore was unfamiliar, but the resemblance was clear. From that distance, the woman's profile, her braided blonde hair, and her manner of walking all looked just like Ursa's, though this woman looked to be taller, more muscled, and older. Before anyone could ask who she was, Ursa stomped away and jumped onto the escalator. The others had to hurry to keep up with her.

When they reached their level and walked toward their quarters, Vega took his life into his hands and pulled Ursa to a stop. The look she gave him was grim, but Vega dared to ask the question on everyone's mind.

"Who was that person? She looked a lot like you." When Ursa didn't immediately answer, Vega reminded her, "Hey, we're a team. If something is wrong, we're here for you."

Ursa seemed to gain control and shook her head. "I was startled. I had no idea she was coming here. That is Asha, my older sister."

Everyone was shocked. Ursa had never mentioned her family, except to say that her parents were supportive of her becoming a protector, but then none of them ever spoke of the family they'd left behind, if they had any. From Ursa's manner, it was very clear that she was not happy to see her older sister at Nebula Headquarters.

During their time in the gym, no one mentioned Ursa's sister, not wanting to upset her. They felt that when Ursa wanted to discuss the situation, she would. As they all made their way back to their quarters to clean up for a late dinner, Phoenix and Ursa received the same message on their communicators. Tomorrow, after breakfast, the Alpha and Beta teams were to meet in Catella's office.

Ursa broke the silence as they all read the message. "Well, we know who this meeting concerns. It is no coincidence that Asha is here; something must be happening on Velland."

"Velland is your home planet, but you don't seem very concerned," Minor observed.

Ursa huffed, "When I left Velland, I had hoped to never hear that name again."

Arris could sense that Ursa did have feelings for her sister and home, just not good ones.

When Ursa left the group and went to her quarters, Minor told the others, "I can hardly wait for tomorrow. The meeting will definitely be interesting."

"Ursa is a protector team leader," Phoenix reminded them, "and if this meeting with her sister doesn't go well, we have to be there to support her."

Everyone agreed, and then they went to their respective quarters.

When Arris arrived in Catella's office, she could sense the tension. The table they all sat around seemed crowded, but the only extra person was Ursa's sister. Spider and Kent sat by Asha, and Catella was at the end. The Alpha and Beta teams sat across from the others. As she sat, Arris felt that Asha had a presence that overshadowed others around her. Even Spider, who generally dominated the room, seemed in second place.

Up close, Asha's face looked hardened, but it wasn't because of the scar that ran down one side. Arris stole a glance at Ursa, whose face now mirrored her sister's. She now understood why Ursa had been pushy and had wanted to be in control when they'd first met at the academy. Growing up under Asha's dominating shadow, Ursa must have developed those behaviors to be noticed.

After everyone was seated, Catella opened the meeting by introducing Asha. "I want to officially welcome Asha. She commands the soldiers that protect the capital city of Cexion on planet Velland, which is in the Volan Galaxy. This group of elite soldiers is made up of the firstborn women from each household. It is an honor and lifelong commitment to join the Vellanites. Now, the Volan Galaxy is a spiral, and communication and visits are limited by the constant spinning of gaseous vapors. Once inside the galaxy, travel between planets can be achieved by spaceship.

"The planets within Volan have been peaceful up until now, but Asha has brought some disturbing news to our attention. Cexion has been attacked, and everyone in it has either been killed or taken captive. Asha thinks they may have been taken off planet, because the army has found no sign of the missing people. The Dakon tribes that inhabit the outer regions pulled the elites from the city with a false report that claimed they were attacking one of the smaller settlements far from the city.

"When the leaders of Cexion received the request from the settlement, they immediately dispatched the elite army. The elites were led into a trap, and while they were fighting the hill tribes, the city fell under attack. These attacks could only have been launched with outside help from one of the other planets, but no one is sure which one. Thus, Asha's here on a secret visit to request our assistance in identifying which planet and who helped the Dakons."

During Catella's speech, Ursa had not said a word but continued to stare at her sister. Once the speech was over, Ursa stood, faced Asha across the table, and demanded, "What of our parents?"

Asha shook her head, and Ursa's face turned white.

"And Illa?" Ursa's voice shook.

"We found no sign of Illa, and it is presumed that she is with the captives." Asha's voice was firm and did not waver.

"How could you let this happen? You are the commander of the elites," Ursa said, her voice rising. Her hands shook at hearing the news of her parents' death and her younger sister's disappearance.

Asha stood and faced her sister. "If you had not blocked all communications from me, I would have informed you sooner." Her words held reproach.

Catella interrupted the scene between the two. "Let us move forward. We have a short window of opportunity, if we decide to honor Asha's request for assistance." After Ursa and Asha sat back down, Catella continued, "Many of the elite soldiers were killed or injured in the trap set by the Dakons, and there are barely enough of them left to protect the city from another attack or even hold it until reinforcements arrive. The Velland military is away on maneuvers and will return as soon as they can. The Space Fleet is under the command of Leader Mallas, and Asha has sent word to him. Once the VSF returns, Cexion will be protected from the Dakon tribes. What we need to determine is if we can assist in identifying who helped the Dakons in this attack and for what purpose. To coordinate the attack took planning, especially for it to have happened when Leader Mallas was away on maneuvers. Volan is a peaceful galaxy, but something must have happened to trigger the attack. And why take such a large number of captives?

"Kent and Spider have been trying to determine which planet the assistance came from, but they require further information. Access to details about trade routes and which spaceships were traveling at the time of the attack is very sporadic, due to interference from the spiraling gases. At the present time, there is no Nebula ambassador assigned to the Volan Galaxy. This is not an oversight but rather one of many positions that need to be filled. Thus, there is no one point of contact through which NAHQ can coordinate with all the planets and gain their cooperation."

"Which planets are we to investigate if we go, and what information does Kent require?" Phoenix asked.

"There are seven planets in the Volan system," Kent answered, "but only two of them have the ability to carry off this type of stealth. If we can get a team on each, I've programmed a communicator to look for the required travel details to determine if it is the planet."

"Alpha can investigate one of the planets and Beta the other," Spider said. "You will portal to Velland and then travel by spaceship. There are a number of trade ships that you can board and not raise suspicion. Once you reach your destination, you will only have a short time on the planet until the trade ship returns. You are to gather information only and report back with your findings. Once we find who generated the attack, we can determine the reason for it and discover why they killed so many and then took the prisoners off Velland."

"What if we find the captives?" Ursa growled. "You just expect us to leave them behind? And how many captives were taken?" Again, Ursa glared daggers at her sister.

Spider responded, "Even if you identify where the captives are being held, you will not have the resources to rescue them. This will be handled by Leader Mallas and his forces."

"If we go, doesn't this put us in the middle of another war?" Vega asked. "With the attack on Cexion and the capture of prisoners, it sure feels like war has started." Vega unconsciously rubbed his arm that had been broken fighting the general.

"Nebula does not engage in wars but does help to prevent them. We hope to intervene here before this attack escalates into a war. At this point, we do not know who is responsible or why. It may be that the governors of these planets have no idea what happened on Velland or don't know that the attack originated from their planet," Catella cautioned the group.

Spider stood up and said, "I will portal to Velland with Alpha and Beta, but I will not travel to the other planets with the teams. I will stay and assist Asha until Leader Mallas arrives with his forces. Are there any objections from the Alpha or Beta team members about this assignment?"

No one spoke.

"OK," Spider said. "We will meet in four hours at the portal dock."

CHAPTER 2

THE ASSIGNMENT

After learning of their assignment, the protectors walked from Catella's office to the transport to return to their quarters and pack.

Unsure what the situation would be once on their planets, Phoenix cautioned, "Be sure to pack as much as possible in your totes. Spider will have any equipment we require, but we need to be prepared for an extended assignment." He looked at Ursa. "Do you want to add anything?"

Ursa's manner had changed since they'd left the meeting. She no longer looked angry but rather deflated, like she was unsure of what to do.

"Ursa," Phoenix said, "if you feel that you cannot continue as leader of Beta, please let us know."

Phoenix's comment brought Ursa around, and she firmly replied, "I am more than ready."

"You've had a major shock," Arris said. "You just learned about your parents and sister. We will understand if you need some time. I never knew my parents, but it was still a shock to finally learn what happened to them."

Ursa turned to Arris. "Thank you," she said and then looked at the others. "I appreciate your concern. Phoenix has covered everything, so let's get packed. Once we've completed packing, we can take our totes and grab a late lunch before we meet Spider in the bay."

Everyone agreed and followed Ursa into the transport.

The protectors arrived together at the portal bay. Both the Alpha and Beta teams were prepared to portal to the Volan Galaxy and assist Asha in finding the missing prisoners. During lunch, Ursa had briefed the others about her home planet and what she knew of the other two planets they were to investigate. Ursa had never been on the other planets, but Kent had sent information about both planets to her and Phoenix's communicators.

The large space dock outside of Cexion was the major trading port for Volan, and it was where transports from the other planets docked to unload and load their cargo. Minerals and other metals from the farthest planets were traded for various items grown on Velland. The three farthest planets were not able to grow food and had to generate their own atmosphere to sustain life. All mining efforts were connected by large tubes that delivered breathable air to the mines and settlements on the planets. The two nearest planets, Bastik and Fexnal, were habitable without the aid of life-supporting generators, which was why Spider and Asha had identified these planets as the source of help for the Dakon attack on Cexion.

Kent was checking something on his comm when the protectors walked up. He looked up and said, "We have a few minutes until the spiral rotates and I can open a portal. You will exit in a field in Cexion where the elites practice.

One of Asha's generals is standing by to open the portal on that end. This is a long portal, and the journey may get a little bumpy, so don't panic."

"Easy for you to say," Vega huffed. He wasn't a big fan of portals.

Arris thought of offering to hold his hand but decided not to.

Kent ignored Vega's comment and continued. "You will not take weapons. Asha will provide you whatever you need for your assignment. I've updated the leads' communicators with maps of the planets, major ports and cities, and areas where a large number of prisoners could be held without being noticed. Alpha will travel to Fexnal, and Beta will travel to Bastik. On your trip to the planet, familiarize yourself with the maps and look to see when your transport returns. If you miss your transport, it won't be easy to secure another passage without proper identification. You will be able to contact Spider, but it will be difficult to get a message to NAHQ. Any questions?"

No one had questions, especially since they didn't know what the situation on their assigned planets would be like.

Kent glanced up. "Here are Spider and Asha."

When the two stepped from the mover, Arris noticed Ursa tense and picked up on her harsh feelings toward her sister.

Spider nodded to everyone and said, "After we exit, we will meet with Asha's generals. They'll brief us about what they have learned since Asha left. Tomorrow, you will leave on a transport to your assigned planets. When the portal opens, Asha and I will go first, followed by Alpha and then Beta. See you on Velland."

"We're stable," Kent announced. "Good hunting and safe return."

When Arris stumbled from the portal onto Velland ground, she wasn't sure if her stomach had caught up yet. Kent had been correct; it was a longer portal and somewhat bumpy. It was like riding in a boat battling high waves that rocked the boat back and forth. Arris stepped forward to be out of Beta team's way and noticed that Vega was still recovering. Vega's face looked more green than brown. Phoenix had moved beside Arris and looked to have fully recovered. Spider and Asha hurried forward to greet the elite general who waited for them in the field. Ursa and Sirus stepped from the portal and seemed to be holding Minor up between them. When Minor's feet touched the ground, his legs started to buckle, and Sirus lifted him back up. Once everyone was out of the portal, the elite general closed her end.

Spider turned and inspected the protectors. Once satisfied they could walk, though maybe not in a straight line, he said, "We need to get out of sight. Follow Asha."

Asha led the group across the large practice field and into a building at the far end. Inside, the building resembled a gymnasium and storage unit for various training equipment. Standing inside were the remaining leaders of the elites. Asha stepped forward and was saluted by her generals. She then clasped hands with each one. The elite leaders were dressed similarly to Asha but with fewer decorations to signify their ranks. Their tunic-style coats hung past their hips, ending where what looked like the pockets of their pants started. Arris realized these weren't, in fact, pockets but holsters without weapons. They must have removed their weapons once they'd come inside. Their pants fit snuggly and outlined well-muscled legs. The uniforms were various shades, from dark gray to the white that Asha wore. All of the elite generals' faces were solemn as they greeted their commander.

Once the formalities were over, the general who had waited in the field said, "We've set up our command center in the back room. We didn't want anyone in the capital to know about it, in case there are spies in the city."

Ursa stepped forward and startled the general when she demanded, "I thought there was no one left alive in the city."

The elite general looked toward Asha for guidance. Asha stepped over and ordered, "General Linn, clarify."

General Linn nodded. "We have the report ready for your review, but there are survivors. A large number, actually."

Before Ursa could speak, Asha asked, "What of our sister, Illa?"

General Linn shook her head no.

The back room had been cleared of equipment, and a long table with enough chairs to seat everyone filled the room. At one end of the room, a screen had been set up, and an elite soldier stood at attention beside a station to display the report. There was food and drink placed before each chair around the table.

"Partake of the refreshments while I report," General Linn said. She nodded to the soldier, and the screen filled with information. "Background details. Six days ago, Leader Mallas led the VSF on maneuvers around the outer ring of planets. The following day, the Cexion council received an urgent report that the remote outpost of Tath was under attack from a Dakon tribe. The transmission was garbled, but the request for aid seemed to be real. So, the council immediately dispatched the elites. Just before we reached the outpost, we were surrounded by Dakon warriors, and both ends of the narrow road were blocked, trapping our troops. The elites were able to drive the warriors away, but not without immense cost. We lost two generals and fifty elite soldiers. Another fifty soldiers were badly wounded.

"Anyone able to fight proceeded to the Tath outpost, where we found that no message had been sent. They had never been under attack. Commander Asha tried to contact the council from Tath, but the transmission was blocked. She could not reach anyone in the city. The elites regrouped and returned to the city only to find that it had been attacked and a number of the citizens had been killed. After a quick search, we found no survivors and no clues as to who had led the attack or where the missing citizens were. The Dakons use primitive weapons and would have left signs, so it was decided that this attack had originated from another planet within Volan.

"After notifying Leader Mallas of the situation, Asha decided to go to Nebula headquarters and request assistance in identifying where the attack came from. Without this information, we do not know who is or isn't our enemy. After Commander Asha left, I gave orders to thoroughly search the city, and that is when we found that many of the residents had been able to get to safety inside the hidden dome located under the elite headquarters building. The only information we could obtain from interviewing the survivors was that the attack came from the direction of the space dock within minutes after the elites had left the city. The attackers were well armed with advanced weapons and carried equipment that blocked all communication. No one in the city received any warning from the dock's security team of the attack, and thus they didn't know what was happening. All the educators and students and most of the residents outside of the main section of the city made it to safety. The attack seemed to be focused on the council members and city leaders. No one was aware that any prisoners were taken. Everyone is greatly concerned that the attackers entered the city from the docks. So, until Leader Mallas returns, all trade has been halted, and the docks have been closed."

When General Linn sat down, the room was quiet. Everyone silently reviewed what they had heard. So intensely had Arris been listening that she had not been aware that she had eaten everything that had been placed in front of her.

Spider broke the silence. "Good report, General Linn. Leader Mallas and the Velland Space Fleet are to dock tomorrow. Once Leader Mallas deems the docks are secure, the trade ships still in dock will be allowed to leave, and others will be allowed to land. When that happens, we will have Nebula teams on board ships going to Fexnal and Bastik to find evidence of which planet is behind the attack and for what purpose." Spider turned to Asha. "Catella and I are very sorry at the loss of your soldiers. Given that they were caught unaware like that and set up to be slaughtered, however, I am relieved that you did not have more losses. If you are ready to review the assignment details with the two Nebula teams, we can begin."

After the mission details were reviewed and Spider agreed with the plan, Asha and her generals returned to their headquarters. Spider gathered the protectors.

"You will report to me every two hours. One beep will indicate you are OK and still searching. Two beeps will indicate that you wish to set up a secure communication. Find someplace safe where we can talk before you send a request so that we won't be overheard. In the morning, disguises and credentials will be delivered here, and then you will be taken to the space dock. Identify your vessel, and when loading resumes, make your way onto your assigned ship. Remember Kent's warning to memorize every detail of the information he uploaded to the communicators, especially the maps and the time schedule. We will stay here tonight, and food will be delivered after dark. There are cots stored in the other room for you to sleep on."

Later that evening, Arris lay on her cot trying to go to sleep. She placed her bed as far away from Vega as possible but could still hear his breathing. Arris felt a sadness for Ursa. Asha had left with her generals without even nodding to her sister. Arris could sense that personal feelings were not encouraged among the elites, only duty. Asha's duty as commander of the elite troops left no room for emotions. Both sisters had lost their parents in the attack, and their younger sister had been taken captive, but this tragedy had not brought the two sisters any closer. Arris wondered what Illa looked like and if she resembled her older sisters, and on that thought, she fell asleep.

Arris didn't feel comfortable in the baggy clothing she wore, but she would blend in with the inhabitants of Fexnal. Phoenix mastered the baggy look. Being tall and slim helped him carry it off. Vega was almost comical in appearance and was too big for the clothes to be baggy. They would have to find a tent for Vega to wear for him to pull off baggy. All three of the Alpha protectors were armed with weapons; each carried a gun with extra ammunition, a knife with a blade that unfolded to double its length, and a flash bomb they could use if they needed to escape capture. Spider cautioned the protectors to make sure to turn away if they threw a flash bomb, or else they wouldn't be able to see for a while. Long sleeves hid their wrist communicators, and Phoenix had the large comm hidden inside a document pouch tied across his chest.

Beta had finished dressing as well, and their gear resembled the Alphas' except not as loose fitting. They were disguised as buyers going to the planet Bastik. They had the same weapons as the Alphas hidden under their clothes. Breakfast was set up at the meeting table, and as they ate, Spider informed them that the VSF had returned and secured the trading docks. When everyone was finished eating, the protectors were taken to the space dock.

Arris gasped when she saw the size of the docks and the number of transports waiting to be loaded. The docks and ships seemed to continue as far as she could see. The ride that carried them stopped, and the soldier disguised as a driver stepped out.

She pointed and said, "Continue to the main dock. The ship to Bastik is on level two and the ship for Fexnal on level five."

As they stepped from the transport, the driver wished them a safe journey.

"This is where we part company," Ursa said as she pointed to the escalator that went to level two. Signs indicated that level-five access was further down the heavily traveled dock.

"Good luck," Phoenix said.

No hugs were possible with their disguises. Traders and sellers hugging good-bye on the docks would definitely stand out.

"Stay safe," Arris told Beta as they walked away.

"Let's go," Phoenix said as he led the way to the level-five access, narrowly avoiding being knocked over by someone running to make his ship.

CHAPTER 3

THE INVESTIGATION

Phoenix stopped at the dock on level five, where the transport to Fexnal was being loaded. The large ship looked battered, like it had made many trips carrying goods between planets. Before Phoenix climbed the narrow steps that led to the ship, he removed three vouchers from the pouch around his neck. Arris followed Phoenix onto the steps, which were secured at the dock and at the transport but floated free between. When Vega stepped onto the floating steps, they swayed from his weight, and Arris grabbed hold of the handrail that ran above to keep from falling off.

When they reached the entrance to the ship, there was an armed guard there to stop anyone from boarding. Phoenix handed the guard the vouchers, and he looked at them and then at the three passengers. Satisfied, he handed the vouchers back to Phoenix and pointed.

"Passenger rooms are belowdecks. Take the stairs on the left."

When Vega walked past the guard, he asked, "How long before the ship departs?"

The guard looked at Vega and shrugged. "When it's loaded."

Once they were inside the ship, Vega mumbled, "When it's loaded. That guard needs to learn how to greet their guests."

Phoenix laughed. "I don't think carrying passengers is how they make their income. Passengers come second to cargo."

"It would be nice to know how long we have to wait before we leave." Vega wasn't ready to give up complaining.

"I see our room up ahead." Phoenix motioned and led the way down the hall. He stopped at the door before he opened it, waiting for Arris and Vega to catch up.

The room was small and sparsely furnished. A small table and six scattered chairs filled the room. Phoenix walked to the table, removed the pouch from around his neck, and laid it down. He then pulled a chair over to the table and sat down. Arris and Vega did the same. When Vega sat down on the chair, it protested with a loud squeak, and Arris grinned. The chairs fit her and Phoenix just fine, but Vega could definitely use a bigger one. Seeing the look Vega gave her, Arris decided not to comment on the chair's protest.

While Phoenix sent a secure message to Spider to let him know they had boarded the ship, Arris noticed a small window, stood up, and walked over to it. She had to stand on her toes to see out but was amazed at all the different ships she could see. She had not taken the time to look around when they were on the dock, anxious not to draw attention while they found their ship.

Arris heard a chair give protest and then sensed Vega standing behind her. "I've never seen this many spaceships before," she said. "They are all so different—some small and others large like the one we are on. The ships that brought supplies to Daedro were all alike and in better condition. It's a wonder that some of these ships are still being used."

"Don't let their looks fool you. It's their engines that count, and I bet each one is fueled and ready to warp," Vega said above her head.

Phoenix's communicator beeped.

"Beta has landed on Bastik," he said.

"That is so not fair. Who knows when we will leave? We could sit here for hours," Vega grumbled.

"Let's spend the time reviewing the maps of Fexnal. There are two major cities and one small town. The cities both have space docks and are not that far from each other. The town is more inland, and I'm not sure of the source of income for its population. Velland is by far the largest planet and has the most inhabitants. There is no official organization between the planets; they seem to trade with each other on an individual basis. That may be the reason there is not a Nebula ambassador assigned to the Volan Galaxy." Phoenix studied the information displayed on the communicator.

After they reviewed all of the data on Fexnal, Alpha team sat at the table and discussed how to begin their investigation. Once on planet, they could rent a vehicle or hire a driver that comes with a vehicle.

"I think we should rent something ourselves," Vega said. "We don't know who we can trust, so I'm not in favor of a driver. We have all the coordinates for where to search, and I can drive anything."

Phoenix agreed. "We'll search the city where we dock first. I'll need to get inside the shipping offices and find out which ships from Fexnal were on Velland when the attack took place and if any of them returned before the dock was locked down. I can use our disguise as sellers and say that I have a complaint about a nondelivery for that day and time. I'm sure they will give me access to their records. Once we get all the information required, we'll move to the next city. Hopefully we can complete all three cities in one day and get to the docks in time for the transport back to Velland."

As the team finalized their plans, the large spaceship shuddered and the engines came to life.

Vega grinned and said, "The loading must be finished."

Once the ship reached warp speed, it seemed only a few minutes passed before it dropped out of warp and reached Fexnal. The ship circled and dropped and then repeated the maneuver until it docked at its assigned space. Overhead speakers announced their arrival.

Phoenix secured the pouch around his neck and walked from the room. Arris and Vega followed. There were only a few passengers on the ship, and it was easy to find the way to the ship's exit. The same guard watched the three make their way off the ship and to the docking area.

Signs posted in the main area gave directions to specific places.

Phoenix stopped in front of one of the signs and said, "The shipping office is directly above. I'm going to go there first. You two go to ground level and secure transportation. I'll contact you when I leave, and you can send me directions to where to meet."

Phoenix climbed the stairs, and Arris and Vega stepped down to ground level.

After looking at several varieties of ground transportation, Vega said, "I think the rovers would suit us best. The roads that connect the cities seem to be in reasonable shape. Many travelers drive rovers, and we will blend in." Vega folded a free map of the area that he had picked up at the dock and put it in his pocket.

"I agree, but I've never driven anything expect in the test simulators at the academy," Arris admitted. "You should decide."

"I'll have to get you on one of the racetracks at Nebula," Vega offered. "There are lots of different vehicles to drive, from cycles to cars. It's exciting to see how fast you can go."

Arris was hesitant. "I'm afraid I'll crash whatever I try to drive."

Vega laughed. "There are safety protocols that prevent accidents. The worst that could happen is your ride will shut down before you end the program."

Vega selected a stall that listed rentals and prices and walked up. After deciding on the vehicle and paying the fee, he was given a round device that would engage the rover. The person at the stall cautioned Vega to not lose the engager. Arris followed Vega around the back of the stall and waited for him to find the rover and pick her up.

When Arris was seated, Vega said, "There's a parking area nearby. We'll wait for Phoenix there."

While they waited for Phoenix, Arris and Vega each ate one of their nutrition bars and drank an energy drink. "One of Spider's many concoctions," Vega had called the drink. To pass the time, they discussed the various transportation modes, from group movers where you stood and held to straps that hung from the roof to small individual rides that had one or two wheels, depending on the size of the riders. Arris laughed and said that Vega and Sirus would require a minimum of three wheels. Vega didn't think the comment was funny.

The atmosphere on Fexnal was hazy but breathable. There was hardly any movement in the air to help clear it. Arris was anxious to see the city and how the inhabitants lived. Most probably stayed inside and out of the stale air.

Vega's wrist comm beeped, and he responded.

"Phoenix is leaving the shipping office," he said. "I said we would pick him up at the main dock exit." Vega turned a switch, and the rover rolled from the parking area.

Phoenix looked excited. After he sat down, he said, "I was able to see the departures and returns for both cities. The agent was very helpful and worried that the shipping agents had done something wrong. I found one possible ship from each spaceport that arrived on Velland and left around the time of the attack. I need to send this info to Spider."

While Phoenix reported in, Vega drove toward one of the major cities on Fexnal.

"Does the city have a proper name?" Arris asked.

"Spaceport One is all I know. The other city is referred to as Spaceport Two." Vega shrugged and then had to swerve to avoid running into a stalled mover, causing Arris to slam against the door.

"Sorry. It was that or run into a mover full of dangling passengers," Vega hastily explained.

From the rear seat, Phoenix said, "There are three areas we are to search to determine if the prisoners are being held there."

"Do we have an actual count, since many of the people found shelter in the dome?" Arris asked. "There may not be that many to rescue."

"Not yet. I'll ask Spider when I report back in two hours," Phoenix replied.

Vega was able to make it to the city without crashing the rover, running over someone, or throwing Arris out of the vehicle. If this is what the race scenarios were like, Arris decided she would avoid Vega's offer. Being jerked forward and backward or side to side wasn't all that fun. But based on how the others on the crowded road drove, Vega was outmaneuvering all of them.

Phoenix didn't seem bothered about the wild ride. He just kept busy checking the communicator.

"When you come to the city, stay to your left, and the road will take us to our first stop," he told Vega.

After Vega stopped in front of a large building that looked made of some type of metal, Phoenix said, "This is the final place Spider asked us to check out."

The building was bustling as people rushed in and out of the open doors.

"This place is definitely busy. The first two were mainly vacant without any noticeable foot traffic. I wonder what is inside that has everyone rushing in and out. They don't seem to be carrying any bags full of purchases," Vega said as he powered down the rover.

"As busy as this place is, I can't see how prisoners could be held here without being noticed," Arris said as she stepped from rover.

"Let's go find out," Phoenix said. He secured the pouch around his neck and joined the others, walking toward the open doors of the building.

"I have to admit, that was the strangest thing I've experienced," Vega said. "These people can purchase anything imaginable and have it delivered. Each of the booths inside sold different items, and after you purchased everything you wanted, you took the list of items to dispatch to be delivered. No packages to carry or worry about. This must be the only place in the city to purchase goods." Vega shook his head.

"It saves a lot of running around. I thought you were going to buy that hat. The vendor kept saying how good it looked on you," Arris teased Vega.

"I was just using the time to look around, but she was persistent. And the hat did look good on me." Vega pretended to adjust the hat.

Phoenix sat down in the back of the rover. "I need to report that the search of SP One is compete and we found no sign of the prisoners. Even after a few discreet conversations where we said that we were looking for the rest of our group, which had become separated, no one admitted to seeing any strangers."

"No one you talked with was being evasive or trying to hide something," Arris added.

"What now? On to Spaceport Two?" Vega asked.

"Yes," Phoenix answered as he finished sending Spider the report.

CHAPTER 4

THE SEARCH CONTINUES

Vega mentioned that they should reach SP Two in an hour, unless someone crashed into them or ran them off the rutted road. The road was heavily traveled, and repairs did not seem to be a priority. Arris hung on to the door, worried that the next pothole would throw her out of the rover. Phoenix rode in the back and seemed to handle the bumps better.

The communicator beeped twice. Phoenix looked down and said, "Find a place to pull off that's secluded. Ursa has sent a request to talk. Maybe Beta found the prisoners."

Vega pulled the rover off the road and behind a small mound and stopped. Phoenix sent a signal to Beta that they were in a secure location and waited.

Ursa's voice sounded scratchy and intermittent over the comm. "Bastik was a bust. We searched the entire city. There is no sign of the prisoners and no record of transports being on Velland at the time of the attack. How is your search going?"

"We completed our search of SP One and found no sign of the prisoners," Phoenix replied, "but we did identify two transports that were on Velland at the time of the attack. We're now en route to SP Two to check it out."

"We'll catch up with you in SP Two. I'll beep when we land," Ursa said.

"Are you sure Spider will approve?" Phoenix asked.

"My sister has been taken and must be on Fexnal. We're coming. I'll let Spider know. If you locate the prisoners, wait for us," Ursa replied.

Phoenix was curious. "How can you get transport this quickly?"

"Don't worry about transport. We'll join you soon." Ursa disconnected.

"It seems Beta has joined our search," Vega said.

"Can you blame Ursa? Her sister is missing. Besides, having Beta with us when we find the prisoners could be helpful," Arris added.

"I'd better get to driving, or Beta will beat us to SP Two, if I know Ursa. I'm sure she knows her way around the docks and how to catch a ride without tickets."

Vega engaged the motor, and the rover bounced back onto the road.

As they neared the spaceport, Phoenix said, "Continue into the city. There is no need to go to the space dock. I have sent the information on the transports to Spider. Asha is checking out who owns the ships, what cargo they were supposed to have been carrying, and whether the cargo was delivered. It would have taken at least twenty heavily armed mercenaries to carry out the attack on Cexion, and they obviously didn't worry about the people they killed.

That's why Spider was hesitant for us to engage if we find the prisoners."

"I don't think Ursa will wait if we find her sister," Vega said as he made the turn to the city, leaving the space dock behind them.

The road into the city was in worse shape than the others, if that was possible.

"I can't believe the commuters put up with these conditions," Arris said.

"It's mostly dock workers and transport crews," Phoenix replied, "and they probably don't care as long as they make it to the city for some downtime. I don't think SP Two is family friendly, from what I read. It's mainly docks for distribution of the cargo that is delivered. The docking facilities are much smaller than those in SP One."

Phoenix continued to review the data on the communicator he held unaffected by the rover's constant bouncing.

As they entered the city, Arris said, "I haven't seen any sign of children. They must attend school away from the cities."

"There are facilities outside of SP One that provide housing for students and faculty. The complex looks quite large. Students must train there and go back to their families during off times," Phoenix explained.

"This city isn't nearly as large as SP One. Where is our first building to search?" Vega asked as the city came into view. He slowed the rover, waiting for instructions.

"Continue straight ahead. The area to search seems large, perhaps multiple buildings," Phoenix replied.

At the slower speed, Arris was able to look at the city, and from the ragged buildings and rough-looking characters, she was glad Vega was with her. Both she and Phoenix could defend themselves from an attacker, but with Vega, anyone would think twice before openly challenging them. It was the weapons that everyone on this planet carried that worried her. It would be hard to defend against them.

"Pull over when you can," Phoenix said. "These buildings are where we are to search." He shut down the communicator, secured it in the pouch, and hung the pouch around his neck.

The building they entered was dark, and the air smelled musty. There were numerous areas sectioned into cubes where hard-looking dock workers sat and drank from bottles while smoke swirled in the dank air above. Arris could tell the three of them stood out from the looks they received. Phoenix walked to a group of workers and began his speech about looking for their comrades from Velland from whom they'd become separated when leaving the docks. Most of the workers shook their heads, saying they had not seen anyone other than the regulars that hung out between jobs or waiting for assignment.

When Phoenix approached the final group of workers to ask the question about missing comrades, Arris noticed a tall figure step back. She watched as he stared at Phoenix, and when one of the workers turned and asked the figure if he had seen anyone from Velland, he spat on the ground and replied, "No one but the scum that hang out here," causing the other workers to laugh.

Arris took Phoenix by the arm and whispered, "We need to leave." She then turned and walked from the building.

When they were outside, she turned to the others and said, "We need to follow that tall worker. He was lying when he said he hadn't seen anyone from Velland. He knows something. Does the layout show doors in the back that lead outside?"

"All the buildings have access in the back for unloading and loading," Phoenix replied. "Let's get the rover and drive around back to watch."

Arris worried that she had made a mistake in identifying the tall dock worker and knew that if they waited much longer, it would soon be dark. She started to tell Phoenix that when Vega whispered, "There are some men leaving out the back. Arris, do you see the worker you mentioned?"

Arris stepped from the rover and walked to the side of the building. She watched one of the men walk away from the group. The worker was tall, mean looking, and hiding the fact that he knew where the prisoners from Velland were being held. She jumped back in the rover and pointed.

"That's him. He's heading for that two-wheeler. We need to follow him."

Vega started the rover and rolled forward, careful to keep the cycle in sight but not be seen. The sky was beginning to darken as the worker rode out of the city.

"Do you know where this road leads?" Vega asked Phoenix.

"According to the map, it's the road to the smaller outpost, but I don't have further information about that town," Phoenix answered.

"I'm going to drive in the dark," Vega said. "If I turn on the lights, the worker will know he is being followed. Arris, watch the road ahead and let me know when to avoid the potholes."

Arris leaned out the window and watched the road, telling Vega when he needed to swerve to miss one of the holes that would cripple the rover.

It wasn't long before they could see a sprinkling of lights ahead. The cycle was still identifiable, thanks to the beam of its headlight.

"Keep the cycle in sight so we can tell where he goes," Phoenix cautioned from the back.

Vega nodded, keeping his attention on the dangerous road.

"Turn here." Arris motioned to the right. "It looks like he is heading to that building up ahead. There's no cover close by where we can hide."

Vega stopped the rover beside a clump of bushes, the only cover between them and the dark building ahead.

When the cycle stopped, the driver got off and walked to the door of the building. Out of the darkness, a shape stepped forward carrying a gun. The two figures stood and talked, but Arris was too far away to hear what was said.

"We need to get closer," Vega said. "We can sneak up in the dark, but I don't see how we can get inside."

Phoenix gave the order to move ahead single file and hide behind a vehicle near the building that looked abandoned. Silently, Vega, Arris, and Phoenix crept forward.

Once they were closer, Arris could hear what was being said.

"They were asking about missing persons from Velland," the tall figure said. "That isn't a coincidence. If Jeris finds out we took prisoners to sell to the mines, he will skin us alive. We were to kill the council and anyone in the capital that could identify us."

"Then we'd better get the prisoners to the outer ring," the guard answered. "Secure a room on a freighter for tomorrow, and we can move them first thing in the morning. Make sure you get a covered ride so no one will see them. I'll drug them tonight so they won't be able to call for help or escape. Once we get them to the outer ring, it will be easy to sell them to the highest bidder."

Arris turned to Phoenix. "We need to get inside and find out how many captives are being held. We can't go back to Velland. By then, the prisoners will have disappeared in the mines in the outer ring."

The tall worker turned his cycle around, and the bright light shone in their direction.

"Hide!" Vega whispered.

The cycle passed.

"I hope he doesn't notice our rover," Vega said, "or if he does, I hope he thinks it has broken down and been left."

The three watched the cycle hurry past the rover, and each gave a sigh.

"Now what?" Vega asked.

Just then, Phoenix's communicator beeped, a signal from Ursa that Beta had arrived and wanted to meet up.

"I'm not sure what to tell Ursa," Phoenix whispered. "If she thinks we found her sister, she'll rush here."

"I'm sure we've found the captives," Arris said. "It looks to be just the one guard, but there could be others inside that we don't know about. We need to get inside and find out before you let Ursa know. Tell her to secure a ride and wait for directions."

"Just how are we getting inside?" Vega asked.

"If you pull the guard from the door, I can get inside. I just need someone to draw his attention for a minute." Arris explained.

"No way are you going inside by yourself." Vega huffed.

Arris looked at Phoenix, "I can get inside without being seen. I just need a couple of minutes without the guard at the door. I'll set my wrist comm on send only and you can hear me. Once inside, I'll verify the number of prisoners and if there are other guards. I'll beep twice when I'm ready and Vega can pull the guard away. We don't have time to waste; we need to let Ursa know if her sister is here."

Phoenix hesitated, "OK. We'll do what you suggest, but signal if you get in trouble."

It sounded like Vega growled, but he didn't say anything. Phoenix was Alpha leader, and if he was willing to risk Arris' life by going inside by herself, then he would support the decision.

CHAPTER 5

THE ESCAPE

When the guard wasn't looking, Arris crept from behind the wrecked vehicle and made her way through the darkness to the side of the building. She pressed her wrist comm once, a signal for Vega to cause a distraction, and waited. The sound of scuffling or something being dragged broke the silence, and she peeked around the building. The guard had heard the sound and was looking toward that direction. The strange sound was repeated, and the guard stepped from the doorway to find out what was making the noise.

Arris ran to the door and stood tight against it. She found the latch, slowly lifted it, and opened the door just enough to squeeze inside. Standing in the dark room, she listened and could hear sounds coming from the back like someone was crying and trying to muffle the noise. She let her eyes adjust to the dark and then looked around. There were two cots with blankets piled on top and a table holding tins of food and containers of drinks. Two chairs sat next to the table. She carefully inspected the floor, looking for signal traps for in case anyone tried to escape but saw none.

In the dark, she blended, allowing her surroundings to conceal her, and slowly walked toward the back. While she was blended, no one would notice her. The room where the prisoners sat on the grimy floor wasn't that large. It looked as if it had been built to secure cargo boxes waiting to be delivered. Bars formed a wall across the front of the room with a door in the middle made from the same bars. Arris inspected the lock. It was simple and easily picked. She counted twenty prisoners locked inside the room, and all of them looked like they had been starved since being taken captive. She did not see any empty cartons of food or water inside their cage.

Arris pushed back the sleeve covering her wrist comm and whispered, "There are no other guards inside. We have twenty prisoners badly in need of food and water. Vega, take out the guard. You may want to interrogate him, but he has not given these people one bit of care. Phoenix, contact Ursa and tell her to bring a transport big enough to carry an additional twenty passengers. Hold on."

Hearing Arris's voice but not seeing anyone, the prisoners had stood up and were huddled together against the back wall.

"Is Illa here?" Arris asked.

From the back, a slim girl stepped forward and weakly said, "I'm Illa."

"Phoenix, tell Ursa we found her sister."

Arris slowly unblended, allowing the prisoners to see her. Just then, Phoenix opened the door for Vega, who pushed the guard forward with a gun shoved under his chin.

Vega pointed toward one of the chairs. "Sit down," he ordered.

Hearing the tone of Vega's voice, the guard quickly complied.

Phoenix propped the door open, and a faint light filtered in from outside. Arris removed the knife from her pocket and picked the lock. She swung the door open.

"If you can walk," she said, "there are drinks on the table. If you need help, raise your hand."

The captives stumbled from the cage, holding on to each other for support, and slowly made their way to the table. Phoenix had already removed the lids from the containers.

"Only take a few sips," he cautioned. "If you drink too much at first, you'll throw up."

After the prisoners finished drinking, most of them sat on the cots, but a few walked to the door, shielding their eyes against the muted evening light.

Illa walked up to Arris and asked, "Who are you, and how were you able to disappear?"

Arris took Illa by the arm and moved the second chair away from the table. The guard glared at Arris but didn't say a word. After Illa sat down, Arris explained.

"We are protectors from Nebula. We came to help Asha find you and the other captives. My name is Arris, he is Phoenix, and the one by the guard is Vega. I didn't actually disappear, but I can blend into my surroundings. That was why you couldn't see me."

Vega looked at Phoenix and said, "This guard's not willing to talk. What should we do with him?"

"Save him for Ursa," Phoenix answered. "She will get any information she wants from him."

Illa exclaimed, "Ursa is here?"

"She is finding transports to get everyone to the space dock and back to Velland," Phoenix said.

"We should hurry," Illa said, her voice shaking. "There are more guards than him. They change out, and I've seen at least four others."

Arris walked to the guard and stared at him. "He is more afraid of someone called Jeris than of you," she told Vega. "But he hasn't met Ursa yet."

Phoenix looked at Vega and said, "Secure this assassin, and then go get the rover and stand watch until Beta arrives. We don't want to be caught off guard."

"Have you contacted Spider, Phoenix?" Arris asked.

"Not yet. We've had our hands full. I think I'll wait for Beta and find out if Ursa secured transport to Velland. She may have contacted Asha to assist."

Arris had doubts about whether Ursa would have contacted her sister, but with the lives of Illa and the other prisoners at stake, she may have. One of the prisoners had taken the tins of food from the table and was passing them around, along with more drink. From the looks of the prisoners, they would need to build up their energy to make it back to Velland alive.

It was easy to tell that Beta was coming from the bouncing lights in the distance. They weren't wasting any time. Arris stepped outside and stood by Vega. Together they watched two large rovers barrel down the rutted road. Minor was driving one with Ursa in the front, and Sirus followed with a second rover.

Dust swirled as the two rovers came to a halt in front of the building.

Ursa jumped out of the transport before it stopped and shouted, "Where's Illa?"

"Illa is inside along with the other prisoners," Arris said.

Ursa rushed past Arris and into the building, looking around until she saw her sister. She hurried over and exclaimed, "Illa, I've been so worried."

Illa raised up from the chair and said, "Ursa. You're really here. It's been years."

Ursa cradled Illa in her arms while she sobbed.

"It was horrible," Illa said. "These men with masks and guns rushed in from all sides and began to shoot everyone in the room. The council was voting on the mining demands. I came with Mother to wait for Father; we were going to go on a trip afterward." Illa gave a final sob.

"After we get everyone back to Velland, we will find the murderers who did this," Ursa promised.

Illa shook her head and said, "But it won't bring Mother or Father back."

Sirus and Minor came into the building and looked around, and then Sirus told Ursa, "We need to get everyone in the rovers and return to the spaceport. Arris said there are more guards that could return any time. We don't want to be here when they get back."

"I contacted Spider and explained the situation," Ursa said. "Asha will have a ship ready to depart when we reach the spaceport. She will send me the dock number as soon as the ship arrives." She glared at the guard secured to the chair, and then looked to Phoenix with a grimace. "What has he told you?"

"He hasn't said a word, even with Vega threatening him. Arris said he is more afraid of someone called Jeris," Phoenix explained.

The guard's face turned white at hearing the name Jeris.

"Get everyone to the transports," Ursa told Phoenix. "I'll be out in a minute."

All three transports carried captives as they rolled away. Vega and Phoenix led the caravan, followed by Minor and Ursa, with Illa seated behind her sister. Arris and Sirus brought up the rear in the largest transport, which could accommodate anyone who had trouble sitting upright.

Refreshed from the drinks and food, most of the captives looked able to make the trip. On the spaceship, they would get medical attention, but first they had to reach the space dock.

"You were lucky to find the prisoners," Sirus said. "Ursa told me they were to be taken to the mines and sold as slaves."

Arris turned around, making sure the captives were still in their seats. "I'm glad you found transports with straps to hold everyone in."

"From what I heard, these men were given orders to kill everyone," Sirus continued.

"Taking them as prisoners actually saved their lives," Arris replied. "It was these brutes' bad luck that one of the prisoners was the sister of Asha and Ursa. Do you know what Ursa learned from the guard?"

Sirus swerved to avoid a pothole. "I'm glad it's becoming light. Easier to see where I'm driving." After another swerve, Sirus said, "Ursa said there was nothing that would help us on Fexnal, but she did get information to give to Asha and Leader Mallas. They will not like what she learned."

"Why did we just leave the guard tied up instead of bringing him back to stand trial?" Arris wondered.

"I wouldn't ask Ursa that question unless you want to know the answer," Sirus said.

As the three rovers raced through the city, they received stares from the hard-looking inhabitants. The rovers had just made it out of the city when five two-wheelers spun onto the road directly behind them. All of the riders had weapons and began shooting as they came near the transports.

"Duck down!" Arris yelled to the captives when bullets began to whiz past. She took out the small weapon she carried and leaned out.

The two-wheelers were swerving back and forth in the road, and that, along with the bumping of the rover, kept Arris from taking a shot at the riders.

She yelled to Sirus, "We need to get off the road and make a stand. I count five riders. We should be able to hold them off, even with these small guns."

Sirus turned off the road and drove toward an area that would provide limited cover. The other rovers followed his maneuver.

"Form a barrier with the rovers and get the captives behind it," Phoenix yelled to Sirus and Minor.

When the dust settled, the captives were secured behind the rovers with the protectors spaced in between. The five riders stopped far enough away to be out of range of the protectors' guns.

One of the riders stepped forward and yelled, "If you want to live, drive away and leave the prisoners."

Ursa yelled, "Fat chance." She stood up and fired two shots at the rider, only missing him because he was out of range of the small pistol.

The rider jumped back and joined his comrades.

"Maybe someone will hear the shooting and come to help," Arris said.

"Not on this planet. There is no law here except to stay alive," Ursa answered.

"I wish we had better weapons than these puny pistols," Vega grumbled.

Minor crawled behind the rover he had driven and lifted down a crate. "Maybe these will help." He opened the crate to reveal the weapons inside. "Ursa figured we might need bigger firepower to make it back to the spaceport."

"This evens things," Vega said as he admired the weapons and selected the largest gun for himself.

As Minor passed out the weapons, Phoenix said, "We need to circle behind the riders and get them in a crossfire. Vega and Minor, if we pull their attention to this side of the rovers, can you get around behind them?"

"We can do it," Vega said. "You just get their attention for a couple of minutes."

Ursa, Phoenix, Sirus, and Arris crawled to the other end of the rovers, where they would stage a fake attack.

"With the one guard back at the building, plus these five, that still leaves another dozen or more that took part in the attack on the Cexion council," Ursa said. "The invaders must have arrived at and left Velland in both of the spaceships that Phoenix identified, or else this bunch would not have been able to take captives. Their ship was the one that came from this spaceport. We need to know where the other ship went when it left Velland. It didn't return to Fexnal; if it had, Phoenix would have found evidence of it."

"When we step out, Ursa and Sirus, shoot high," Phoenix said. "Arris and I will stay low. This way it will be hard for the assailants to return fire. When they regroup, we will move behind the rovers. This should give Vega and Minor time to circle behind them." Phoenix admired his new gun. "I won't ask how you obtained these weapons, Ursa, but I'm glad you did."

Ursa grinned slyly.

"It shouldn't take us long to reach the spaceport, unless we have another ambush," Vega said. He and Minor had returned to the rovers after making sure the assailants who had attacked them would not be following. They had searched each of the attackers but hadn't found any identification or information about who had hired them.

"They were mercenaries hired for the job. That's why they were able to take prisoners after being told to kill everyone," Ursa said, her voice holding no hint of regret about the deaths of the five assailants.

"That was a good plan, getting them in a crossfire, Phoenix," Minor said.

"A little Spider strategy," Phoenix replied. "Now, let's get this group to the space dock and home to Velland."

CHAPTER 6

THE RETURN

Arris glanced into the room where two of the elite soldiers were busy clearing the table, loading empty plates from breakfast, baskets of breads, and drinking cups onto carts to return them to the kitchen. Breakfast had been hot, and there had been plenty of it. Even Sirus and Vega had eaten their fill. After arriving back on Velland and getting the captives safely home, the protectors had returned to the gym, where they cleaned up. A good night's sleep, clean uniforms, and the hot breakfast had refreshed them.

Arris was anxious to learn the latest updates from Commander Asha and Leader Mallas. As soon as the large room was cleaned, the update on attack would begin. The elite generals who had attended the meeting back when the protectors had first arrived were waiting in the gym to take their places. Additional chairs had been carried in for Leader Mallas and his staff.

Illa entered the room with Asha. Illa looked like she had recovered from being held captive. Seeing Illa in clean clothes with her hair combed, Arris observed that she was a

45

younger, prettier, daintier version of her sisters. Illa had still lived at home with her parents, but with them gone, Arris wondered what she would do. Asha lived in the elite military complex, and Ursa at Nebula Headquarters.

Spider entered the gym and told the protectors, "The meeting is ready to begin. We have seats reserved on one end."

The room was full. After everyone was seated, Asha walked to the front.

"This is a sad time for the residents of Cexion. Due to a well-planned and well-executed attack on the Cexion council and the elite infantry, we lost many loved and valuable citizens. Both Leader Mallas and I will give our full effort to identifying and bringing to justice the ones who did this.

"I want to thank Catella of the Nebula Association for allowing Spider and the protectors to assist us with finding the prisoners that were taken off planet. The performance of protector teams Alpha and Beta was outstanding. They located the spaceships that carried the raiders, found and rescued the prisoners, and defended the prisoners from an attack by the very ones that had taken them, and they did all this at risk to their own lives. If I have one positive piece of news, it is that six of the assailants from Fexnal were killed."

Asha paused as cheers filled the room, and the elite generals nodded a silent thank-you to the team from Nebula.

"The transports that carried the assassins have been identified. Both came from Fexnal. The ship from Spaceport Two was hired for the purpose of bringing goods back from Velland. The person who made the transaction does not exist, and the crew from the ship cannot be found. The crew may have been the same people who attacked the protectors. Therefore, Spaceport Two has no further information.

"The ship from Spaceport One arrived from the outer ring, but any information about where it originated from or who owns it has been erased. When that ship left Velland, it did not go to Fexnal or Bastik and therefore must have returned to the outer ring. Three of the planets in the ring are being mined, and each has several mining settlements and shipping docks. We don't have much information about these planets, even though the metals they produce are delivered to the Velland spaceport for sale or trade.

"There were demands made by the mining owners, and the Cexion council was voting on them the day of the attack. It was no secret that these demands were to be voted down. The council felt the demands were not in the interest of Velland, and if Velland turned down the demands, Fexnal and Bastik would follow suit. I do not have a list of all the demands, but one of them was that there would be no inspection of ships from the mines and no tracking of who the deliveries were for. These measures would have allowed ships to land on Velland with the Cexion council having no way of knowing what their cargo was or who it was for. Also, the price of the metals mined in the outer ring has tripled.

"Ursa, the Beta team leader, interrogated one of the assassins and learned that the leader of the attack was called Jeris. It was he who hired the assassins from Fexnal. We cannot find any information about Jeris. The assassin said Jeris is planning to take control of the space docks on Velland, Fexnal, and Bastik. Then he would own all shipping, selling, and trading rights within the Volan Galaxy.

"Finally, how do the Dakon tribes fit in with the attack? From our latest report, it seems the tribes have organized under a single leader. They have never operated like this before and would previously have fought each other for any reason. The attack on the elite army was planned and carried out by more than one tribe.

"Tomorrow there will be an election of new council members. Once the council is reestablished, it will open dialogues with the councils of Fexnal and Bastik to discuss the situation. That is all I have to report. When more information becomes available, it will be distributed to those in this room only. There is still a concern that there may be spies in Cexion that report to Jeris and the Dakons."

Asha looked exhausted as she turned to shake Leader Mallas's hand, ending the meeting.

The protectors followed Spider into the gym and to the area where they slept. Spider motioned for them to gather round.

"Asha has requested that we stay and guard the new council. After the elections are over, the new members will resume work on the issues the previous council was dealing with. After the Dakon ambush, the elites' numbers are down one third. The soldiers who were injured will not be able to resume their duties for some time. There have been reports from all the settlements that warriors have been spotted, and there is concern that the Dakons may be preparing for a coordinated attack on all of the settlements at once. If Catella agrees to our protecting the council, then we could stay on Velland for some time.

"Asha and Leader Mallas have met, and the elites will continue to guard Cexion and the settlements. Leader

Mallas will have his space fleet on alert to watch for any unscheduled ships requesting to dock. Mallas has also been in contact with the docks on Fexnal and Bastik regarding the attack and has requested any information they may have about Jeris. He asked if any additional ships from the outer rings are in port. This action will more than likely alert Jeris that the Velland Space Fleet knows of his part in the attack on Cexion. Transmissions to Nebula are intermittent, and until the planet rotates, we can't contact Catella. Until we have our orders, stay close and stay alert."

After Spider left, Phoenix asked Ursa, "I know it has been sometime since you lived in Cexion, but would you give us a tour of the city? If we are to guard the council, we need to learn the layout and points of entry. I'm certain that Catella will allow us to stay and protect the new council until the situation in Volan becomes stable."

Ursa agreed that it was a good idea, and the protectors spent the remainder of the day touring the city. Ursa pointed out the various buildings and their uses, the main roads in and out of the city, the elites' compound, and the council chambers inside one of the taller buildings.

While they were inside the council chambers deciding the best positions for the protectors to stand guard, Illa came into the room. She walked over to Ursa and pointed to one side.

"Over there was where I was sitting with Mother, and the attackers entered from that door. At first, we thought it was a drill, seeing all the masked men carrying guns. The leader pointed at the table where the council was seated and gave orders, and then the shooting started."

Illa shuddered, and Ursa placed her arm around Illa's shoulders.

"Mother told me to run and pushed me toward that door over there to escape. All I remember hearing was gunfire and screams. I ran into that room and hid. The ones taken captive were the ones who escaped into that room. I think we were found as they searched the building on their way out looking for something to steal, because the shooting had stopped by then. We were held in the room for a while, and then we were marched outside and loaded into a military-looking vehicle."

"The attackers were using military ground transport; that explains how these killers could get to the city from the spaceport so fast," Ursa clarified.

Illa looked around. "I'm glad the room has been cleaned up and the table and chairs replaced. I've just come from a meeting with the others who are posting for council seats, and everyone agrees that the new council will meet in here and carry on."

Sirus walked over. "Are you posting for council?"

Illa looked up at Sirus and nodded. "Yes. I've completed all my training for Cexion administration and leadership. I had planned to start working with Father on council matters, but now I hope to carry on in his place."

"Best of luck," Sirus said. "You will make a good council member."

"Will you live alone in Cexion?" Arris asked.

Illa's look was sad. "I plan on staying at home. It's the only place I've ever lived, and I don't want to move. I have plenty of friends, and if I'm elected to the council, I'll be very busy."

That evening after dinner, Arris wandered outside. She was tired but not enough to go to bed. She walked around the gym and leaned on the fence that surrounded the elites' training field. She saw two figures walking side by side, so engrossed in what they were talking about that they didn't notice her. Arris was shocked when she realized it was Sirus and Asha. "That's interesting," she mumbled to herself.

Vega came up behind her. "What's interesting?" he asked and then realized who Arris was watching. "Now, that is interesting. Asha almost looks small next to Sirus."

Arris didn't want to say anything further, even though she had sensed something when the two had passed by. It was like a strong companionship or respect. Both Asha and Sirus were soldiers, and they held the same beliefs, but was there something more.

Arris turned to go back into the gym, but Vega stepped in front of her.

"What aren't you saying, little sister?"

Arris shook her head. No way was she going to tell Vega what she thought, because Vega would not let it go without trying to find out for himself. If Vega invaded Sirus's private space, who knew what could happen. Later that night, after she was in bed, she heard Sirus return to the gym and go to bed.

Arris had known Sirus for years—he was like her big brother—and everything she had learned about Asha left Arris wondering how two individuals as dedicated to their positions as Sirus and Asha were had formed an instant bond. Sirus was a caring person, but his size and looks hid that side of him. Asha wore a protective shell around her emotions. This allowed her to perform her duty as commander of the elites and make the hard decisions that others could not. Somehow, Sirus and Asha had instantly developed feelings toward each other.

The following morning, the protectors began developing a strategy on how to protect the council from another attack, deciding on the best places to watch the road into the city and the entrances into the building where the council met. Phoenix suggested, after they completed their plans, that they should go investigate the space dock and become familiar with its operations. After letting Spider know where they were going, the protectors walked from the gym toward the elite headquarters.

When they reached headquarters, General Linn was seated behind a desk. She stood up when they entered. "Welcome to elite headquarters."

"Is Asha here?" Ursa asked, not signifying her relationship to her sister.

"Commander Asha should return shortly. She wanted to attend the council vote this morning," General Linn explained.

"We wanted to borrow a vehicle to drive to the space dock," Asha said.

"I'm sure the commander would approve. If you will wait out front, I'll have a rover brought around."

After thanking General Linn, the protectors stepped outside.

While they waited, a sleek-looking military rover rolled up. Asha was driving, and seated next to her was Illa, who looked like she was bursting with excitement. Her face glowed and she wore a large grin. Before the vehicle stopped, Illa jumped out and ran to Ursa.

"I did it. I was elected to fill Father's seat on the council." Illa grabbed both of Ursa hands and pulled her around in a circle. It looked like the two sisters had done this dance many times before.

Ursa's face now mirrored her young sister's. "Congratulations, Illa!" she exclaimed.

The other protectors gathered round Illa and Ursa, adding their congratulations.

Asha stepped from the rover and stood by, watching her sisters' rejoicing. Arris noticed the loving look on Asha's face, but she was the only one, because the look disappeared as quickly as it had appeared, safely hidden behind her shell.

Sirus detached himself from the celebration and walked over to Asha. He spoke quietly to her, and Asha smiled and nodded at his words.

CHAPTER 7

ELITE RITES

"I'm glad Catella approved of our staying in Cexion. I like it here. The food's good, and everyone in the city is friendly," Minor said as the protectors walked from the gym.

They had met with Spider and learned that he had been able to contact Catella and gain approval for their extended stay. The protectors would do what they had trained for and protect the new Cexion council, which would hold its first meeting tomorrow. Everyone had been relieved when Spider had told them of Catella's decision, but Sirus had looked the most relieved. Arris sensed that as long as Asha needed help, Sirus would be there for her.

The protectors were on their way to the elites' parade ground, where bleachers had been erected for the last rites ceremony for the soldiers killed in the Dakon ambush. Everyone living in Cexion would attend the ceremony. When the protectors reached the reviewing area, the bleachers were packed with attendees.

"Let's go on this side. There are still a few seats available." Vega pointed and led the way.

Once the protectors were seated, Arris looked around at the large crowd of people that filled the bleachers. Everyone looked well groomed and well dressed. When the protectors had toured Cexion, they had seen no areas that were not maintained. All of the streets had been free of debris, and there had been no evidence of anyone living on the streets, like she'd seen in the cities on Fexnal. According to Ursa, Bastik was even more primitive than Fexnal.

Off to the side where the protectors were seated, individual chairs on wheels and with arm supports were being pushed forward and placed in a line in front of the bleachers. The elite soldiers who had been wounded in the attack sat in the chairs. Many of them should still have been in the hospital and were not able to sit up, instead slumping to the side. Even with their injuries, these soldiers knew they were fortunate not to be part of the last rites ceremony to honor their fallen comrades. An announcement came from speakers, signaling that the ceremony was about to begin.

A trio of elite soldiers carrying horns marched to the front and began to play an anthem. Everyone stood up, except for the wounded who were not able. Commander Asha and General Linn marched from behind the bleachers and climbed to their seats in the review area. Asha was dressed in a white uniform adorned with gold braiding and four stars. General Linn also wore a white uniform but with less braiding and only two stars. When the anthem was finished, everyone waited until Commander Asha sat down before they took their seats.

"Elites present," came from the speakers and echoed around the arena.

It was an amazing spectacle to see the six elite generals who reported to General Linn march forward. The six generals were dressed in light-gray uniforms adorned with gray braiding, and each had a single star on her uniform. Marching beside each general was a soldier carrying a long spear. Each spear was painted a different color and pattern. One by one, the generals each led a brigade of elite soldiers. The soldiers were dressed in gray uniforms adorned with braiding the color of their unit's spear. They wore shiny black boots that reached mid-calf, and every soldier had a sword attached to one side. When each brigade passed the reviewing stand, the general and the soldiers saluted Commander Asha.

Behind each brigade came a military truck with an open bed, and sitting on the bed were shiny silver containers adorned with the color of the brigade. When the ceremony was over, the containers would be placed with honor in the memorial building on the compound. Each soldier's name and rank would be printed under the container that held their remains.

When the final brigade passed, Vega whispered to Arris, "The elites are still three hundred strong. I wouldn't want to come against them. No wonder the Dakons set a trap to box them in. If they hadn't, they wouldn't have stood a chance."

When the solemn ceremony was over, the protectors silently made their way back to the gym.

The following morning, the protectors dressed in their Nebula uniforms and carried weapons. The new council would hold its first meeting today, and the protectors would arrive early and take their assigned positions. "Not on our watch" was their mantra. The families of the council members who had been killed had suffered a great loss, and the protectors vowed it would not be repeated.

When they stepped outside, two military rovers with drivers were waiting. One was for the protectors, with the exception of Phoenix. Phoenix was to go to the space dock and access the data. Kent had asked Spider to get records of all the spaceships that had arrived from the outer rings going back at least one year. If they could get the same information from the docks on Fexnal and Bastik, Kent would try to find a pattern of when ships arrived without delivery documents or did not list any cargo upon leaving. It was a long shot, but Spider wanted Kent to try to find out when Jeris had been on these planets, whether there were any records about meetings concerning mining shipments, and who had attended these meetings. Spider would start tracking Jeris by tracking the ones that were working for him.

Spider rode with Phoenix to the space dock. He was joining Leader Mallas and the captains of the VSF on Mallas's command ship. Little information was known about Jeris, and Mallas wanted to develop a defense strategy and define the next steps in the investigation of the attack on Cexion. From the information the mercenary had given Ursa, the attack on the council had been only the first part of Jeris's greater plan.

"Good luck. Hopefully you will find information that Kent can use," Spider told Phoenix when they parted ways at the space dock.

"Thanks. I just wish Kent were here. He's much faster than I am at data mining," Phoenix said as he walked toward the shipping office.

The command ship of the Velland Space Fleet was huge and gleamed in the daylight. When Spider came on board, he was greeted by a member of the ship's crew, who would take him to the conference room. The inside of the ship gleamed as much as the outside, showing the care the crew gave the large vessel. When Spider entered the conference room, it was filled with men in uniforms with the VSF insignia on one side. The various pins and medals on the other side signified their ranks within the fleet. Leader Mallas stopped talking and greeted Spider.

"Attention, everyone. I would like to introduce Spider from the Nebula Association. He is here at Commander Asha's request. As you already know, the teams from Nebula quickly found those who were taken hostage, and we are very grateful for our citizens' safe return. I have asked Spider to join our team as we decide on the best method to protect Velland from the madman called Jeris. If everyone will find a seat at the table, we will begin." Leader Mallas motioned for Spider to take the chair next to his.

When Spider learned there were only seven ships in the space fleet, he worried about whether they would be enough to hold off another coordinated attack. If the other six ships were the size of the command ship and had experienced officers in charge of them, they still made a considerable force. Spider was impressed with the officers who reported to Mallas and knew they would defend Velland with their lives.

The planets of Fexnal and Bastik did not have a military space fleet, only security teams that tried to protect the docks and cities. Both planets did have councils to manage the docks, but from the comments Spider heard around the table, management and security were lacking on both planets. Fexnal and Bastik did have transport vessels that flew between the three planets, buying, selling, or trading goods. The councils on Fexnal and Bastik had tried to implement shipping regulations but could not enforce them. That had allowed Jeris to come and go without record.

By the end of the meeting, they had decided how the fleet would be deployed and what matters to investigate. First, Mallas would request meetings with the councils on Fexnal and Bastik. He wanted to find out if anyone had information about Jeris. Mallas requested that Spider attend these meetings to help him determine if anyone was aligned with Jeris. Mallas had learned from Asha that Spider had no equal in strategy or in battle. Spider asked that Arris join them and told Mallas in secret of Arris's abilities. Mallas agreed to Arris's participation.

Three of the VSF warships would circle Velland, watching for any signs of an attack from space. No vessels would be allowed to dock at the spaceport without proper documentation or without first being cleared by the dock security team. One warship would stay docked in case of an emergency.

Tomorrow, the final two warships would secretly leave for the outer ring to look for transport ships that were not part of the trading fleet. These VSF ships would not be allowed to dock on the ring planets without clearance, and it was doubtful that they would get it. But they could circle the three planets that were being mined and determine if there was a buildup of spaceships. The fourth small planet was not being mined and had no settlements, so it was not considered in the search.

One concerning factor was that once the two ships were inside the ring, communication with the command ship would be difficult. A timetable had been created that called for the two ships to be inside the ring for two days before coming out and contacting the command ship with updates. The ships were to stay together at all times. The fear was that if they became separated inside the gaseous rings, they may not be able to find each other if something went wrong.

All of the VSF warships would be monitored by Mallas from the command ship. After thanking everyone for attending, Leader Mallas ended the meeting.

That evening after dinner, Spider and the protectors stayed at the table. Spider wanted to hear about their first day guarding the council. He asked if they had any concerns or problems. Ursa reported that the day had been quiet and nothing had seemed out of the ordinary. When Ursa mentioned that the council had voted to send an emissary to Fexnal and Bastik to discuss the mining issues, Spider told them of Leader Mallas's plan to visit both planets to look for information on Jeris.

Ursa said a new leader of the council had been voted in—Daji Adain, whose father had been killed in the attack. Daji had attended many previous council meetings and was familiar with the issues and how to run the council. Ursa had known Daji since she was a child and said he would be a good council leader.

Spider decided to contact Mallas and combine the visits. This would give the emissary the protection of the VSF in case of a threat. Before Spider left the room to contact Mallas, he told the protectors that Arris would be joining him in the meetings on the other planets.

When Spider returned, Phoenix updated the teams on the information he'd found at the spaceport. The officials had been very helpful, especially after having been contacted by Leader Mallas. Phoenix had sent the information to Kent while at the spaceport.

After he was done recounting what he'd learned, he asked Spider, "Will you try to get the same information from the ports on Fexnal and Bastik?"

"Yes. I will contact the port authorities myself, along with Arris. If they try to lie to me, Arris will know, and I'll put pressure on them." Spider didn't explain what pressure the dock authorities would receive, but Phoenix had no doubt Spider would get all of the information available.

Just before the meeting was over, Spider's comm beeped, and he told Arris, "Be ready to leave tomorrow, and be prepared to be away for two days."

After the meeting, Spider and Sirus left the gym together. Arris knew that Sirus was going to meet with Asha, but where was Spider going?

That night before going to sleep, the protectors discussed the next day's assignments.

"Do you still want me to patrol the city?" Vega asked Ursa. "If an attack comes from the spaceport, the fleet will be aware and contact us. If the Dakons try to attack the city, the elites have guards posted around the city."

"With Arris away for two days, Phoenix can monitor the main entrance, and you and Minor can guard the council chambers. We need to switch places every few hours so we don't become distracted staying in one area," Ursa responded.

"It's good that both Spider and Arris will be part of the meetings," Phoenix added. "They can keep watch on the emissary the council sends."

While they were talking, Sirus entered the gym and came over.

"Where did you and Spider go?" Minor asked.

Sirus sat down on his bunk. "We met with Asha and discussed scenarios for if the tribes attack all the settlements at once."

"Why don't those living in the settlements move into the city until everything settles down?" Minor suggested.

"They can't leave the farms and animals unguarded," Ursa explained. "Whenever there is an attack, the settlements send for help and hold off the tribes until the elites arrive. If the settlers leave, the tribes will raid the crops and eat the animals. They could even burn the settlements. These tribes are nomadic and live off the land, which is the reason they raid. It's an easy way for them to get food."

"Asha said the settlers have weapons and are well trained," Sirus added. "It's only when they are attacked by large bands of warriors that they need help from the elites. With the elite soldiers down in numbers, Asha is trying to decide whether she should deploy one of the battalions at the settlements, since each has reported of being watched. She could post ten soldiers at each of the five settlements, but that would weaken the force guarding Cexion. And would ten soldiers be enough to hold off a large attack on a settlement?

"Until Cexion is deemed safe from another invasion by Jeris, Asha is unwilling to send more soldiers away from the city. Asha has a lot to deal with right now in determining the best way to deploy the elites. It was difficult burying so many soldiers at one time, and with a number of elites still injured, Asha has to protect the city and the settlements with depleted numbers."

The protectors, including Ursa, had no answers for Sirus. Understanding Asha's responsibility as commander of the elites kept them silent.

CHAPTER 8

THE SPY

The meeting was held after dark in the gym where the protectors slept. Asha was concerned; she wasn't sure who to trust. After finding out about Jeris and his plan to take over all trading in the Volan Galaxy, along with the coordinated Dakon attack on the elites, Asha was certain there were spies in Cexion and at the space dock. For everyone's safety, a curfew had been put in place, and after-dark patrols guarded the streets. Until Cexion was deemed safe from further attacks, the curfew would stay in place.

The elite generals, Spider, Ursa, Sirus, and Arris sat around the table, waiting for Asha to call the meeting to order. Phoenix, Vega, and Minor were on patrol, making sure the citizens of Cexion were safe inside their homes. The three were also looking for escape routes in case of another attack by Jeris or the tribes. If the council was in session when an attack happened, the protectors wanted several ways to get them to safety. They had identified three places in the city to take the council. Each of the hideouts was easily defended and would provide protection for the protectors. If an attack did happen, the protectors would get the council to safety.

Asha walked to the front and called the meeting to order. "We have two issues to resolve. First, we cannot leave Cexion unprotected. We know what happened last time and will not allow this to happen again. The Cexion dock is the hub for the other planets to buy from and trade with Velland. If Jeris takes control of the city, then we could lose the space dock and even the settlements. Our citizens would not survive if this were to happen.

"Second, all of the settlements are being watched by the Dakons. So far, there has been no sign of the tribes gathering for an attack. It was suggested that they are waiting for orders from Jeris. The settlements provide crops and meat not only for Velland but for Fexnal, Bastik, and the mining colonies in the outer ring as well."

Asha paused to allow everyone to understand how critical the situation was.

"We are certain that Jeris has spies in Cexion and at the space dock. Otherwise, he would not have been able to land unnoticed and convince the Dakons to work with or for him. I'm sure he has promised to give the tribes the settlements if they help him. The elites are down in numbers, and I am concerned about sending even one battalion outside the city. We need to decide whether to stay with our current strategy of having the settlements send for help if attacked or to deploy one battalion between the five major settlements."

The room was quiet until Spider asked, "Do you have a count of the number of tribes and how many raiders there are within each tribe?"

"No," Asha replied. "The tribes are nomadic and move around. For years, there have been a couple of raids each year for food, always involving around twenty raiders. Up until this last attack, their weapons and vehicles had been scavenged and pieced together. Based on what we saw during the attack on the elites, their weapons and vehicles appear to be new and military-like. Somehow, Jeris has secretly supplied the tribes with military equipment."

"You need to do reconnaissance to find out the number of tribes and raiders and how they are equipped before you can plan any battle tactics," Spider said. "Perhaps the protectors can assist with this."

Ursa spoke up. "Count the protectors among your elites. We will protect the council and obtain recon on the tribes."

Asha looked at Ursa and nodded. "Thank you. I'll have one of the generals who is familiar with the tribes coordinate with you. The sooner we get this information, the sooner we can decide how to deploy the elites. Leader Mallas will be visiting Fexnal and Bastik to determine these planets' involvement with Jeris. We must learn more about Jeris and how he was able to join the tribes."

When the meeting was over, one of the elite generals came over to Ursa and introduced herself.

"I'm General Cane, and I grew up in the settlements. Tomorrow after curfew, I will meet here with you and the protectors you will deploy. Have them ready to leave after our meeting, and make sure they are prepared to be gone at least three days."

General Cane's looks were different from the other generals, who mirrored Asha's tall, blond appearance.

General Cane was shorter with sandy-brown hair and hazel eyes. Her arms were tanned from spending time outside.

The following morning after Spider and Arris left for the spaceport, Ursa told Vega and Minor of their new assignment.

"How do we find a tribe, and how do we blend in?" Vega asked.

"General Cane will take you and have clothing for you like the tribes wear," Ursa explained. "She will meet us tonight after curfew, and the three of you will leave after the meeting. Now, let's get to our posts before the council arrives."

After curfew, the protectors waited for General Cane to arrive.

Ursa told Phoenix, "Asha has assigned two elite soldiers to help guard the council until Vega and Minor return."

"Will we be armed?" Vega was concerned about the recon on the tribes.

"There is no way you will go without weapons," Ursa said. "These tribes are wild and unruly. I've heard stories of fighting within tribes, and the tribes have always clashed with each other."

Vega let out a sigh. "Now I feel better." The scowl that had been on his face since hearing of the assignment lifted. He looked at Minor and grinned. "Now it sounds like fun, wild and unruly fun."

General Cane opened the door to the gym. She looked like she had been running. The general breathed out. "Sorry I'm late, but I needed to make sure my troops knew where to deploy while I'm away."

After Phoenix and Sirus left to assist with the night patrols, Ursa, followed by General Cane, Vega, and Minor, walked to the table and sat down.

"General Cane," Vega asked, "will you give us a little history of the tribes and tell us what to expect?"

General Cane looked at Vega. "You will be hard to disguise because of your size. The warriors are skinny but tough, like twisted wire. They don't respect anything and think they can take whatever they want. I remember them raiding the settlement where I came from. The only warning we'd have was the cloud of dust from their carriers. They would drive through the settlement, grab what they could, and be gone before the settlers could arm. You must understand that each settlement is like a small city.

"The tribes, like the inhabitants of the settlements, are the descendants of the settlers who moved away from the city to grow crops and raise livestock. When the majority of the settlers agreed to become part of the Velland trade system, those who were against the new regulations moved further away. With their opposition to any sort of rules or government, they were not able to get along or settle down or grow their own food. As their numbers grew, they separated into what they call tribes. Each tribe has a name, but I don't know them. They started calling the men *warriors*, but *raiders* is a better term. These are hardened men who don't care about anything but surviving, even at the expense of others' lives. You will be going to a place where you will need to be extra vigilant to stay alive."

"Sounds like forsaken," Minor said.

When the meeting was over, Vega and Minor were each given a gun and a wrist comm. General Cane was also given a wrist comm to stay in communication with them. Ursa did not want them to use the elites' communication devices in case the Dakon spies now had access to the system.

Outside, a small two-seat rover with large, knobbed tires waited.

"Sorry, but one of you will have to ride in the back. This is the best transport for off-road," General Cane explained.

Vega took the seat next to General Cane, and Minor sat behind them facing backward.

"You sure you can find your way off-road and in the dark?" Vega asked

"No problem. I grew up in the settlements and know my way around. I like the open country better than the city, which is why I volunteered for settlement protection." The general pulled her night vision goggles over her eyes and started the rover.

Phoenix and Sirus had returned from their patrol and now stood by Ursa as General Cane rode away with her two passengers.

"I'm not sure about Vega and Minor being on their own," Phoenix said.

Ursa looked worried. "They were the only ones that could be spared."

"Let's hope they stay out of trouble and make it back in one piece," Phoenix replied.

Ursa nodded her agreement, and Sirus said, "Those two will do fine. I think."

Spider and Arris sat at a table in a conference room in the VSF command ship while they waited for Leader

Mallas. He had specific orders to give to the ship crew and the soldiers who were assigned to protect the large Velland space dock. Mallas wanted to make sure that no ship landed at the dock without the proper paperwork, and each ship was to be inspected by the dock security team before it was allowed to unload its cargo. When Mallas returned to the command ship, they would depart for the planets of Fexnal and Bastik, where they would try to discover information that would lead them to Jeris.

The door to the room opened, and Illa walked in, followed by an older-looking man. He appeared scruffy, with a balding head and a protruding belly. Arris instantly did not trust this person and wondered who he was. Illa answered her unspoken question.

"Spider and Arris, I would like to introduce Rod Hinds, Cexion council emissary. Rod will meet with the councils on Fexnal and Bastik concerning the mining consortium's demands."

Rod seemed to be making an extra effort to be friendly as he smiled and nodded to Spider and Arris. "I am happy that you are part of the team," he said. "I know we will soon get matters resolved." He walked over to a table that held refreshments, filled a plate, and picked up a drink. He then sat down at the table and began to eat.

Arris could tell that Rod's words did not convey how he really felt. When Illa said she needed to return to the council, Arris followed her out of the room.

Once they were down the hall and could not be overheard, Arris asked, "Illa, will you give me some background on Rod, since he is joining the team?"

Illa paused before she replied, and Arris could tell she was trying to find words that did not say what she really felt.

"Rod would come to the council meetings when there were issues that concerned the docks. He was the dock security lead and managed the security team. Before that, he tried to join the VSF but was turned down. Rod posted for one of the council seats, and I was surprised when he was voted in. I was also surprised by who voted for him."

"What aren't you telling me?" Arris probed.

Illa sighed. "Father never really liked him. He once said that Rod had a reputation at the docks; if someone didn't agree with him, something always to happen to that person. He felt Rod wasn't to be trusted."

Silently Arris agreed with Illa's father's assessment of Rod and wondered if Rod was the link to Jeris and the reason he was able to get on Velland unnoticed.

Arris returned to the conference room, sat down by Spider, and signaled that they needed to talk.

Spider asked her, "Do you know how to reach the main deck? I would like to talk to the navigator."

Arris knew the request was a way to get them out of the room without Rod becoming suspicious. Once they were out of the room, Arris filled Spider in on what she sensed and on Illa's comments about Rod.

It was their second day, and they were on their way to Bastik. Spider and Arris sat alone and discussed the lack of information they'd found on Fexnal.

"Either Jeris is very devious or he has his spies in charge of the docks," Spider said. "I didn't find anything to show he has been on this planet. Everyone was cooperative, and I sent Kent what I found, but the data is lacking. The docks on Fexnal need to have someone in charge who will make sure the regulations are followed. It's for the planet's own good."

"At the council session I attended with Rod," Arris reported, "I did not sense anyone from Fexnal was being devious. The council members were shocked to learn of the attack on Cexion. Rod, however, did not accurately convey the mining demands but rather presented them in a way that made them seem like a good idea. I know he is the link to Jeris, but how do we get him to admit it?"

"I think it would take an extra dose of serum to get him to admit to anything," Spider said. "He has been at this game a long time. The best strategy with him is to assign someone to watch him and find out who he is meeting with. He could not have coordinated the Cexion attack and united the Dakons himself. Rod is more of an enforcer, someone to get people to cooperate, which makes me wonder if he threatened those who voted for him."

When the VSF command ship docked on Bastik, Leader Mallas and his crew did not receive a warm welcome. It was apparent that they were not wanted there. Spider and Arris hung back and left with Rod to attend the Bastik council meeting. Spider did not want to draw attention to himself or Arris, so they acted as Rod's assistants. From the greeting Rod received, it was apparent he was known on Bastik. He did not receive the glares that Mallas had. A rover awaited Rod to carry him and his assistants to the city.

On the ride, Spider told Arris to stay with Rod and get the names of those she sensed were aligned with him. Spider was going to sneak back to the dock and see what information he could find. In one of his pockets, packed in a small box, were pins he could use to "encourage" the dock workers to tell him what he needed in case they refused.

During the Bastik council meeting, it was apparent to Arris that the council members were not happy at having the VSF on site searching for clues concerning Jeris and the attack on Cexion. One member said that the Velland commander did not have the council's permission to investigate. Arris did not have to rely on her senses to get the feel of the council. When Rod presented the mining demands, every council member voted to go along with them. On the ride back to the space dock, Rod was in a jovial mood and didn't notice that Spider was missing.

When Leader Mallas stormed into the room where Spider and Arris were to meet privately with him, his ears were red, and if it were possible, his eyes would have popped out of his head.

"I can't believe it. Right under my nose!" he shouted.

As Mallas paced the room with fists clenched, Spider shrugged at Arris's questioning look. He had no idea what had upset Mallas.

Mallas opened a comm and yelled to the ship's crew, "Ready the ship for return to Velland." Only then did he acknowledge Spider and Arris seated in the room. He wiped his brow and turned to them. "I just found out that the shipbuilder on Velland is no longer there. His whole operation has been moved to Bastik. It was pure luck that I recognized the man when I was searching the city and followed him to his new building. All the orders the VSF had placed for ships have been scrapped. I had a team on Velland go look, and there is nothing left of his old shop. Even his home has been gutted, and his family are gone. I approached him and asked why I wasn't informed, and he said that it was his business and he could move it when he wanted. I almost choked the man. I'd thought he was to be trusted, so I hadn't followed up on our ship orders."

"That is concerning," Spider said. "Did you learn who he is building ships for on Bastik?"

"From what I could see, the ships resembled mining vessels." Mallas huffed.

"And his family, any sign of them on Bastik?" Spider asked.

Mallas shook his head.

"I suspect they could be living in one of the mining settlements," Spider said, "perhaps against their wishes. You need to find a way to meet with this builder in secret. He may have been forced to move his operation to keep his family alive. You need to find out how many ships of what kind he has delivered in the past year. We know who they were built for."

Spider's comm beeped. Kent had been able to get a message through, and from the data Spider sent, he'd determined that one spaceship seemed to be arriving without any paperwork. Kent found notes in the spaceport logs that referred to the spaceship as the *Dark Matter* and said it was assigned to the mining fleet. Kent found no record of who was on board or what cargo it carried. Spider closed his comm. This was the first solid link to Jeris.

CHAPTER 9

A PRISONER

It was a long, bumpy ride, and Minor, who was seated in the back, had to hold on to keep from being thrown out. General Cane kept the rover at a fast pace till they reached the ravine, where she stopped. There wasn't time for talking. At the speed General Cane drove, Vega had had to constantly watch ahead so they could avoid crashing into a boulder or running into a ravine. Dawn was fast approaching, and the opportunity for Vega and Minor to sneak into the distant camp would be lost once it was light out. Stiffly, Minor climbed from the back and joined Vega and General Cane as they looked over a small knoll through night vision goggles.

"Behind the pens are trees where you can hide. Once you're hidden, you can decide the best way to infiltrate the camp. As I said, the tribes are nomadic, and I don't think anyone keeps track of who is sleeping in camp. Try to avoid direct contact with the warriors. Especially you," General Cane said, gesturing at Vega.

Minor coughed. "What is that smell?"

"In the pens are the tribes' livestock. The long-haired cattle are used for milk and meat. The smaller animals are wild boar and goats that roam the hills. The warriors go on drives and chase the animals into these pens. Then they make camp around the pens until the animals are eaten, at which point they will build a pen in new area and go on another drive. They move the camp to the new area and leave all their stench and filth behind. You can find old camps like these all over the mountains." The general sounded disgusted.

In the distance, the dying embers of a few campfires still glowed. The camp consisted of huts, lean-tos, and tents. From where they stood, it was difficult to see anyone sleeping outside or in the lean-tos. Parked away from the camp were old, beat-up rovers and two-wheelers, but there were six military trucks close to the camp. Each could hold a dozen warriors. All of these trucks looked new and in good shape. Beside the largest tent sat a large rover like the one Asha drove.

"You need to hurry to reach the trees before dawn. Stay hidden as much as possible, because if you are captured, you will be killed," General Cane cautioned. "How will you signal me?"

"If you receive two beeps on your comm, come quickly. If you receive three beeps, come quicker," Vega answered. "And if you receive one beep …"

The general looked confused. "What does one beep mean?"

"We're dead."

Minor chuckled, but General Cane didn't. Humor was not encouraged within the elite ranks.

Minor looked at Vega and said, "I'm not sure how you are going to blend in. You could disguise yourself as a tent with legs, or I could put a blanket over your back and ride you in to camp."

"Or I could put a leash around your neck, and you could be my pet Minor," Vega growled.

General Cane shook her head as she started the rover to drive back to the nearest settlement to wait.

Vega and Minor reached the safety of the trees just as dawn lightened the sky. They had taken time to scout ahead in case the tribe had guards posted but had not seen any. When they'd neared the pens, though, a few of the long-haired cows had snorted at a new scent. Vega removed the robe he wore, took out his gun, inspected it, and secured it under his belt. Now that it was light, he could see the dark-colored markings that General Cane had drawn across Minor's face. Vega's face was also tattooed. After they made their small camp, Vega and Minor crawled to the edge of the trees to watch as the tribal camp awakened.

Logs were tossed into the main fire pit and quickly caught fire. Men and women came from the tents and lean-tos. There were three huts, and in front of each hut sat a well-armed guard. The huts seemed to be used for purposes other than sleeping. Vega motioned to Minor, pointed to the huts, and made the sign for weapons. One of the women walked up to a hut, and the guard stood up and moved aside to allow her to enter. They watched the woman come back out carrying a leg of meat and other foods to cook breakfast for the tribe. So, the huts were used to store weapons and food and were well-guarded.

It was easy to see why General Cane had described the men as "wiry." They were about Minor's height but weighed less. As some of the men pulled on ragged shirts, Vega could count their ribs. Activity increased around the camp as the men waited for their first meal of the day. Vega and Minor watched two men walk to a large tent. Words were spoken, but they were too far away to hear. Finally, the men were allow to enter the tent.

"That must be the tribe leader's tent," Vega whispered. "That is where we will find information, if there is any to be found."

The women cooked in pans hung over the fire, and the men stood around waiting. After the food was prepared, a platter was filled with meat and other foods and carried to the large tent. Then the men and children were fed. Vega and Minor retreated to the safety of the trees.

"The only guns I saw were carried by the guards. The men carry knives but no guns. Apparently, all firepower and food is kept locked inside the huts to control the tribe," Vega said.

"It's hard to tell the men from the women. They all wear the same ragged clothes, and everyone's face is tattooed. Even the children's faces are painted," Minor observed.

"How we are going to get inside that big tent?" Vega asked, worried.

Suddenly, something that sounded like a truck horn bellowed three times. Vega and Minor crept to the edge of the trees to see what was happening. There was mass movement in the camp. The women hurried inside the tents, taking the children with them. The men gathered around the fire pit. From the large tent walked a tall man dressed in a uniform. It was apparent he was the leader of the tribe, but he was not from the tribe. He had a military bearing in the way he walked and in his posture. The man stood in the front and spoke, but his words did not carry above the sounds of the animals. When the man turned and walked back to his tent, the other men formed a line in front of one of the huts.

"It looks like they are arming to raid," Minor whispered.

"When they leave, we can get in the tent," Vega said.

It wasn't long before one of the guards walked to the hut and opened the door. Standing in the doorway, he began to pass out guns as the warriors stepped forward. The guns were made for long-range shooting, and each warrior was given an extra cartridge of bullets. The number of armed warriors made Vega concerned, but he had no way to warn General Cane.

After the warriors received their weapons, they walked to the military trucks, climbed into the back, and sat down. In teams of two, guards climbed into the front of the trucks.

"One driver and one lookout for each truck," Vega said.

The uniformed leader walked from the large tent and climbed into the rover. He said something to his waiting driver, and the rover jumped to life and sped away, leaving a dust trail. The trucks, filled with armed warriors, formed a straight line behind the rover. Once out of the camp, the convoy headed in the opposite direction from the settlement where General Cane waited.

Minor exhaled. "At least they aren't headed toward the settlement."

"But where are they going armed for battle?" Vega wondered.

"Maybe training or target practice with their new weapons?" Minor guessed.

After the dust settled and the convoy was out of sight, Vega and Minor crept from their hiding place to the front of the pens. Silently, they watched the campsite. No one came outside, so they snuck into the camp, being careful not to cross in front of the tents but rather staying hidden behind them. The lean-tos were empty. They seemed to be used by the warriors who did not have families. They heard voices from inside the tents, but still no one came outside. With the warriors away, perhaps the women and children were ordered to stay inside until they returned.

Quickly, they reached the large tent. The two snuck around front and listened. Hearing no sound from inside, Vega lifted the flap and looked in. The tent was empty. He motioned Minor inside and then followed and lowered the flap behind him.

Vega was shocked. The tent was filled with communication devices. Tacked on boards were maps of each settlement. A list of the crops, along with the various animals, ran down the side. Written across the bottom were the numbers of men, women, and children, and this worried Vega more than anything.

Vega studied the equipment, trying to determine each one's purpose. He sat down in front of a station with a monitor and keypad. "Keep watch. I'm going to see if I can access any information. We only have a few minutes before we need to get out."

Minor moved to the back of the large tent where it was dark, listening for any sign that the warriors were returning.

After a couple of tries, a list of documents filled the screen. Vega gasped as he read the first one, and then he read the next one. Finally, he turned off the monitor and pushed back the keypad. He had just turned around to tell Minor they needed to get out when the tent flap opened and a guard stepped inside. The guard paused, giving his eyes time to adjust to the dark interior.

Vega stood up and faced the guard, who startled and pointed his gun at him. Vega started to tell Minor thanks a lot for warning him, but Minor began to fade. Vega cleared his throat to keep the guard looking at him, giving Minor time to blend with the tent.

"Jeris sent me to check on things," Vega said. It was the first thing that came into his head.

The mention of Jeris confused the guard, so the guard had met or knew of Jeris.

"If Jeris sent you, why aren't you wearing one of his uniforms?" The guard stepped closer to Vega and glared up at him. "Why are you dressed like a warrior with paint on your face?"

"My paint job looks better than your stupid face," Vega huffed, taking the guard by surprise because he did not show any fear. Even if Vega stood a head taller and was twice the man's size, the guard had a gun, and it was pointed at Vega.

Minor slowly stepped from the back of the tent.

"I should shoot you and feed you to the swine," the guard hissed at Vega.

Minor stepped behind the guard.

Vega shrugged. "If you feel the need."

The guard started to say something just as Minor delivered a chopping blow to both sides of his neck, causing the guard to collapse onto the floor, unconscious. Vega jumped forward and caught the gun before it hit the ground, stopping any chance of it firing, since it was still aimed at him.

"That was close. What are we going to do with him?" Minor whispered.

"Thanks for the warning." Vega just had to say it. "We could tie him up and question him later. He doesn't look heavy."

It didn't take long to tie the guard's arms and legs and gag his mouth. As quickly as possible, Vega and Minor carried their prisoner back to their camp. By the time they made it to the trees, the guard had started to squirm. After securing the guard to one of the trees, Vega and Minor heard the sound of motors. The caravan was rolling back into camp.

"Do you think they will miss the guard?" Minor asked.

"If General Cane is right, it will take some time before anyone is missed, unless this new leader has instituted a roll call. As soon as it's dark, we can signal General Cane. I need to get to Cexion and let Asha know about the settlements being tracked and what I read on the monitor." Vega removed his knife and held it to the guard's neck. "I'm going to remove your gag, and you are going to answer some questions."

The guard glared at Vega as he pulled the gag away. Before Vega could begin, the guard spit at him. Startled, Vega punched the guard on the side of his head, knocking him over. The guard moaned as Vega secured the gag once again. Question time was over.

When it became dark and the warriors found their beds, Vega sent General Cane three beeps. He and Minor would make their way to their meeting place as fast as they could. Vega was worried that the elites could not protect both the capital and the settlements with the tribes joined and the warriors armed.

"We can't leave him here. If he's found, he will tell the leader about us," Minor said.

"Let's feed him to the swine," Vega answered, making sure the guard heard. It earned him another glare. Vega leaned his face close to the guard's. "Can't spit with that gag in your mouth." Making a decision, Vega turned back to Minor. "Let's take him with us. He won't be missed before he tells us everything."

This caused the guard to violently shake his head from side to side.

Vega smirked. "I think our new friend would like a date with a spider."

Vega's comm beeped. General Cane was on her way. With the guard secured between them, Vega and Minor crept from their camp, leaving no sign they were ever there.

"I thought you had run into trouble," General Cane said when Vega and Minor reached the small knoll were she waited. She startled when she saw what they carried between them. The guard had given up his struggles and hung limply. He would not walk, making them carry him.

"Where are we going to put him?" General Cane asked when Minor said they were taking their prisoner to Spider.

"I have an idea." Vega picked up the guard and slung him over the hood of the rover. "We just need to secure his hands and feet to the fenders."

The guard struggled as his feet and hands were tied, and once he was secured, the general drove away in the dark.

General Cane giggled. "It feels like when I was a little girl hunting with my father. He would tie the animals he caught to the front of the rover to bring them home."

Before they reached the gym, Vega told General Cane to stop. He got out of the rover, took a sack, and tied it over the guard's head.

"I don't want this guy to see anything. The less he sees, the less he knows."

"It's a good idea, in case he escapes," General Cane agreed.

"No one is to know he is here except the protectors and Asha's staff. We don't know who is reporting to Jeris," Vega cautioned.

That evening, as he walked into the gym, Spider exclaimed, "Vega and Minor captured a prisoner?"

Asha walked beside him. "According to General Cane. And they have him secured in the gym. No one else knows about this, and we don't want it getting out. It could jumpstart something Jeris has planned, and we need time to figure it out."

"Nothing those two do should surprise me," Spider mumbled.

Asha couldn't hide her smile. "As soon as the other generals arrive, we can start the meeting."

Spider and Arris had returned from their trip with Leader Mallas, and Spider was waiting until the meeting to tell Asha what he had learned at the spaceports and the information Kent had discovered.

The protectors stood around the hooded man tied to a post in the corner of the gym.

"It was bring him or kill him and feed him to the swine," Vega explained when Ursa asked why they had brought the guard with them.

"Has he told you anything?" Ursa asked.

"No. He just spits a lot. I figured Spider would like a try," Vega answered, and Ursa sighed.

Asha called the meeting to order. The protectors and the elite generals were seated around the table. Leader Mallas was not present. He had other matters to attend to, and the first was to find out how the shipbuilder had been able to move his operation off planet without him knowing about it. He was also meeting with his ship captains to figure out a way to monitor the other planets' space docks without anyone being aware. In a private conversation, Spider had told Mallas not to trust Rod Hinds or the council on Bastik—and really not to trust anyone outside of his staff and Asha until the spies in Cexion were identified.

After Spider updated everyone about Jeris and his ship, the *Dark Matter*, he identified Rod Hinds as the spy on the Cexion council. Asha said she would assign two of her soldiers to follow Rod and find out who he was meeting with. The difficult part would be when Rod went to the docks. Spider said he would contact Mallas to make sure Rod was watched when he came to the space dock. Then the meeting was turned over to General Cane, Vega, and Minor.

When Vega told everyone about the settlements being mapped, down to crop, animal, and individual, the table went silent. When he told them what he'd seen on the monitor, gasps were heard. The document had listed four major tribes, numbered one through four, and underneath each tribe was a list of its warriors. Jeris had placed one of his men in charge of each tribe and provided guards, and he had equipped them with communication equipment like what Vega had seen in the tent. Every tribe now had the latest weapons and trucks to transport the armed warriors, and they could be activated whenever Jeris was ready to strike.

CHAPTER 10

DECEPTION

Spider had finished his "talk" with the Dakon guard that Vega and Minor had captured. The guard was now locked away in a secure room in the elites' compound, snoring loudly. Asha made sure only the elite soldiers, who would take turns watching the guard, knew about him. After locking the door, one of the elite soldiers mentioned that when the warrior woke up, he would not have any idea what had happened or where he was.

When the guard's hood had been removed and he'd seen Spider, any thought of spitting at this fierce-looking individual, the likes of whom he had never before seen, vanished. His eyes bugged when Spider removed the small pins from their case and told the warrior he had a few questions for him. Of course, the warrior, shaking with fear, refused, and Spider bit him with one of the pins. After the warrior willingly answered all of his questions, Spider bit him again. The second pin would erase his memory of the past few days. Spider had explained all this to the elite soldiers who had carried the unconscious guard to his private room.

The guard had been very talkative, and Spider had learned that Jeris had been coming to Velland for over two years, meeting with the tribes and forging an alliance with them. Jeris had promised the tribes control of the settlements and the profits from the distribution of crops and meat from the space dock to the other planets within Volan. The tribes would become very rich and the settlers their slaves. Each settlement had been infiltrated by Dakons posing as field hands, working the crops, and tending the animals. That had allowed them to gather information for Jeris.

Cexion, the beautiful capital of Velland, would be Jeris's new headquarters, from where he would rule the Volan Galaxy. Jeris had it all planned out. The Dakons would manage the settlements, and he had already gained control of the mining colonies without anyone being aware. The planet of Bastik was under his rule, and Fexnal would comply once they lost the protection of Leader Mallas and the Velland Space Fleet. With the new ships the builder had delivered, Jeris's fleet now equaled the VSF ships. When Jeris made his move to take over the Volan Galaxy, Leader Mallas would be caught off guard and easily defeated.

Asha and Spider received a secure communication from Mallas asking them to meet him on the command ship. It was dark, and the city was under curfew when Asha drove the rover to the space dock with Spider seated next to her. The large dock seemed eerily quiet as they walked to the command ship. They were careful not to talk so as not to give away their presence or allow anyone who might be watching them to overhear what was said. Once they gained entrance to the command ship, they were ushered to Mallas's private office, where he waited. Mallas pointed to the chairs across from his desk and began speaking before Asha and Spider sat down.

"Everything's in a scramble," Mallas exclaimed. "I secretly met with the shipbuilder and learned he is being watched by Jeris. If he doesn't do what he's told, he won't see his family again. It's like Spider said; his family has been taken to one of the mining colonies. The builder has delivered four ships to Jeris during the past two years, and none of them are mining vessels. They're all military."

Mallas paused and pounded his desk with his fist in frustration.

"I've lost one of our ships in the outer ring," he continued. "I sent two ships to scout the mining planets, and one has disappeared. The other ship finally gave up trying to locate the missing ship and came out of the ring to contact command and find out what to do. According to the commander, the three mining planets appeared to be operating normally, and they didn't see any sign of Jeris building an army. They were not allowed to dock on these planets because only mining vessels have permission. That doesn't make me feel comfortable after hearing of the builder's family being held prisoner.

"The missing commander was in an opposite orbit when he notified the second ship that he was seeing activity around the fourth small planet, which has never been colonized. He went to investigate and never returned. This small planet is surrounded by a black mist, so it's only speculation what happened. I sent the one ship back inside the outer ring to patrol between the planets and keep trying to contact our missing ship. Until I know more, I am not willing to send this ship into the black mist to investigate."

Mallas turned and poured himself a drink. Once refreshed, he continued.

"We did manage to sneak our own spies onto the docks in Fexnal and Bastik. It's like we thought. After dark, there is activity happening that is not being recorded. Both docks on Fexnal and the one on Bastik receive nightly communications in their shipping offices. This must be how Jeris is giving his orders and getting his new warships off planet. If the commanders did not seen any new ships on the mining planets, the ships must have been flown to the small planet, where they are hidden by the black mist. That is what I wanted to tell you without being overheard. Thanks for coming on short notice." He sighed loudly. "I'm not sure where to deploy the fleet, since I don't know what Jeris is planning or the number of fighting vessels he has. And now our fleet is down one military vessel."

After Mallas calmed down, Asha updated him on what had been discovered about the Dakon tribes—their alliance with Jeris and one of his soldiers being installed as leader in each of the four tribes; each tribe having communication equipment so Jeris can coordinate attacks; the tribes being heavily armed and having new military transports for the warriors; and Jeris's plans to give the settlements to the Dakons and make Cexion his headquarters to rule the Volan Galaxy.

Mallas now looked even more dazed and mumbled, "All of Volan is under attack. No planet is safe, and Cexion and the settlements are in jeopardy. How do we defend against multiple attacks?"

Spider had stayed silent throughout the meeting, listening and processing all the information. Now, he finally spoke.

"We take the fight to him."

Both Mallas and Asha stared at Spider. Neither knew what to say.

"We need to coordinate attacks against all four tribes at the same time and disable their communications with Jeris so he won't know what's happening. Then we need to take out their weapons and vehicles and the soldiers Jeris has put in charge. Without weapons and someone giving orders, I believe these tribes will scatter like they have always done.

"Each of the settlements must find out who is spying for Jeris and remove these threats. Once the Dakons are no longer a threat, Asha can concentrate on protecting Cexion against another attack, and I am certain Jeris is planning one. Anyone Rod Hinds has met with during the past days must be picked up and interviewed, and make sure Arris is there. If they are helping Rod, they must be dealt with.

"Velland and the other planets in Volan are in critical danger, and you, Leader Mallas, must prepare the VSF for a full-scale attack. Volan is at war, and we must act before Jeris does."

Spider looked at the alarmed faces of Asha and Mallas, knowing they were aware what would happen if they failed to stop Jeris. The fate of Volan was in their hands.

"We have a number of issues to deal with and not much time to put plans in place," Asha told her generals, who were seated around the table.

The meeting had been set up in secret and was not listed on any of the generals' schedules. Spider and the protectors had joined the meeting after making sure the council members arrived home before curfew.

"We have had Rod Hinds under watch since learning of his deception and have a list of everyone he has met with. Tomorrow, General Linn will have these individuals picked up and brought to headquarters to be interviewed. She will say it's about elite recruitment, as all of these men have daughters. This should not cause Rod any concern when he hears about the interviews. General Linn will conduct the interviews and ask each one about Jeris to determine his reaction. Arris will be in the meeting acting as a scribe, and she will know if their answers are truthful. If these men are innocent, they will be released, but if they are working with Jeris they will be detained until we find out the extent of their involvement.

"Illa has made a list of the citizens who voted Rod onto the council, and she has set up a meeting with them tomorrow before the council meets. Arris will be in the room standing guard. Again, the meeting agenda is a ruse to get these individuals away from Rod and find out if they or their families were threatened in any way. If any of them are working with Rod to overthrow Cexion, they will also be detained. This is the first step toward determining the number of spies Jeris has reporting to him and the extent of the breach in Cexion.

"After curfew, Rod goes to the space dock shipping office. There he reports what he has learned to Jeris. We have given Rod false information to pass along, which he has done. Leader Mallas has installed listening devices in the office, and a copy of anything Rod inputs into the data logger is sent to the command ship. Rod is under constant surveillance until we decide to bring him in and charge him with treason.

"We have learned that the Dakons have spies in each of the settlements. In secret, General Cane has contacted the settlement leaders and told them about the spies. Once identified, these spies will be captured and brought to elite headquarters for questioning.

"Now for the real purpose for this meeting. We need to develop a plan to attack all four Dakon tribes simultaneously in two days."

Asha waited for the generals to recover. Only General Cane looked pleased at the announcement.

After Asha brought the generals current on all the information about the tribes, she said, "Spider and General Cane will be in charge of planning and coordinating the attacks. The Alpha and Beta protectors, along with twenty of General Cane's soldiers that are familiar with the tribes, will make up the team. With the tribes no longer a threat, the elites will be able to concentrate on protecting Cexion and its citizens. Leader Mallas and I are aware that Jeris will attack Velland and try to take Cexion for his headquarters, and we must be prepared."

One of the generals raised her hand. "From the count we received, it will be our thirty fighters against three hundred Dakon warriors. That is poor odds and does not offer much of a chance for success."

Ursa looked across the table at the general. "That sounds like a fair fight, actually"

Spider and the other protectors nodded their agreement. Asha glanced proudly at her sister, but only Arris noticed.

After the meeting was over, the protectors returned to their sleeping area in the gym and discussed their mission with Spider.

"Black Snake? That's a scary name. If all the leaders Jeris put in charge of the tribes are as mean as our prisoner said Black Snake is, it's no wonder the tribes are cooperating," Minor said after being told by Spider to make sure Jeris's soldiers in charge of the tribes don't get away.

"When we saw him at the camp, the warriors did what they were told," Vega added.

"I'm glad Spider will be the one going against Black Snake," Minor admitted.

As everyone climbed into their bedrolls, Ursa looked around and asked, "Where's Sirus?"

No one answered, but Vega's expression caused Ursa to stare at him.

"You know something."

Vega shook his head in denial. "My mind is a blank."

"Finally something we can agree on," Ursa said, causing Minor to laugh and Arris to hide her smile. No one wanted to tell Ursa that Sirus was meeting with Asha.

"Get a good night's sleep, everyone," Phoenix said. "Tomorrow will be busy with all the interviews, helping Spider finish building the communication blockers, and packing our gear to be ready to leave after curfew."

It was late into the night when Arris sensed Sirus enter the gym. As much as Vega teased her about needing her sleep, it seemed her senses didn't need that much. When Vega went to sleep, it was lights out, and nothing could wake him, not even his own snoring.

CHAPTER 11

STEALTH

Eight desert-ready rovers were loaded and ready to leave after curfew. Spider did not want to alert anyone of their leaving; he was unsure about the spies' ability to keep watch on the elites' compound.

They'd learned from the interviews that had taken place that day that all but two of the men who had voted for Rod for the new council had been threatened. They'd been told that if they didn't vote for him, their families would have an accident. The two remaining men, who were part of Jeris's network of spies, were now detained in individual cells in the elites' compound. Arris had shivered when she'd sensed these men's hatred toward Illa. When Illa had questioned them about Jeris, both men had vehemently denied knowing him, trying their best to make Illa believe them. These two men had been given a special assignment, or so Illa had reported to the council with Rod in attendance. Their special assignment was to be questioned by Spider, but only a few knew about it. Rod had had a smug look on his face after hearing Illa's report, certain he would have more information to pass on to Jeris.

It had turned out that the men Rod had met with in Cexion and at the space dock were allies of his, but they were not aware of Jeris or of Rod's deception. Arris had been able to sense these men's confusion when General Linn questioned them about Jeris, although they had admitted to passing information to Rod. One man had stated that it was safer to do what Rod asked than to refuse.

That evening, Spider gave the protectors instructions on the correct way to set up the communication blockers he had built. It was the first thing that must be done when they reached the camps, and the blockers needed to be near the main tents when they were activated. There was no way for Spider to test the blocking range for the equipment Jeris had installed.

The day before, Asha had sent her own spies to each of the camps to gather needed information. Now, each team knew where the huts were located, which huts to target, where the main tent with the communication equipment was located, and the number and location of all the new military vehicles. Spider and General Cane used this information to finalize their plans.

The four teams were ready, and Spider had gone over the details with them again in order to coordinate the attack. Team one consisted of Spider, Arris, and five elite soldiers; team two was General Cane, Vega, and five elites; team three was Phoenix, Minor, and five elites; and team four was Ursa, Sirus, and five elites. The team members were all dressed in desert-camouflage fatigues, and their pockets were filled with flash bombs and extra ammo. Everyone carried two weapons, one long rifle and one pistol. Spider wanted to ensure they were armed for any situation. They would run silent and dark and had night vision goggles slung around their necks.

General Cane had met with her soldiers, giving them specific instructions about which huts to set the explosives on. One of the soldiers had questioned the orders, asking why they didn't blow up the food as well. These were the enemy that had killed their comrades in the deadly trap. General Cane had said she understood the feeling but that women, children, and the food supply were not the mission's targets. She'd told them that the warriors were not armed, except the few guards at each camp, and said to only open fire on the warriors if they were attacked. If given the chance to escape, the warriors would run away and not stand and fight. This would help to even the overwhelming odds.

"Remember," Spider said, "one beep when your communication blocker is activated. When all four camps communications are blocked, I'll send two beeps to signal you to begin placing explosives on the huts and trucks. Team leads, make sure all the explosives are in place before you set them off. When that happens, be ready to breach the main tent and take out the leader. Elites, don't take any chances after the explosives have taken out the weapons and military vehicles. If the warriors try to fight, defend yourself. If one of the teams run into trouble, signal me with multiple beeps. I'll open a link and determine how to help. These camps are not close, and it may take an hour before I can get you help. Follow the plan and do not deviate. Does everyone understand?" Spider looked around making sure everyone was prepared. It was a huge task, but surprise was on their side.

The rovers drove single file away from the compound. They would run together for about an hour and then separate, each team heading to the camp they would attack. General Cane and the elites drove the rovers and were skilled in off-roading. Vega sat next to General Cane, comfortable with her driving in the dark, unlike during the first trip. The rovers made little noise, their engines muffled. There was faint light from the night sky, which hid their departure from Cexion and would hide their approach to the camps.

Asha and the other generals had seen them off, making comments like "Good hunting," and "Stay safe," and "Watch your six," as they drove away.

Asha had walked to the rover where Ursa and Sirus were seated and said, "Come back safe." Both Ursa and Sirus had nodded to Asha. Arris had wondered which of the two the comment had actually been for and then decided it had been for both.

Arris was now seated behind Spider in the rover and could sense his concern. It wasn't worry. The protectors were trained for what lay ahead. The elite soldiers were also more than ready to take revenge on the tribes, and she couldn't blame them.

Spider and General Cane were certain their plan would work. The major concern was Jeris's commanders. That was the reason they were to enter the main tents in teams of two. After learning of the cruelty of Black Snake, Spider was concerned that the commanders would have set traps for their protection. Black Snake had once shot one of the warriors for no other reason than to install fear within the tribe. Spider personally knew this type of fear would only last so long before the warriors would want revenge.

The two rovers slowed and came to a stop behind a small knoll. The elite drivers signaled for everyone to get out. They would go on foot from here. Spider untied the communication blocker and lifted it from the back of the rover. He placed it on the ground, pulled two straps from his belt, and secured them around the device to serve as handles. He and Arris would carry the blocker into camp while the elites made ready the explosives. Two elites would place explosives around the huts filled with weapons, and the other three would do the same for the military trucks. It was the quiet just before dawn when the raiding party crept toward the sleeping enemy camp.

They made no sound and moved in the dark, so no one noticed the team approach the camp. Spider halted and signaled to the elites to stay hidden until the blocker had been activated. Then he and Arris continued into the camp. It was easy to make out the large tent. Spider stopped and motioned to Arris to ask if she could sense others. She motioned no. When they were within a few steps of the large tent where Black Snake was sleeping, Spider took a couple of minutes to set up and activate the blocker. Then, he and Arris crept back from the tent. Spider had not seen any motion sensors, but that didn't mean Black Snake did not have them hidden closer to his tent.

The silence felt ominous, and it seemed to Arris that they waited forever. Spider watched his comm for the signal from the other teams. Finally, he receive the third beep. All the blockers were activated. Spider sent two beeps to each of the team leads. He then motioned to the waiting elite soldiers to place the explosives. When all the explosives were in place, they would set them off in unison, creating havoc in the camp and giving Spider and Arris time to meet Black Snake.

The sudden booming explosion, which shook the camp and set fire to the weapons huts, made Arris jump. Spider leaped toward Black Snake's tent, not trying to hide his approach. Arris hurried after him as one by one the military trucks exploded. Spider was already inside the tent when Arris reached it. There was no sound from inside, and this worried her.

The camp was now awake with warriors shouting, women screaming, and frightened children crying. Arris knew the elite soldiers had found cover and were ready to fight off any attacks by the warriors. The elites would stay hidden, waiting to see what the warriors would do.

Slowly, Arris lifted the flap of the tent and looked inside. Spider and Black Snake were circling the inside of the dark tent, each holding a knife. It looked like the death dance by two Cillian vipers she had watched during protector training. The lesson had been about how animals could instinctively recognize their enemy and fight to the death to protect their own. One of the vipers had invaded the nesting place of the other with the intent of eating the eggs in the nest. It had been a violent, hissing battle as the mother protected her eggs.

Black Snake looked bigger, but Spider was crouched low as he matched Black Snake's steps. Arris aimed her gun, ready to shoot the snake, but sensed Spider telling her to wait. This was a battle between two fierce soldiers, both willing to fight to the death.

Arris crouched at the tent opening, ready to shoot any warrior that tried to breach its entrance. From the noisy din outside, consisting in part of the elites firing their weapons, it seemed the warriors had troubles of their own.

Black Snake swung his arms as he circled, waiting for the chance to cut Spider. Spider stayed crouched in their circle dance of the tent. Suddenly, the snake struck, and Spider leaped aside, taking the snake by surprise. Black Snake had never encountered an opponent like this one before. He snarled as he turned to face Spider across the tent, and Spider jumped feet first. The impact was hard enough to knock the snake to the ground, causing him to drop his knife. Black Snake scrambled to reach his knife to continue the fight, but he was not fast enough. Spider struck, and the snake withered on the tent floor before dying.

Spider made sure the man was dead and then quickly gave Arris orders. "Destroy all of the equipment and set fire to the tent. We don't know what other devices Black Snake may have hidden. Then, go help the elites. I need to watch for signals from the other teams."

Spider ran from the tent as Arris sprayed bullets at the equipment Jeris had setup, shattering all of it to pieces. She pulled a fire stick from her belt and broke off the top. Flames erupted from its end. She threw the stick onto the cot where Black Snake had slept and watched the blankets catch fire. Flames reached for the tent sides. Satisfied, she lifted the flap, looked around, and ran toward two of the elites crouched behind the main fire pit.

The tribe was making a mass exodus from the camp. The women carried some of the children and led others by the hand, escaping the billowing smoke from the fire that had engulfed the ammunition hut. The guns and ammo stored inside began to explode, and it sounded like a fierce battle was taking place.

Over the noise of the exploding weapons, Arris could hear the cough of motors. The old, beat-up rovers were being started. Each rover's engine sputtered in protest at carrying double the number of riders in the escape. A couple of the armed guards took aim at the elites but were shot first. With the guards down, the warriors knew their knives did not stand a chance against the elites' firepower. They also realized that they were being allowed to escape, along with their families.

When the camp emptied out, Arris and the five elite soldiers made sure all of the weapons and military trucks were destroyed, never to be used again. The few tents that had not caught fire were searched. All of the animals had escaped. Panicked from the explosions, the animals had broken down their pens and run to safety.

One hut remained standing. It was filled with various foods for the tribe. The elites helped themselves to a few of the vegetables that only grew in the desert and were never served at meals in the compound. Arris took a bite from one of the purple gourds and made a face; it tasted bitter to her.

Arris looked around the campsite. The silent attack had been a success and had gone as Spider had planned, but what about the other teams. Arris hurried to find Spider.

Spider had opened a link and was taking to Phoenix. "Are you sure she can make it back to the compound?"

"Yes. Minor did a good job stopping the bleeding. The bullet is still in her shoulder, but she is stable," Phoenix said.

"Watch for the coordinates from General Cane, and we'll meet you there," Spider replied.

"We'll be there."

Spider turned to Arris and the five elite soldiers and said, "Good job."

"What about the other teams?" Arris quickly asked.

"All teams completed their tasks and reported that the warriors scattered as expected. One elite soldier on Phoenix's team was shot, but her wounds are not fatal. She'll be able to return to the compound."

On hearing Spider's words, Arris and the other elites all breathed a sigh of relief.

Ursa's team was the last to reach the area where they were to meet so they could travel back to Cexion together.

When the rovers stopped and everyone stepped out, General Cane announced, "Elites assemble."

Instantly, the elite soldiers formed a line in front of their general, even the soldier that was wounded.

"Soldiers, I could not be prouder of you. The odds were not in our favor on this mission, but each of you was willing to go. You have performed beyond expectation, and I thank you. Now, let's go home."

The elites proudly saluted their general, broke ranks, and returned to the rovers for the victory ride home.

Spider closed his comm and looked at the protectors. "Asha said good work. She will meet us when we return."

"What about the tribes? Is anyone going to keep watch on them?" Minor asked.

General Cane came over at that moment and said, "It will take them a while to regroup, especially without threats from Jeris's commanders. I will suggest a recon be set up to watch them, but for now, the Dakons are no longer a threat."

"Did anyone have trouble taking out Jeris's commanders? You should have seen the look on our guy's face when he saw Sirus enter the tent. I thought he was going to cry and not fight." Ursa laughed.

General Cane spoke first. "Vega dispatched ours quite quickly." She grinned at, Vega who grinned back.

"Phoenix didn't ask any questions before he fired," Minor said.

"Good job, everyone," Spider said. "Let's get back to Cexion. Taking out the Dakons was the easy part; Jeris is another kind of trouble."

CHAPTER 12

BATTLE PLANS

The meeting was after curfew in the back of the gym. That afternoon, Mallas had sent an urgent message to Asha asking her to schedule the meeting. He had received a distress signal from the men he had watching the spaceports on Fexnal and Bastik. When he'd tried to contact his men, all communication had been blocked on both planets.

After receiving Leader Mallas's urgent message, Asha gave orders to have Rod Hinds picked up. The time for his deception had come to an end. When the elites watching his house went to arrest him, Rod wasn't there. Somehow, Rod had found out he was being watched and had slipped away unseen. Rod had not gone to the space dock, or else his entry would have been reported to Mallas. VSF soldiers were now in control of dock security, replacing Rod's old crew.

Mallas looked more harried than the last time Arris had seen him. The stress of worrying about multiple attacks from Jeris's warships—and not knowing where or when these attacks would occur—was taking its toll on the VSF leader. Mallas had two of his commanders with him, and they were seated on each side of him. Asha and the elite generals were there, along with Spider and the Alpha and Beta protectors. There were no empty chairs around the long table.

"When Jeris lost contact with the Dakons, he probably alerted Rod, and Rod went into hiding," Spider suggested when Asha reported that Rod had disappeared.

"What concerns me is that we don't know if there are others in Cexion that are helping Jeris," Asha replied. "And Rod must have had a hiding place set up."

"What we do know is that the spaceports on Bastik and Fexnal are now under Jeris's control," Mallas said. "He had men on both planets waiting to take over when given the signal. The soldier that was watching the Fexnal dock was able to secure a transport and get off planet thanks to one of the Fexnal council members. When the dock was seized, the council member was there and almost killed. Our soldier rescued him, and both escaped. When the soldier admitted he was spying for me, the council member took him to his private dock and told him to take his ship. The council member has sent a message asking for help. Apparently, the Fexnal council does not agree with what Jeris is doing."

"Should we close our dock until we know more about what Jeris is planning?" General Linn asked.

"That will be difficult; there are ships from the other planets waiting to dock and unload. Also, we need to ship food and other goods on schedule before they expire and become unusable. Completely closing the Velland dock would affect all of Volan," Mallas answered.

"Do you dare send part of the fleet to Fexnal and take back the port from Jeris's men?" Spider asked.

"At this time, without knowing the current situation at the docks or what firepower Jeris has installed there, I'm not willing. We also don't know the situation in the city or know if the Fexnal security team is still under council control," Mallas admitted.

Spider outlined the situation. "First, we must make sure that Cexion and Velland are safe. After they are secure, we can figure out how to free Fexnal. Jeris has had Bastik under his control for a while, so that will be a harder task. Finally, I would send a discovery team to the outer ring and find out the situation on each planet. You will have to defeat Jeris one planet at a time. He has had time to infiltrate the planets and set up his own army, making him hard to defeat."

"The settlements are safe, and the elites will protect Cexion. This frees the VSF to battle Jeris's fleet for control of Volan," Asha said.

Mallas nodded to Asha and the elite generals. "I'll have my commanders develop a plan prioritizing Velland first, Fexnal second, Bastik third, and the outer ring last. It will be a huge undertaking, but we can do this if you feel Cexion will be safe."

"We've got this," Asha firmly replied, and her generals agreed.

The meeting adjourned with Mallas telling Spider, "Your input will be welcome in designing a strategy to battle Jeris and his warships to free Volan."

Spider agreed to join Mallas and his commanders in the morning on the command ship. First, though, he needed to meet with the protectors. Asha would need their help to defend Cexion.

Spider had altered two of the communication blockers used against the Dakons so that they would beep when near any device emitting a high-voltage signal. If Rod was in contact with Jeris—and Spider had decided that was why Rod had gone into hiding—he would need a strong, high-voltage signal like the one used at the space dock. The plan was for Vega and Sirus to drive through the city with the modified blockers and search for a signal. When they found the signal, they were to track it to the source and stop it. Vega would search half of Cexion, and Sirus the other half.

Asha was deploying the main body of the elite soldiers along the two main roads into Cexion. The plan was to allow Jeris's army to come so far and then block the road behind and in front of the mercenaries while the elites attacked— the same trap that the Dakons had used. Following Spider's suggestion, metal shields were being hidden along both sides of the road to give the elite soldiers added protection. Spider was serious when he told Asha to plant bombs in the road and set them off after the road was blocked. He knew Jeris would bring every weapon at his disposal; Jeris had plans to make Cexion his new headquarters, and he would come prepared.

The council had been alerted to the coming attack. Using the emergency protocols, they warned every citizen of Cexion to quickly make their way to the underground dome when the alarm sounded. The dome was being prepared for another attack; drinks, food, medical supplies, and folding cots were now stored inside. Many of the people volunteered to help with the preparations, vividly recalling the first attack.

The protectors were dressed in their Nebula uniforms and openly carried weapons. They had positioned themselves around the room where the council was meeting. When council leader Daji Adain told the others about Rod, some members were shocked but not many. Those who had known Rod for years weren't surprised at his betrayal.

One of the elite generals presented the protection plan to the council, and one of the council members asked, "What if the elites can't hold off an attack? What will happen then?"

Ursa was in the room and stepped forward. "Once everyone is inside the dome, it will be sealed from the inside. The protectors will defend Cexion alongside the elites. Don't forget, the VSF will be protecting the space dock, and Jeris's army may never make it to the city."

The looks on the council members' faces ranged from doubtful to hopeful after hearing Ursa's words.

It was almost time for the curfew to begin when Sirus stopped the rover. His legs had started to cramp up, so he stepped out and stretched. Both he and Vega had been driving around since morning, circling the streets of Cexion looking for Rod and waiting for the device to beep that it had picked up a signal.

Sirus contacted Vega via his wrist comm. "Have you found anything?"

"Nothing so far," Vega's voice came back. "I'm beginning to wonder if Rod is running scared and not in contact with Jeris."

"Could be the situation. I'll circle a few more times and then head in."

"I'll do the same."

Sirus was tired as he turned the rover down the last road before he headed back to the compound. The device next to him suddenly beeped, causing him to jerk the steering wheel to one side and run the rover off the road. He grabbed the device to keep it from tumbling out of the vehicle.

The device beeped again. Sirus looked around. He was in the outskirts of the city, and buildings were scarce. He studied each of the buildings. All were either shut down for curfew or boarded up, not being used. There was one building with all the windows boarded up and the front door tightly shut but with a faint light flickering through the cracks around an upstairs window.

Sirus picked up the device and walked toward the building. The closer he came, the quicker the beeps sounded. Sirus set the device on the ground and turned it off. If this was where Rod was hiding, he didn't want to signal his approach.

The area was dark, which helped to hide his approach. Sirus decided to verify that it was Rob before he signaled Vega. Silently, he ran to the building. The front door had boards nailed across it to stop anyone from getting inside. He crept around to the back of the building. A small door in back had recently been used, from the scuff marks on the ground. Sirus remove his gun and opened the door.

When he entered the back of the building, he could hear voices filtering down from above and then footsteps coming down the stairs. There were at least two others in the building.

When a man reached the bottom of the stairs, Sirus stepped out and said, "Stop where you are."

The man startled at seeing Sirus and yelled to someone above, "We've been found. Send the signal." Then he pulled a weapon.

But before he could shoot, Sirus shot him and bolted up the stairs, taking them three at a time. He had to reach the man in the room above before he could send the signal.

The upstairs had been furnished with a table and chairs. Two cots were pushed against the wall. Stacks of garbage gave the room a stench; the hideout had been in use for a while. In a small room off to one side, Sirus spotted Rod rapidly entering data into a communication device like the Dakons had used.

"Stop what you're doing and place your hands on your head," Sirus warned.

Rod didn't pause in his effort, so Sirus rushed forward and knocked Rod to the floor.

Rod wiped blood from his nose and smirked. "You're too late to stop the attack."

"You traitor," Sirus growled and hit Ron on the side of his head, knocking him out cold.

Sirus hurried to the communication device. Whatever Rod had been typing had been sent, and the device was now idle.

Sirus opened a comm line to the protectors. "I have Rod in custody, and the device he was using to contact Jeris is the same as those the Dakons used. The only thing Rod said was that I was too late to stop the attack."

Asha's voice came from the comm; she still wore the one Spider had given her. "Where are you?" Sirus gave his location, and Asha said, "I'll be right there."

Rod Hinds sat cuffed in one of the elites' rover, leaning to one side and moaning. When asked about the attack, he just mumbled, "Too late." That was all they were able to get from him. Rod would be taken to the compound and locked away with the other traitors.

Asha looked down at the man Sirus had shot. "He looks familiar, perhaps from the dock."

"He's been here for some time and was the main contact for Jeris. Rod was just a gofer doing Jeris's errands," Sirus said.

The soldier manning the elite communication center called Asha on her communicator. She sounded panicked as she reported.

"Commander, I just received an urgent message from the space dock. A trade ship from Bastik was given clearance to land after all paperwork was confirmed, but when the ship entered to dock, it continued to where the road into Cexion separates. According to the dock security lead, the ship hovered and dropped military vehicles with parachutes to the ground. The vehicles split up at the crossroad, and there are a dozen vehicles carrying armed soldiers on each road headed for Cexion."

"Sound the alarm to warn the citizens to get underground and alert the generals to prepare for the attack," Asha quickly ordered. Then she rushed from the building with Sirus following. She turned to Sirus. "You need to join the protectors."

Sirus looked at Asha and shook his head. "I'm staying by you."

Asha could tell there would be no way to change his mind and stated, "I'm proud to have you fight beside me."

When the emergency siren sounded, all the street lights in Cexion were lit, and residents of the city crowded the streets to reach the underground shelter. The protectors had gathered at the broad entrance to the path that ran downward to the dome's doors, which were wide open.

"It's like organized panic," Minor noted as the people rushed down the streets to reach safety.

"As soon as the last of the residents are inside, Daji will signal and seal the entrance," Ursa told the other protectors.

"Take your assigned positions and hold them unless you receive an order from me or Ursa," Phoenix ordered.

"We're ready," Vega responded, noting that there were only the five of them. Sirus had not returned.

CHAPTER 13

THE BATTLE BEGINS

"Take out that transport. Don't let it get away," Mallas barked to his fleet. He was angry at having been deceived by Jeris and having given the transport from Bastik clearance to land. He turned to the lieutenant standing beside him on the bridge of the command ship. "Contact dock security and close the dock. Tell them to send all transports back to their home ports until further notice. No vessel will be allowed inside Velland space, no exceptions. Any ship entering Velland space will be shot down."

The soldier sitting at the communication station turned in his seat to face Leader Mallas. "Defender Two is giving chase with orders to shoot. If the vessel reaches Bastik space, what are your orders?"

"Tell Commander Reel that the ship had better not reach Bastik space," Mallas growled, his face red with frustration.

"Yes sir," the communication specialist responded.

"What is the status of the fleet?" Mallas asked his second in command.

"Defenders One, Three, and Four are hovering above Cexion. Defender Two is giving chase to the vessel from Bastik. Defender Five has gone back inside the outer ring to locate the missing Defender Six. That's our current status, sir," the lieutenant responded.

"Sir, Commander Reel is reporting that the vessel from Bastik is no longer a threat and will not reach Bastik space." The communication specialist grinned.

"Finally, some good news," Mallas huffed.

"Sir, are we to stay docked or join the defenders?" the lieutenant asked.

Mallas thought before he answered. "Until I figure out what Jeris's next move is, we'll stay in port. Make sure all of the defenders are on full alert. There are no limits to Jeris's deception."

"Sir, I have a request from Commander Asha," the specialist said. "She is asking to have Spider contact the Nebula protectors. They haven't been able to reach him."

Mallas shook his head and replied, "Spider left the command ship when he heard about the attack on Cexion. I've had no contact with him since."

"Thank you, sir. I'll relay this to the elite commander." The specialist turned back around and sent the message.

Mallas paced the bridge. "I hate waiting around for something to happen."

"The wait may be over, sir." The communication specialist looked stunned. "Defender Five has sent a message from the ring, or just outside of it. It's garbled from interference, but Commander Ternek reports that seven warships have left the ring and are heading our way."

Leader Mallas took a deep breath. "Lieutenant, prepare the command ship for departure. Notify the fleet commanders of the situation and tell them to assume a defense formation to protect Velland. We will join them and coordinate the fleet's defense against the coming attack. I'm sure Jeris knows he outnumbers us by two warships, and that's the reason he's attacking now."

"How much time do we have?" the lieutenant asked.

"I would guess less than a day with the latest hyper technology," Mallas replied.

After all of the residents reached the underground dome, Daji sent Ursa a message that he was securing the doors. The doors could only be opened from the inside, unless Jeris's soldiers used explosives to blow them open. Ursa responded to say she received the message and updated the protectors.

Each of the protectors' wrist comms beeped, and Sirus said, "I'm with Asha guarding the entrance to Cexion. Leader Mallas responded that Spider left the command ship when he heard about the attack on the city. No one has heard from him. The elites watching the road have signaled that the military trucks have crossed the first defense line. When the last truck crosses, the roads will be sealed ahead of and behind the trucks. If the invaders break through the defenses, I'll signal you. Stay alert."

"How do we keep getting ourselves in the middle of wars?" Vega grumbled. "I thought we were protectors and protected individuals."

"Isn't that what we're doing, only on a larger scale?" Minor responded.

"I just hope this scale isn't too large. If Jeris's attackers break through the barriers, the five of us won't be able to hold them off for very long," Vega said.

"Stay behind cover and don't expose yourself," Phoenix ordered. "It's our best option. If we break cover and try to get away, the open area will make us easy targets."

Sirus could hear the roar of the trucks before he saw them. He watched from behind the barrier, and Asha stood beside him, waiting for the signal to close off the roads. As the first truck rolled by, Sirus knew that Jeris had his soldiers well prepared and wondered where Jeris had learned military strategy. He must have had specialized training to pull off what he had been doing the past few years and do it without being discovered.

The invaders were heavily armed and wore protective vests. Each military vehicle had metal shielding surrounding it, protecting the wheels and engine. A dozen men were in the back of each truck, and none had seen the elites hidden along both sides of the road. Asha was in charge of the elites on this road, and General Linn was in charge of those on the other road.

Asha's comm vibrated, and she opened a link.

"The final truck has passed the barrier. Both roads are ready to seal off," the elite in the communication center reported.

Asha sent the signal to deploy the barriers and block the roads.

The military convoy did not slow but continued down the road. Sirus knew they must have heard the heavy barriers being moved into place. The scraping noise rose above the sound of the engines. He and Asha ran up the road, staying hidden behind the barriers, and stopped before they were exposed. Elite soldiers hid behind the barriers. Each one was armed, but none had the protective vests the invaders wore.

The lead truck slowed finally as it approached the barrier, which was made of heavy metal railing that the trucks could not break through and wire mesh to stop the soldiers from crawling between the rails. When the lead truck stopped, so did the convoy.

"Elites, open fire," Asha ordered, and the elites stepped up to the barriers and began firing at the men in the trucks.

Sirus watched as the elites shot at the men and told Asha, "Tell your soldiers to aim for the head, arms, and legs. Their bullets are being deflected by the vests."

The elites' bullets were not deterring the invaders.

"Blow the bombs," Asha ordered.

A dozen bombs exploded along the road, knocking over three of the trucks. The invaders scattered and began to fire back at the elites, but their bullets were deflected by the barriers. Sirus heard one of the invaders shout, "Engage grenades." He watched as half of the soldiers stopped firing and removed grenades from behind their vests, which they began throwing behind the barriers.

Sirus yelled to Asha, "Tell the elites to move back."

The first of the grenades exploded amid a group of elites.

"Get the medics!" Sirus yelled as he raced toward the barrier.

Every elite behind the barrier had been injured. The ones not badly hurt were trying to carry the more seriously injured away from the rain of grenades. Sirus raced up, picked up two unconscious elites, and ran. When away from the grenades' reach, he laid the wounded soldiers on the ground and returned to help the rest of the injured escape.

Medics in rovers rolled up and began to treat the wounded. Sirus looked at the injured elites and could tell many were in critical condition. If they lived, it would be without an arm or a leg. He could do no more for these elites, so he ran back to where Asha watched.

"It looks like they are reading a rocket to fire at the barricade!" Asha exclaimed.

"You can't let them fire the rocket. If they breach the barrier, they will get inside the city," Sirus shouted. "Have the elites aim at the men in the back of the lead truck."

Asha gave the order, and the elites moved to higher ground, where the grenades could not reach. Using long-range rifles, they began to fire at the lead truck, taking aim at places where the enemy's armor didn't reach. The invaders began to stumble from their wounds. They took cover beneath the truck, and stopped readying the rocket to launch.

"Do you have rockets or anything powerful enough to blow the trucks?" Sirus yelled to Asha.

Asha shook her head. "We've never had a reason. Our enemy has always been the Dakons, and guns and rifles were enough to keep them away."

As the battle raged, Sirus began to worry. Asha pointed down the road at three trucks coming fast. At the barrier, the lead truck and the one behind it turned and drove to each side of the road.

Asha pointed. "What are they planning?"

"They're making a shield for the middle truck," Sirus answered.

The soldiers in the side trucks stood up and lifted the metal plates to create a shield to protect the soldiers in the middle truck, who were getting ready to launch a rocket at the barrier.

Asha's comm beeped, and General Linn yelled, "They used rockets on the barrier and are entering the city on foot. We are grouping to give chase. Warn the protectors that troops are entering the city."

A rocket was launched from the truck and blasted a hole in the barrier. When the smoke from the explosion cleared, the invaders ran toward the opening. Several invaders stopped at the barrier and placed grenades around it. They ran for cover as the barrier was broken into pieces.

"They'll be able to drive the trucks through!" Asha sounded panicked. "I have to let Ursa know."

Sirus counted in his head. The numbers of elites and invaders were about the same, but Jeris's men wore protective vests and had greater firepower. Had Jeris known the current number of the elite soldiers? Sirus knew that Rod must have passed that information and decided he would pay Rod a secret visit as soon as Jeris was defeated.

CHAPTER 74

BATTLE FOR CEXION

After Asha sent word to the protectors that Jeris's invaders were entering the city from both roads, Ursa order the protectors to shoot on site.

"Don't let the enemy get near the dome entrance," she said. "With the information Jeris has been given by Rod, I'm sure he knows this is where the council and citizens are hiding."

Sirus was riding beside Asha in the rover and told her, "Order that all the street lights be kept on. Jeris's soldiers have night vision and your elites do not. One advantage we have is that the elites know the city. They know how to get around and where to mount a defense."

Sirus held his gun, ready to shoot when they caught up with the invaders. Asha's comm beeped.

"The invaders are heading to the central part of the city and not bothering to set up any defense lines," General Linn reported. "We are in pursuit."

"They are planning to take control of the major buildings first. Once the buildings are secure, they will regroup and try to take the city block by block," Sirus yelled over the sound of gunfire. It was easy for Sirus to see the strategy Jeris had developed.

Jeris's troops raced directly toward the hub of the city, where all the businesses were managed, with the elites in pursuit. If Jeris took control of the exchange trade, it would cripple Cexion.

Asha opened a link to elite headquarters. "Sergeant, send a message to all the elites telling them to form a line around city central and defend from there."

The entrance to the underground dome was not far from the city's hub, and Sirus knew the protectors were in trouble. He yelled to Asha, "You've got to deploy a squad of elites to the entrance of the dome. The protectors will not be able to hold out for long."

When Jeris's soldiers reached the city hub, they halted and formed a defensive position against the approaching elites. The squad leader then immediately dispatched two-man teams into each of the buildings. The remaining soldiers were given orders to form ten-man squads and clear the city of the elites. The invaders all shouted when given orders to kill the elites—no prisoners would be taken.

The invaders separated into squads and started down the four main streets to confront the elites, and the battle began. The elites took cover where they could find it, shooting at the invaders coming down the streets. A few of the military trucks had been driven through the barriers and were being used to shield the invaders from the elites' bullets. Between the protection of the military trucks, the bullet-proof vests, and the enemy's greater firepower, the elites were at a disadvantage against Jeris's army.

"Here they come," Phoenix warned the protectors.

He and Vega were deployed to the front. Ursa, Arris, and Minor were hidden where the entrance began to slope downward.

"Aim for areas that aren't protected by the vests," Ursa reminded them.

When the first of Jeris's soldiers appeared, Phoenix and Vega opened fire, and the invaders, caught off-guard, ran for cover.

As the fighting to protect the dome's entrance became more intense, Phoenix's and Vega's positions were too open, so they retreated to where the other protectors were hidden. Thanks to skilled shooting by the protectors, the first wave of invaders received multiple wounds in arms, legs, and heads. They called for reinforcements, and a second squad arrived, hidden behind one of the trucks.

"We won't be able to hold out against that truck, and I can't see a way to take it out," Minor yelled to the others. All their wrist comms were set to send and receive.

"Hold your positions," Ursa ordered. "I wish Sirus were here with that rocket launcher he used on Daedro."

"Hold on a bit longer. I'm coming," Sirus's voice echoed from their wrist comms.

"You can't get here too soon," Vega yelled as he reloaded and continued firing at the coming menace.

When they approached the city, Sirus had Asha stop. One of the military trucks had been left behind, and he wanted to check it out. The truck had been damaged by one of the buried bombs, and the seepage of fluids underneath the truck was the reason it had been abandoned. Sirus climbed into the back of the truck and inspected the rocket launcher.

Asha's communicator beeped.

"My soldiers are not able to hold their positions," General Linn reported over sounds of gunfire.

Asha contacted the command center and learned that both elite battalions were losing the fight against the heavily armed assassins. Realizing their current positions were in jeopardy, Asha ordered, "Elites, pull back and regroup."

"Do you want to drive or shoot?" Sirus asked after Asha closed her communicator.

"I'll drive. I know how to get around the city better than you." Asha climbed into the rover that now had a rocket launcher secured in back.

"Let's go on a truck hunt." Sirus grinned as he climbed in back and lifted the launcher to the top of the rover.

Asha sped toward the city hub along back streets to avoid being seen by Jeris's men. She spotted the first truck being used as a cover for the enemy, drove up an alley to get as close as she dared, and stopped. Sirus aimed the launcher and fired. The truck exploded, and among the invaders using it for cover, those who escaped injury panicked and ran. Hidden elite soldiers stepped out and fired their guns, stopping their escape.

Asha turned and drove toward the underground entrance. Sirus wanted to take out that truck next and help the protectors. Before they reached the street, Asha's comm beeped.

General Linn's voice was shaking. "The enemy breached our defenses. I've lost a number of elites and have others wounded. I'm signaling the retreat to the compound. We can defend from there. We're too outnumbered."

Before Asha could respond, static echoed from both her elite communicator and the protector wrist comms that she and Sirus wore. The voice was broken up by static but recognizable.

"Don't shoot me or the Dakon warriors riding with me. They are coming to fight Jeris. I have one hundred armed warriors, and we are entering the city from the desert side." Spider's voice went silent and then came back. "There are another hundred sharpshooters from the settlements entering from behind the elite compound. Have General Cane meet them and deploy them in the buildings. The higher the better for them to shoot from. We will reach the city in five minutes."

"Elites you heard the message from Spider," Asha said immediately. "Keep the invaders your targets. Do not shoot the Dakons or Spider. General Cane, meet the sharpshooters and deploy them as near the city hub as possible. Elites, do not give up. Help is on the way."

"This fight is about to get interesting for Jeris's goons," Sirus yelled as Asha sped toward the city hub. "Now let's give the protectors some assistance."

"The Dakons and settlers put the odds in our favor," Asha shouted as she drove, "assuming we can trust the Dakons."

"You can trust Spider. He would not have brought them if they were a threat. That was why no one could reach him. He was convincing the Dakons to fight Jeris and sending the sharpshooters from the settlements. What a terrific plan.

General Cane said at long distances, the shooters never miss with their rifles."

Asha took a corner on two wheels, almost throwing Sirus and the launcher out of the rover.

"Sorry," she yelled as she straightened the rover.

"No problem," Sirus yelled back.

"Get ready. It's the next turn off this alley."

The rover bounced from the alley and onto the road that led to the dome. Sirus heard gunfire; the protectors were trying to keep the enemy away from the dome entrance. One blast from the rocket mounted on the enemy military truck heading toward the entrance was all it would take to blow open the dome doors.

Asha drove onto the road and stopped the rover. The invaders hiding behind the truck turned and stared, unsure what was happening. Sirus pointed the rocket launcher at the truck, adjusted the sight until the truck filled the crosshairs, and then fired. The truck exploded, raining fire down on the invaders crowded behind it.

The invaders' uniforms caught fire, and they dropped their weapons and began to slap at the flames. In that instant, the protectors stepped out and began to shoot in unison. Sirus and Asha joined them, firing from the opposite end of the road. The invaders were trapped, and though they tried to escape, none did.

Sirus and Vega cleared the road, making sure the enemy was no longer a threat.

"Good work," Phoenix said when everyone gathered in the center of the road. "We should be able to hold our position without the threat of the truck."

"What do you want to do now?" Sirus asked Asha.

Asha started to reply when her communicator beeped and one of the elite generals reported.

"You won't believe this. There are at least twenty old rovers and a dozen two-wheelers entering the city filled with Dakon warriors. Spider signaled that they will continue until they meet up with Jeris's soldiers. Apparently, the Dakons have a score to settle. Spider asked that we give him and the Dakons backup."

While the general reported, shrill war cries could be heard in the distance and rolling clouds of dust began to appear.

"Do as asked. We'll watch for the Dakons and defend Cexion from here," Asha responded.

Asha's communicator beeped again, and General Cane said, "I am leading the sharpshooters from the compound. I'll try to get as close to the center as I can before I deploy them."

"You'll be able to get to the dome entrance. We have it secured and will watch for you," Asha replied.

Fierce war cries began to echo around the city as the Dakons rode in, looking like wraiths from the desert floor. All the warriors had red paint streaked across their faces and were armed with rifles, spears, and knives.

General Cane ran down the road followed by men dressed in buckskin. Moccasins muffled their entrance, and many wore hats made from animal skins. Each man carried a long rifle.

General Cane raced up and said, "This is Terylen, leader of the sharpshooters." She bent over to catch her breath before continuing. "Which buildings do you want him to deploy the shooters in?"

After Asha gave Terylen instructions, she turned to Sirus. "I need to get to elite headquarters and command from there. You stay and help guard the dome." Sirus started to protest, and Asha placed her hand on his arm. "I'll be fine and will see you afterward." Then she jumped into the rover and drove away.

The Dakons entered the city and roared past the elites, who had retreated behind a building. Jeris's men were caught by surprise, thinking the Dakons were under Jeris's control and not a threat. They were wrong. Before they could defend themselves, the wiry Dakons leaped from their rides and wreaked their revenge. Up close, the invaders' guns and vests were no match for the Dakons' razor-sharp knives. The invaders who managed to escape ran toward the city hub and were shot by the sharpshooters leaning out of the high windows. The few invaders who reached the city hub, thinking they would be safe, were greeted by the protectors and not their comrades. The sharpshooters had already cleared the city streets of Jeris's men.

The battle for Cexion was over. Spider rode up to the dome entrance in one of the Dakons old rovers. The warriors followed behind him. Spider stepped from the rover, turned to the Dakons, and raised his hand.

"Thank you, brothers. You helped prevent a terrible tragedy. If Jeris had been able to take control of Cexion, all of Velland would have been lost. He had no intention of honoring his word and giving you the settlements. Return to you tribes and remember your promise to meet with the settlers. Go in peace."

The Dakon warriors nodded to Spider in agreement and then turned and rode out of the city.

Ursa walked up. "How did you get the Dakons to fight?"

"They realized that Jeris had no intention of honoring his word or freeing those he'd taken from each village. That was how he'd gained control, through false promises and threats. After our raid on the villages, seeing that we did not harm the women, children, or food supplies, the Dakons knew the elites were not their enemy. The tribes have agreed to talk with the settlements and to work for food instead of stealing it. Many of the tribe members with families would like to find permanent homes."

Ursa shook her head in amazement as Spider explained.

With the city under elite control again, the protectors and Spider returned to the elite compound and entered headquarters. Their uniforms were torn and dirty, their faces smeared with dirt, but none had been wounded, which made Vega very happy. They were exhausted but also jubilant.

Asha hurried over and greeted them. "I can't thank you enough." She turned to Spider. "I'm still in shock that the Dakons fought for Cexion, but I'm glad they did."

One of the elite soldiers walked in and saluted. "Commander, there are a few of Jeris's men still alive, but none are willing to talk."

"Secure them in cells until we decide what to do with them," Asha ordered.

"Is the dock safe?" Spider asked.

"So far," Asha replied, "but Jeris has left the ring with seven warships. Mallas and the VSF have gone to meet him. I don't have an update on the situation."

CHAPTER 15

SPIDER STRIKES

"We need to strike while Jeris is engaged with the attack on the space fleet," Spider told Asha. Spider and the protectors were seated in Asha's office in the elites' compound.

"But we don't know the situation on Fexnal or Bastik or how many men Jeris has in control of the space docks," Asha protested.

Spider was not willing to give up. "The council member has sent a request for help, and if we can get onto Fexnal without being noticed, we can locate him and find these things out."

Asha tapped on her desk with pencil while she thought. "I can't send an elite patrol. Considering the losses we took while stopping the attack, including those who are injured and out of commission, I need to keep the elites who can fight in Cexion. I must protect the city."

"I wasn't considering an elite attack," Spider said. "The council member's spacecraft is still in dock and could land on Fexnal without drawing attention, since that is its home port. The craft is built to carry ten passengers, but I only need seven seats for the raiding party."

Asha looked up, realizing Spider's plan was to take the protectors with him to free Fexnal. She started to protest but then glanced at Sirus and could tell that not only he but all of the protectors were ready to follow Spider.

"My reasoning is, we have been on Fexnal a number of times and know where to go and not to go. If we wear disguises like before, we will not be noticed. From talking with your generals, we've learned that many of Jeris's soldiers came from Fexnal and Bastik, and a few had markings on their foreheads to show they were felons exiled to the mining colonies. There may only be a few of Jeris's men guarding the docks. If we take them out and put the Fexnal council in control, that is one less battle for Leader Mallas," Spider explained.

"I agree," Asha said. "With Jeris engaged and all of his soldiers that weren't killed locked up, now is the time to strike. I doubt he has learned the outcome of his attack on Cexion. I'll send word to have the spaceship readied for travel, and General Cane will supply you with weapons. There is still a communication shield around Fexnal; make sure to take that down." Asha stood up and faced Spider and the protectors. "Remember, you don't know who to trust, so be careful."

"But we have a secret weapon," Ursa pointed out. "If anyone isn't telling the truth, Arris's nose will light up."

Ursa's words caused everyone to laugh except Arris and Asha. Arris scowled when she sensed that Asha wanted to break protocol and laugh but didn't.

It was night when Minor broke hyperspeed and brought the spaceship to hover over the Fexnal dock. He waited to be hailed by the docking team, but no one seemed to have noticed the unlit ship.

"Take the ship to the far end and dock in one of the empty spaces," Spider ordered. "Running without lights, we haven't been seen."

It took little time for the protectors to exit the spaceship, secure a rover, and make their way into the city, following Phoenix's directions.

"Are you positive this is the building where the councilor lives?" Spider asked as Phoenix studied the communicator he'd carried when they rescued the prisoners.

"Yes. Kent downloaded all of the information on Fexnal, and Councillor Bellan lives here."

"OK. Let's make our way to the back and enter the building. Sirus, guard the door; no one enters after us."

Spider stepped from the rover they had borrowed at the space dock and silently crept around the building. The protectors followed single file. He opened a door that led inside to a stairway. Making no sound, the group began to climb the stairs. On the fourth floor, they stopped and waited for Phoenix to identify the councilor's living quarters. It took Minor no time to pick the lock and open the door, and everyone slipped inside.

"I'll find where Councillor Bellan is sleeping," Spider whispered. "Wait here and guard the door."

Muffled noises were heard, and then Spider led a tousled-looking man into the living room. The man was shaken from waking up with Spider standing over him with his hand over his mouth to stifle his screams.

Spider whispered, "I'm sorry to shock you awake, Councillor Bellan, but I had no choice. You remember Arris and I attended the meeting with Rod Hinds?"

Bellan nodded while trying to control his shaking legs.

"We are here in answer to your request for assistance. Yesterday, Jeris's soldiers attacked Cexion but were defeated. Jeris is on his way with a fleet of seven warships, and the VSF has gone to meet him. I have no further information regarding this matter. When we docked, there were only a handful of men guarding the dock, and none of them looked like soldiers. We plan to take back the dock and return it to Fexnal's control. Is your security team trustworthy and able to hold the dock once it is freed?" Spider waited for Bellan to answer, knowing it was a lot of information for him to absorb at once.

Bellan breathed deeply and steadied himself. "Our security team was told that if they interfered with Jeris's men, they would be killed. They are under house arrest in their barracks not far from here. If we free the docks from Jeris's men, Fexnal security will keep the docks secure. We were all caught by surprise, unaware of the spies Jeris had on Fexnal."

Spider and the protectors waited for Councillor Bellan to get dressed, and then they accompanied him to the barracks where the security team bunked.

Asha's comm beeped. She saw it was Spider and opened a link.

"The docks on Fexnal are secured, and the communication shield is down. Fexnal security is in control of both docks and under Councillor Bellan's command. There were only a handful of Jeris's men at the docks, and they didn't put up a fight when they saw the security team and the protectors were there to take the docks back. Jeris must have thought threatening to come back and kill them would be enough to keep their allegiance. Anyone identified as working for Jeris, either on the council or at the docks, has been arrested and locked up. Fexnal is free from Jeris's control."

"Good work. Will you return to Cexion?" Asha responded.

Spider hesitated and then said, "I have one more stop before we return."

"Do I want to know, and will I worry?" Asha asked.

"Probably not and yes. Any word from Mallas?" Spider replied.

"I've received no reports from our fleet. Stay safe and return as soon as you can."

"You have the coordinates for the shipbuilder's dock?" Spider asked Minor.

"Good to go," Minor said, and the small spaceship lifted away from the dock.

After they'd freed the Fexnal docks, Councillor Bellan had told Spider to use his ship as long as he needed it. Spider knew that Fexnal had been an easy win; surprise had been on their side. He wasn't sure about Bastik.

The dock used by the shipbuilder looked dark and deserted when Minor landed the ship.

"Night vision and stay alert," Spider cautioned as he led the way from the small dock. "The builder lives in the back of the building behind the hangers."

"What if he's not here?" Vega whispered.

"We'll find out where they have taken him. He's too important to Jeris's plans," Spider said.

"If Jeris's warships need repairs, this is where they'll come," Sirus agreed.

When they reached the back of the huge building, there were two guards standing outside, and light filtered from inside. Spider signaled for Vega to circle around and get the guards trapped between them and to beep once he was in place. Then they would take down the guards.

"That was too easy," Vega said as he rejoined Spider and the protectors. Neither guard had been on watch. They'd been smoking and talking when they were knocked out. The guards were tied up with their mouths gaged and propped up against a tree.

Spider crouched low and crept to the door. He signaled for Arris. "Can you tell if there are others inside?"

Arris leaned against the door and listened. "I can hear someone sleeping but no one else."

Spider motioned for them to breach the door, and Sirus kicked it in. The protectors stormed inside with weapons ready. The crashing noise woke the man sleeping on a cot pushed against the wall. The man sat up, looking frightened.

"Are you the shipbuilder friend of Mallas?" Spider asked while the protectors secured the room.

The man nodded his head.

"Other than the two guards outside, is there anyone else here?"

The builder shook his head no.

"We're secure," Spider said. Once the builder was awake enough to answer questions, Spider asked, "Do you know the status on the space dock? There is a communication shield that we need to take down."

"Based on what the guards have said, most of the men left to invade Cexion. Besides these two guards, there are perhaps four or five more. They rotate out but are not friendly. They know what I think of Jeris."

"Do the guards use rovers to get to the dock?" Spider asked.

"Yes. There are two parked on the other side of hangar three."

"Vega and Minor, retrieve the rovers."

When Minor and Vega drove up, Spider said, "Minor, take the builder to the ship and ready the ship for takeoff. Vega and Phoenix will drive the rovers. I doubt we will be noticed, since these rovers are used by the guards. We will assess the situation on the dock and locate the shield. If we can take out the dock guards, we will, but our main target is the shield. Asha feels there are others living on Bastik who don't go along with Jeris and that's the reason for the shield. Minor, I'll signal you if we are returning or if you are to come to the space dock."

"Make sure your weapons are reloaded," Spider told the protectors when they were ready to leave. "Fexnal required little ammo after Jeris's hoods saw us and the security team coming. The security lead was correct when he said that the men were small-time crooks and would run before they would fight."

The first rover pulled away from the hangar with Spider sitting beside Phoenix and Arris riding in the back. Vega drove the second rover. Ursa sat in front by Vega, and Sirus filled the back seat. Using their night vision goggles, Vega and Phoenix drove without running lights. The sound of the small engines broke the darkness around them. Phoenix had studied the maps Kent had downloaded on Bastik and knew which road to take to bypass the city. They should reach the space dock without raising any alarms.

Spider sat down in the control office of the space dock on Bastik and looked around. The dock had been guarded by four men, who had decided to resist when Spider ordered them to surrender. The four would no longer be a problem. Spider opened a communication link and sent a signal to the Cexion space dock.

The security lead answered, and Spider told him, "The Bastik shield is down and in pieces. Unless there is a replacement shield, communications will stay open. Patch me through to the elite commander."

When Asha acknowledged, Spider said, "Let the Cexion council leader know that communication with Bastik is now open. I don't know the status of the city. We came directly to the dock to take down the shield, and there are no guards working for Jeris at the dock. Jeris may not have any men left on Bastik. As soon as Minor arrives to pick us up, we are heading back to Cexion. I have a couple of extra passengers that I want to interrogate. They were guarding the shipbuilder and didn't want to share. The shipbuilder is safe and coming with us."

"I'll let Daji know; he has friends on Bastik and will contact them to find out the situation in the city. Great work, and I'll see you soon." Asha signed off.

Spider told the protectors, "Get ready. Minor is docking, and it's time for us to get back to Cexion."

CHAPTER 16

THE DARK MATTER

Leader Mallas positioned the space fleet in a V-formation just beyond the Velland atmosphere. From this position, he could deploy the ships where the need was most critical after Jeris arrived. The space fleet hovered, awaiting the arrival of the warships from the outer ring. The Velland commanders knew they were outnumbered, but they stood ready to defend their planet.

"Any word from Defender Five?" Mallas asked his communication operator.

The comm tech swiveled around in his chair and answered, "No word, sir." Then he turned back to watch the screen for any incoming signals from the ship.

When Defender Five had emerged from the ring to signal that Jeris and his warships were on the way, Mallas had not ordered Commander Ternek to return to the fleet. Since then, Mallas had decided to recall Defender Five to join the fleet, but the ship had not yet responded to his request. Mallas was worried that before the battle with Jeris had even begun, he was down two spaceships.

"Sir, there are ships coming out of hyper and entering Velland space," the second in command said.

Mallas stepped to the large viewing screen to watch the arrival of Jeris's fleet. Swirling clouds of smoke appeared, and a dark-gray warship broke from hyper speed in the space beyond the VSF command ship. Mallas knew this was Jeris's ship, the *Dark Matter*, he was looking at. The viewing window of the warship was black, hiding the evil that stood behind it. When the clouds of smoke dissipated, Mallas gasped. The ship was larger than the VSF command ship. Curved horns rose from the top, and steam spiraled from the horns. Jagged black lines spread outward from the command deck and across the ship. Just the size of the ship alone would cause anyone facing Jeris to shrink with fear, and there was still the added threat of the weapons that lined the expanse below the command deck. But Mallas stood firm.

One by one, the six warships broke hyper and dropped in behind the *Dark Matter* in a V-formation. These warships were smaller than the *Dark Matter* but looked just as deadly. The warships were painted the same dark gray with jagged black lines. Each warship had multiple weapons mounted underneath the command deck.

"Hold your positions," Mallas ordered the VSF commanders.

It was a waiting game to see who would make a move first. Finally, a voice echoed over the communication system in each of the VSF ships.

"You must surrender; you will not survive. You are outnumbered and cannot win this battle." The threat of the words was backed by the menace in the voice that echoed throughout the fleet.

The comm specialist turned around and exclaimed, "How did Jeris break our communication protocols?"

Leader Mallas grimaced. "It is easy, especially if you helped develop it." Then he stepped from the viewing panel over to the communication speaker.

"Jerrad, show yourself," he said over the comm. "Your foul game is over."

Behind Mallas, people gasped, and over the open speaker, the VSF commanders exclaimed, "It can't be him."

Finally, the black screen on the *Dark Matter* opened, exposing the man who stood there. He was dressed all in black and was tall, like Mallas. His features mirrored Mallas's, but the face was hardened and mean looking and his eyes were filled with hatred.

Jeris's words were cynical when he loudly rasped, "How did you know it was me, dear brother?"

Mallas stood with folded arms and looked back at Jeris. "It was easy when I saw your ship and the way the warships were deployed. You drew ships like that when you were growing up. You learned tactical strategy while training to be a fleet commander. Your knowledge of Cexion and the Dakons and the other planets explains how you were able to implement all your evil plans."

Jeris sneered. "I have you to thank, brother. You trained me, took me to the other planets, and then exiled me as a criminal to the mining colonies."

"Your own actions exiled your from Velland," Mallas replied.

"And you never did one thing to help me!" Jeris screamed back at his brother.

Mallas didn't answer Jeris's rage but shook his head in disbelief at all his younger brother had been able to accomplish without anyone being aware of it or of who was behind all the destruction.

Jeris leaned closer to the window. "After I organized the other exiles and took over the mining colonies," he hissed, "the rest was easy. You were too busy playing your space games to notice. And my name is Jeris. Jerrad died years ago. You have two minutes to surrender … or else."

The comm went silent, and the black shield again covered the window, hiding Jeris's shaking form.

"Ready for attack," Mallas ordered the VSF commanders. "Defenders Three and Four, deploy your weapons in a swivel motion. My brother will try to surround us."

As Jeris began to seek his revenge against his brother, the two warships at the end of the v-formation moved to surround the space fleet. The *Dark Matter* began firing its weapons at the VSF command ship. The warships on each side of the *Dark Matter* aimed their weapons at the fleet ships. The space fleet, expecting the attack, made a tactical move up and away and fired back. Weapons fire from the warships and the space fleet exploded in the sky like fireworks.

"Defender Two, cover Defender Four. Defender One, move beside Defender Four and cover the flank." Mallas continued to reposition the fleet, blocking the warships from entering Velland space.

"Defender Three is surrounded and taking fire," Mallas's second in command yelled.

"Position the command ship to intercept and protect," Mallas ordered.

Before the VSF command ship could be repositioned, Defender Three's commander reported, "Our weapons have been taken out."

"Return to dock," Mallas ordered the crippled ship.

"Defender One has blown up one of the warships," Mallas's second reported, "but it is having to defend against two warships.

"Where is Defender Four?" Mallas asked, trying to determine a way to aid Defender One in fending off multiple attacks.

At that moment, the command ship was hit, causing Mallas to grab hold of a railing to avoid falling down.

"How bad was the strike?" he yelled to his second in command over the noise of the impact.

"We've lost all weapons on port side," the second reported. "Sir, each of the defenders now has two warships attacking it, and the *Dark Matter* is moving toward us. What are your orders?" The second's voice was tense with worry.

Mallas was concerned. Jerrad was good at strategy games, and he had come prepared. He was well armed and had brought two extra warships to the battle.

"Tell the defenders to hold their positions and to aim for the weapons mounted underneath the command decks." Mallas was trying to outsmart his brother. During Jerrad's youth, they had played many strategy games like this one.

"Sir, Defender Two has been crippled, and the commander is not sure if he can make it back to dock," the second reported. More bad news.

Mallas opened the comm link. "VSF commanders, hold your positions as long as possible."

With all the warships determined to cripple the space fleet, neither Jeris nor his commanders noticed when Defenders Five and Six broke from hyper speed and positioned themselves directly behind the warships.

After warning Leader Mallas that Jeris had left the ring, Defender Five had gone back inside and flown straight toward the small planet hidden by the black mist. It was the only place where they had not searched for the missing defender. Just as Defender Five had neared the small planet, Commander Ternek had been stunned to see Defender Six appear from the black mist. Both he and his crew had cheered when they'd seen the missing ship.

Defender Five had opened a comm link to Defender Six, and Command Ternek had requested a status update.

Commander Marico had responded, "When Jeris led his pack of wolves from the planet, the ones left behind to guard weren't up to the task of fighting VSF soldiers. These curs were used to weakened men not able to fight back. Jeris's men have been taken out and the planet turned over to the few slaves that survived the mining pits."

"Good job, Commander Marico," Commander Ternek had shouted. "Now let's go join the VSF and help remove the menace of Jeris and his wolf pack."

Both VSF defenders had jumped to hyper speed as soon as they'd flown from the gaseous ring, anxious to join the fleet and the battle against Jeris's warships.

Defender Five and Six hovered at the far edge of the battle to assess the situation. Then VSF Commanders Ternek and Marico opened fire on the warships that surrounded the fleet. Being caught unaware by the surprise attack, two of Jeris's warship were instantly blown to pieces. The remaining warships were now caught in the cross fire between the VSF defender ships and were quickly dispatched.

Commander Ternek's voice echoed from the comm. "Defenders Five and Six reporting. All the warships have been defeated. The black command ship is the only remaining vessel. Commander Marico and Commander Ternek are on deck awaiting further orders."

The worry instantly left Mallas's face, replaced by a wide grin. Mallas responded, "You arrived just in time, Defender Five and Defender Six. Defenders, surround the *Dark Matter*." He turned to his comm tech. "Hail the *Dark Matter*."

"The comm is open sir, but they aren't responding," the tech reported after several attempts to contact Jeris.

"Jerrad, the game is over. All of your warships have been destroyed. You can't hold out against the fleet."

Mallas waited, but still no reply came from the *Dark Matter*.

"Open fire and take out those ridiculous looking horns," Mallas told his second in command.

The second nodded. "Yes sir." He issued orders to the gunner to aim at the *Dark Matter*'s smoking horns.

When the *Dark Matter* was hit, both horns exploded, and the black shield lifted. Jeris stood at the window.

"Well, brother, you win again. I have no intention of surrendering and being exiled again. I would rather die."

The *Dark Matter* shuttered and then exploded into pieces.

"Jerrad!" Mallas yelled as he watched the destruction. He collapsed and was caught by his second. "Why?" He sobbed out loud.

CHAPTER 17

VOLAN FREEDOM

The elite communication center had kept an open link to the VSF. Asha and the elite generals were seated in their briefing room, and Spider and the protectors had joined them. Everyone was tense as they listened to the communications during the battle, knowing there was nothing they could do to help Leader Mallas and the space fleet.

They all gasped when they learned Jeris's true identity and cheered when Defenders Five and Six joined the fleet. When the *Dark Matter* exploded, no tears were shed in the room for Jeris or his followers.

"Jeris was actually the younger brother of Leader Mallas?" Vega couldn't believe it.

"Yes," Asha answered, trying to keep the sadness out of her voice. "He was brilliant, like Leader Mallas, and excelled in completing all VSF training in record time. It makes sense now how Jerrad could get around without being noticed. He knew Rod Hinds from the academy and was familiar with the space docks on the other planets. Jerrad had created quite a large organization that took bribes and exploited others before he was finally caught. His court martial was attended by everyone in Cexion. I felt sorry for Leader Mallas, having to pass sentence on his own brother."

Ursa mumbled something under her breath, and from the look on Asha's face, she had heard what Ursa had said.

"What will happen next?" Phoenix asked.

"According to Illa, the Cexion council will assist the Fexnal and Bastik councils in reestablishing control on their planets. I have been asked to develop a training center at the compound and train the security teams for both councils," Asha explained.

"Congratulations," Spider said, and all the protectors echoed his comment, except Ursa.

Asha continued. "Leader Mallas is sending Defenders Five and Six back to the outer ring to free the shipbuilder's family and the Dakons who were taken prisoner by Jerrad and to make sure there are no allies of Jerrad left in control. Before trading begins again with the mining colonies, Mallas will go meet with them to establish a trade council with members from each mining colony."

Spider stood up. "I need to contact Nebula and let them know that we can portal back as soon as it is possible. There is no need for further assistance on Velland."

When everyone rose to walk from the room, Asha said, "Ursa, please wait. I would like to discuss something with you."

As the protectors left elite headquarters, Minor commented, "That will be one discussion best to avoid."

After everyone but Ursa had left the room, Asha stepped over and closed the door. She turned and faced Ursa.

"I heard what you said about me. Do you really think that I would allow anyone to harm you or Illa?"

"You have never cared about anything but being an elite," Ursa said, her hands on her hips. "Father doted on you and never gave me or Illa a nod. Why do you think I left Cexion? I was tired of being in your shadow."

Asha looked stunned. "Is that what you think? I didn't have a choice. I was five when I entered the elite program and was only allowed to come home twice a year. I missed my parents, and when you and Illa were born, you were all I cared about. I couldn't wait to see you again. You and Illa had lives. You both were so pretty and got to wear pretty clothes and attend school with other children. Watching you and Illa play made me happy. I never got to laugh or dance or act silly. If you think I didn't care, you are so wrong. Showing emotions is one of the first things they take away from us."

Ursa was speechless and didn't know what to say. "Father always made such a big deal when you came home; he had to show you off to all his friends. It was like he only had one child."

"Ursa, I am sorry about Father's behavior. I know he was proud of you when you left for the academy. If he didn't tell you, he should have." Asha caught her breath and then huffed, "Father should have been the elite, not me."

Ursa grinned on hearing Asha's comment. "Father would have made a good elite. He was always so military-like at home. He gave Illa and me orders daily and made sure we carried them out. Illa and I would try to find ways to get out of doing them. It became a game for us."

Asha laughed out loud. "I can see him marching in a parade in uniform."

Ursa joined her sister in laughing until tears ran down their faces.

Asha stepped forward and took Ursa's hands. "You mean everything to me. You and Illa are my family. I thought you didn't like me, and that's the reason I didn't tell you this before. When you blocked all communications from me, I was hurt."

"I'm sorry. I should never have done that. I let my jealousy determine my actions," Ursa admitted, looking into her sister's eyes.

Asha smiled. "I'm just happy we could clear things up. You were jealous of me, and I was jealous of you. Perhaps going forward, we can be sisters and friends."

Ursa smiled back as she held Asha's hands. "Deal."

Spider looked into the room and asked, "Is everyone packed? Kent signaled he will be able to open a portal in one hour."

"Everyone is packed and ready to portal," Phoenix reported.

Spider nodded and left the gym, saying he wanted to say good-bye to the elite generals.

The protectors carried their packs to the open field where the portal would open and set them on the ground. Arris noticed Sirus walk off and knew he was meeting Asha. When Sirus returned, Arris could sense that Sirus was sad. She walked over to him and slipped her hand into his.

"I know you will leave your heart in Cexion."

Sirus frowned at Arris. "You know too much, little sister."

"Well, we are a family and care about each other," Arris replied.

As the protectors waited, Asha drove up with Illa riding beside her.

"Ursa!" Illa yelled. "You can't leave without saying good-bye." Illa jumped out of the rover and hurried to Ursa.

"I knew Asha was bringing you to say good-bye," Ursa replied as Illa grabbed her around the neck and tightly squeezed.

Asha stepped from the rover and joined her sisters.

When Illa loosened her hold on Ursa, Asha stepped forward and gave Ursa a hug. "Stay safe, sister, and stay in touch."

Ursa smiled. "I promise."

A portal began to swirl.

Spider said, "It's time," and stepped into the portal.

Arris took Sirus by the hand and said, "Let's go home, big brother."

The End

BOOK 5

CATELLA'S MYSTERY

CHAPTER 7

A SECRET MESSAGE

Since their return from the Volan Galaxy, the protectors had been away on assignments, their help having been specifically requested by Nebula ambassadors who were dealing with difficult situations in their galaxies. But now, both the Alpha and Beta teams had returned to Nebula headquarters and were enjoying some well-deserved downtime.

Catella and Spider had highly praised them in front of the Nebula council for the support they had provided during the Volan wars. Commander Asha of the elite forces had sent an official document to NAHQ, signed by her and Leader Mallas of the Velland Space Fleet, commending the protectors for their performance and courage.

Kent and Arris had met for lunch and were catching up on the past few months.

"Ursa stays in contact with Asha and Illa," Arris said, "and she seems happier since getting matters settled with her sister. Sirus is in touch with Asha, and Vega with General Cane. I'm glad we've made new friends on Volan." Arris got a faraway look in her eye and sighed. "I had one friend growing up, but she moved away, and we lost contact. I sometimes think about Katy and wonder why she never wrote to me."

Kent concentrated on eating, stirring something on his plate.

Arris watched him for a minute and asked, "Is something bothering you?"

Kent shook his head without looking up and continued to push food around his plate with his fork.

Arris laid her fork on the table and stared at Kent, sensing that something was bothering him. She sat and watched him stir his food.

Kent heaved a sigh and looked up, knowing that Arris wouldn't give up. "About Katy not writing," he finally said. Then he paused and took a deep breath, hoping it would not be his last. "She did write to you. Two letters. Andra was concerned about you staying in contact with Katy, so she destroyed the letters. She told Catella about the letters, and he also thought you should not stay in contact with her." Seeing the glare he received from Arris, Kent hastened to explain. "It was for your safety and maybe Katy's. It was a thread that needed to be cut."

Arris didn't know whether to be mad because she hadn't been given Katy's letters or glad because Katy had kept her promise to write. Learning that Katy had written to her, Arris's mood lifted. Arris had experienced the danger of being hunted by the general and understood the need to keep Katy from harm. She pondered this.

"I wonder how Katy is," she said. "She would be out of school by now." Arris looked at Kent. "Thanks for telling me. I won't mention it to Andra. Maybe Katy thought we had moved and I hadn't gotten her letters and that was the reason I never wrote back."

Their conversation was interrupted by a group of individuals in brown uniforms with "Nebula Animal Habitat" stenciled on the front. As the noisy group sat down, one of the men noticed Kent and leaned over.

"Hi, Kent," he said. "Haven't seen you for a while. Are you still working in communications?"

Kent smiled and responded in a teasing voice, "Hey, Cabe. I'm still communicating, and I see you are still working at the zoo."

Cabe laughed. "It's a zoo all right. We finally have the latest shipment of animals logged in and have set up a feeding and exercise schedule. Now the trainers can begin working with them."

As the group began eating their lunch, Arris said, "I didn't know there was a zoo here. I never noticed anything like that on the plans when I was helping Catella."

"It's not a really zoo but rather a collection of select animals that are part of a special training program," Kent explained. "They teach them, for example, to go into certain areas and make sure it is safe before we send a person in. Things like that. A lot of residents staying here volunteer to help out because of their love for animals. There is a variety of animals if you are interested."

Growing up, Arris had never had pets, and all dogs scared her. When she'd been playing at the park one day, a large black dog had snarled and lunged at her. Thankfully, the snarling beast had been on a short leash. That experience had left her not wanting to get too close to any dog, because all dogs have sharp, pointy teeth. She had liked to visit the pet store and look at the different animals, though. Arris had never asked for a pet apart from one time when she'd asked for a goldfish. Her request had been denied with the excuse that it would be too much work for Andra. Arris had wondered how much work having a goldfish would be. But with the fast escape from her apartment, Arris had realized why she couldn't have a goldfish. It would have been left behind with no one to care for it.

Kent's wrist comm beeped, and he read the message. "I need to get back to communications. Let's meet up tomorrow and do something."

Arris grinned and responded, "Maybe we could go to the zoo."

After lunch the following day, Kent and Arris waited for a carrier to take them to the animal habitat.

When they exited the carrier, Kent told her, "Cabe is an animal care specialist and has a special bond with all the animals. Like you, he can sense when they are happy or upset. Catella brought him to Nebula to be in charge of the animal training program specifically for that reason."

They came to a set of tall doors, which were sealed shut, with a keypad to one side. Kent entered a set of numbers, and both doors slid to the side to open. The extra-wide doorway would allow very large cages to be brought inside the habitat. Arris paused before she stepped inside, not sure if she should be worried.

Arris was shocked when she walked into a vast area filled with everything from tall pens to small cages. Paths ran throughout the space, many ending in large fenced-in sections that were filled with animals and their trainers. The trainers varied in looks and size, depending on the planets they came from. From watching them, it was easy to tell they all had the same devotion to the animals under their care as Cabe.

"This way." Kent motioned and led the way toward a row of offices running along the wall.

Cabe's office was big but looked cramped because of the number of shelves covered with various items. Pictures of every animal in the training program lined the walls with number codes written underneath each picture. The animals ranged from huge, hairy beasts that could eat you to small, cuddly ones. Arris knew there was no way she would go near the large, hairy ones.

Cabe hurried into his office and huffed, "I'm sorry I'm late, but we just moved that last of the animals into its own cage. This one has been a nightmare because of its constant noise. The handler named it Echo because it keeps repeating the same sounds over and over. If it weren't so darn cute, I think we would put it outside." Cabe grinned at his own joke.

When their tour of the zoo was over, Arris thanked Cabe and then added, "I never knew this place was here. I really enjoyed seeing how the trainers work with the animals."

Cabe responded, "Whenever you want to help out, we'll put you to work. The handlers do all the feeding and keep the cages clean; this frees the trainers to work with the animals."

Arris quickly refused because of being on constant assignment. That was the excuse she used, at least, instead of admitting to fearing the animals because all of them had teeth.

Two days later, Catella received a private communication from Cabe requesting his presence in the zoo. There was something concerning that needed his attention.

When Catella stepped from the carrier, Cabe was waiting for him. After Cabe opened the double doors to the habitat, he said, "We need to go to the back section of the habitat."

As Cabe led the way, he explained the situation. "Several weeks ago, we received a large shipment of animals, and we finally have their specific training requirements logged. There was one small animal that arrived with no paperwork or any indication of where it had come from. It was not part of any orders that were placed by the trainers either. Special food was packed with it, and because of its gentle nature, it was set aside until the other animals that we knew what to do with were processed.

"It is a furry little guy with large eyes and a bushy tail. We could not find any other animal like it in our database to match it to. Once it arrived, it began to repeat the same sounds over and over, and the constant noise is driving the handler crazy. The handler named the little guy Echo because of its constant repeating. We finally placed him in his new home, thinking it was the cramped cage that was causing his constant noise, but the larger cage didn't help."

Cabe stopped, unlocked a storage room, and walked in. He pointed to a small cage sitting on a bench.

"This is what I wanted you to see. Only the handler and I have seen what he found when he was cleaning out Echo's cage."

Catella walked over and looked at the cage, the bottom of which was now cleaned of shipping material. The name "Catella" was scratched into the floor of the cage.

Catella turned to Cabe and asked, "May I see this animal?"

"This way," Cabe said, and he led the way from the storage room to a medium-sized cage built into the back wall of the habitat. Cabe opened the door of the cage, and a small creature with red fur skittered from the back and ran into his hands, all the while making the same sounds over and over.

Catella reached out and petted the small animal. "I haven't seen the likes of you in many years." He pushed a button on his wrist comm and said, "Kent, will you come to the zoo and make a recording of one of the animals. You need to see if you can figure out what it keeps repeating."

Within a few minutes, Kent hurried in. He looked at Cabe and asked, "Is this the animal you were telling me about? Echo, I think you called him."

Cabe nodded and held up the animal so that Kent could make a recording of the sounds being repeated.

"That should do it. I'll go back to the command center and see if I can match the sound pattern and figure out what this little guy is trying to tell us," Kent said as he stopped the recorder.

Cabe walked Catella and Kent to the carrier.

"Let's not make anyone else aware of the situation until we figure out what is going on," Catella said to Cabe. "You should run a search of the Hydris Galaxy, specifically the planet Hyrila, for animal species that may match Echo. Echo could also be a hybrid and modified from his origin."

Cabe said he would let Catella know if he found a species that matched Echo.

The following day, Kent reported what he had found to Catella. "I've run the sound pattern that Echo is making through a universal code decipherer, and it came up with a pattern that is repeated, like ones and zeros. When I ran the numbers, they resulted in what would be considered an SOS. I'm not sure what to do next."

Catella thought for a minute and then said, "Try to match the pattern against the Hyrilian dialect in the Hydris Galaxy. We may not have much in our data archives regarding this galaxy. It has been ages since I've had contact with anyone from there."

The next day, Kent walked into Catella's office. "I found a few sources of the Hyrilian dialect in our database to match to, and the result is not very clear. I want you to hear it before I tell you what I think it means."

Kent placed the recorder he'd used to record Echo's sounds on Catella's desk and pushed a button. A monotone computer-generated voice said, "Help me. Help me."

Catella looked at Kent and nodded that he agreed with him—the message was a call to Nebula for help.

After Kent left, Catella rode his personal carrier to the zoo. Cabe was waiting for him when he exited the carrier.

"Thank you for meeting me on short notice. I would like to see the animal again," Catella said.

When Cabe opened Echo's cage, the small ferret-like animal scurried out, and Catella picked him up.

Catella petted the animal and said, "I have received your message. Thank you."

Instantly, Echo stopped his noisy repetition, cuddled up in Catella's arms, and began making a purring noise.

CHAPTER 2

THE PUZZLE

Catella sat across the table in his office from Spider, and Kent had joined them. After explaining Echo's call for help to Spider, Catella wanted his advice on what to do next.

"Before I met you, Spider, or even had the idea of forming the Nebula Association," Catella said, "I spent my early years in the Hydris Galaxy. There was a scientist on the planet Hyrila working on his ideas and inventions. He was looked on as being 'out there' or different by the other scientists. Hyrila had set up a multilevel complex dedicated to scientific experiments. I formed a friendship with this scientist, because many times, I too have been looked on as being 'out there.' When trying to get the idea of Nebula realized, I received many unneeded and unwelcome comments."

Catella stopped for a moment, lost in thought about days long past.

"Kent," he finally continued, "will you download everything we have on the Hydris Galaxy and scan the data to see if a person named Kohlo is mentioned in any of the logs. It has been so long; I am surprised that he remembers me or even knows how to contact me. He must have learned of NAHQ and of our mission, even though we have never been involved with the Hydris Galaxy. I did contact them to join, but the planets' leaders were not in conflict with one another and not interested in the Nebula mission.

"The fact that Kohlo, if it is him, sent this message and did so in this hidden way makes me wonder what has happened in Hydris since I left and lost contact with him. I remember Kohlo did have animals that resembled Echo that he was working with to get them to repeat and respond to specific sounds. Our little guy certainly did his job well." Catella looked at Kent and chuckled. "The handlers almost put him in a soundproof cage because of his constant clamor. Since he has stopped all the noise, he has become a favorite of the handlers, and they all agree he is highly intelligent. During the day, Echo has the run of the habitat."

"That's great news," Kent replied. "Echo is certainly one of the cutest animals they have. I'm sure he'll find a permanent home in the zoo."

Catella nodded and said, "Back to the reason for this meeting. After Kent gathers the data, I was thinking of sending an investigator to Hydris to see if he can locate Kohlo and determine the reason for his call for help. This mission must be kept secret, because the galaxy is not part of Nebula and we could be looked upon as interfering."

"While Kent gets the data ready," Spider said, "I'll work on a way to get an investigator to one of the planets in Hydris. Once in the galaxy, he will be able to move around the planets to locate Kohlo. I'll have a cover story for the investigator to use by the time Kent has the data available."

Later the following week, the protectors had finished their daily workout in the gym. They were covered with sweat and congratulating each other on having completed the latest routine that Sirus had challenged them with.

"I really think that Sirus is trying to kill us," Minor wheezed, still chasing his breath after completing the final sprint.

"What doesn't kill you makes you stronger," reminded Sirus.

"That's easy for you to say," retorted Minor, who was bent over and sucking air.

Sirus laughed. "You surprised yourself today. When I gave out the routine, you said you would never complete it."

"Death drill number … what number is this one? You must stay away at nights trying to find ways to do us in." Minor straightened up, but his legs were still shaky.

All their wrist communicators beeped at once, and they stopped talking to read the message.

Vega groaned. "Downtime is officially over."

"I'm glad," Ursa said. "I was becoming bored just hanging out."

Vega huffed. "But hanging out doesn't get you shot at. I bet there is a situation on some planet that just can't solve its problems without our assistance."

"That's why we trained to become protectors," Phoenix interjected. "Vega, you like to grumble, but you'll be the first to volunteer if Spider asks."

"Catella, Spider, and Kent will be in the meeting too," Ursa said. "Something big must have come up to get them all there."

"I haven't seen Catella since we returned," Arris said. "Kent said he was busy, so I didn't want to bother him, although Kent said Catella does keep tabs on me."

Sirus spoke up. "You are special to Catella, like a protégé, and he has watched out for you since you were left on Earth by your parents."

Arris nodded her head in agreement. As long as she could remember, Catella had been there, and knowing that Catella was there gave her comfort.

"Let's meet for breakfast, and then we can go to the meeting together," Ursa suggested, and the others agreed.

Each of the protectors' workout suits were drenched with sweat as they headed to their rooms for a hot shower.

The following morning after breakfast, the protectors walked into communication room 32. They looked rested following a night's sleep, and all were wearing clean uniforms.

As they sat down at the table, Vega mumbled, "Well, here we go again."

Kent was already seated and said, "It may not be as bad as Volan."

Vega sat down, but before he could make a comment about Volan, Catella and Spider came into the room. Catella stopped and nodded to the protectors seated at the table. Then he and Spider took their places.

"I trust you have enjoyed your well-earned rest," Catella said in his formal way of speaking.

The protectors agreed that they had, and Ursa added, "We're ready to get back to work."

Vega groaned.

"The reason I called this meeting and asked Alpha and Beta teams to join us is that there is a concerning situation in the Hydris Galaxy." Catella paused when he noticed Phoenix look confused. "Years ago, I had a close acquaintance on the planet Hyrila, and I believe that he sent me a secret message for help. Even though Hydris is not part of NAHQ, I did send an investigator to try to make contact with him. The investigator arrived on the planet and then vanished, and there has been no further contact from him."

Catella waited, in case the protectors had questions. When no one spoke, he continued, "I would like to send both teams on a secret mission to Hydris. I understand that you could be put at greater risk since Hydris is not part of Nebula. If you would rather not participate, I will understand. In that case, please leave now before we begin discussing assignment details."

Not one of the protectors stood up.

Catella smiled. "Kent has gathered all the information we have regarding Hydris. There are three habitable planets: Hyrila, Hytura, and Hydea. If I am correct, you will find my former acquaintance Kohlo and our missing investigator on Hyrila. Kohlo was studying animals, such as the one he used to contact me, when I was there a long time ago. Spider will develop a cover story for each team to explain why you are on the planet. Alpha and Beta teams, I must stress that you should not become separated from your team members. Years ago, some of the experiments the scientists were working on were quite questionable, and if they were developed and implemented, that would cause me to be concerned for your safety."

"Can you tell us what some of these experiments were?" Arris asked. She still vividly recalled the n-real clone of her mother. A shiver ran down her back.

Catella hesitated. "The experiments were all over the spectrum, but many involved animals being bred for size and strength. Mind control was being used to combat fears, and there were some scientists trying to combine species. That is one of the reasons I left Hydris. The leaders were allowing these scientists too much latitude." Catella shuddered. "I do not want to lose contact with another Nebula associate and hope that you will find our missing investigator in one piece. Please be careful."

"I will accompany you," Spider told the protectors, "but I will not take part in your teams' missions. I'll monitor from a central location and track your signals at all time. I will also watch for the investigator's signal. These signals are not designed to work across long distances, but if he is in the city or close by, we can find him. Please be ready to leave in two days."

The following day after breakfast, the protectors sat in the open area by the hallway that led to their rooms. Kent had forwarded what information he was able to find on the Hydris Galaxy to their communicators, and they were now reviewing the data.

"Kent is concerned that much of the data is out of date and can't be verified," Phoenix said. "The situation on planet may be very different from what Catella remembers. Given the call for help, we could be going into a hostile situation without anyone on planet to contact for assistance."

"Spider will be with us to monitor our situations," Ursa reminded everyone.

"He'll have our backs at all times," Sirus added, "and if one of our teams run into trouble, he can send the other team to help."

"Too bad there isn't a way to know what the planet is like before we get there," Vega mused. "If some of the experiments that had been taking place when Catella was there were implemented, we could become the hunted and not the hunters." Vega made his voice shake and quiver in a low, eerie tone.

Minor retorted, "You always bring up the worst possible scenario."

Vega grinned. "Hope for the best, prepare for the worst."

Phoenix brought everyone back to what they needed to accomplish. "We meet with Spider soon, so let's make sure we have reviewed everything Kent sent."

After a late lunch, the protectors went to room 32 to wait for Spider. They had done a final review of the data Kent had sent and were prepared as much as they could be, given the outdated information. Spider hurried into the room, followed by Kent, and they quickly sat down.

Spider glanced around the table and said, "I trust you have gleaned all you could from the data on Hydris. I was able to contact an acquaintance who has recently visited Hydris to trade. He told me he was on the planets Hytura and Hydea and made contacts to begin trading, but he was not able to find any contact on Hyrila. Nor was he allowed on planet. Each of the three planets in Hydris is self-governed, and they don't rely on each other, so no one seemed concerned that there has been no official communication with Hyrila for some time. It may be years since the other planets had any contact with Hyrila, according to my source. From this information, I've designated Hyrila as our destination to begin searching."

Spider nodded to Kent, and a holo of the Hydris Galaxy appeared above the table showing the three major planets in the galaxy. Each planet had either one or two moons.

"The investigator portaled to Hytura, and there, he hired a private ship to take him to Hyrila. The ship's captain confirmed the investigator got off at the port, after which the captain returned to Hytura. The investigator has not made contact with NAHQ since arriving on Hyrila. I asked Kent if he could find a way for us to get onto the planet without alerting anyone. Kent has found an old, unused portal that connects to Hyrila. For us to make use of this portal will require a two-portal hop. The outermost planet in the Riddan Galaxy, where NAHQ is centered, is Bankos. Kent contacted the planet's intergalactic monitor, who he knows, and had him verify that the portal is stable. The monitor, whose name is Calais, will assist Kent in managing our portals there and back. The plan is to have Calais available each day at a designated time to watch for portal activity. Calais will update Kent when we return to Bankos, and Kent will open the NAHQ portal for our return to HQ. I will work out the details with Kent and Calais before we leave.

"We are not sure where exactly we will exit the portal on Hyrila, so be prepared. With all of the scientific projects that were being done, Catella thinks that this portal must have been used in the past and forgotten about. Catella said the scientific laboratories were located outside a major metropolis on the planet. When you return to your rooms you will find clothing for your assignment. The uniforms will not have any reference to NAHQ, nor will you carry any identification. We have three objectives: first, find our missing investigator; second, find Kohlo; and third, assess the situation on Hyrila and report back to Catella. I plan on this assignment being completed in three days. Any questions?" Spider looked at the protectors.

No one had any questions. Even Vega stayed silent.

The following day, the protectors waited in the large receiving area by the portal entrance. They were dressed in uniforms that were made to look worn but were actually the latest design for wear in battlefield situations. Hidden pockets concealed small guns and hand weapons that Sirus had passed out once they'd arrived at the portal. Alpha team was dressed in brown jumpsuits that somewhat resembled the ones that trainers at the animal habitat wore. Beta's outfits were similar in look but gray in color. Each protector had packed a small tote with items that would sustain them for the three days they planned to be away.

Even their distressed apparel could not hide that fact that they were all in great physical shape. They stayed in optimum condition, thanks to Sirus's daily death drills. Arris was the shortest of the protectors, shorter than Minor by an inch. Sirus was even taller and wider than Vega overall. Phoenix and Ursa were both tall and svelte, their muscles exposed by their one-piece suits. Phoenix's hair was a shade whiter and his eyes a lighter blue that Ursa's. Arris had secured her auburn hair in a single braid that hung down her back and sparkled with red highlights, offsetting her almond-shaped eyes. Minor's curly brown hair fell over his ears, hiding the fact that they were pointed at the top. Each protector looked different from the others and excelled at different skills that, when combined, made each team a force that would be prepared for any situation they encountered.

CHAPTER 3

THE SEARCH BEGINS

Arris stepped from the portal and to the side to wait for Vega. Minor moved forward to join Spider and the other protectors. Vega, not a big fan of portals, had looked slightly green when Arris had entered with Minor, leaving Vega to wait a couple of minutes before he portaled. Vega was bringing up the rear. Spider and Sirus had gone first, in case they stepped from the portal and into a hostile situation. Phoenix and Ursa had waited the number of minutes Spider had specified and then stepped through. Arris and Minor had counted down and then stepped into the portal themselves. Arris had full confidence in Kent, and when Kent had said the portal was stable, even if it had not been used for some time, that was all the assurance she'd needed. When Vega stepped out, Arris thought that he might kneel down and kiss the solid ground beneath his feet. Arris took Vega's arm and guided him to where the others waited.

It was dark, but the sky was beginning to lighten. In the distance, animal sounds could be heard. Spider was moving the scanner he'd brought with him around, getting a readout of the landscape.

"There looks to be a building not far away, and it appears empty. I don't see any signs of life on the monitor. Follow me," Spider said in a whisper.

Spider led the way, and when they were close enough to make out crumbling walls surrounded by a broken-down fence, he stopped and motioned to Vega and Sirus to scout ahead. Everyone waited in silence as the sky lightened. The sounds of animals awaking increased; roars grew louder, howling became more intense, and a strange screeching sound echoed.

Vega silently returned and reported, "The building is empty. It looks like it was once used to house animals. There's a lot of scat still left on the ground, so watch your step."

Once they reached the structure, it was light enough to see that it had been abandoned long ago.

Spider glanced around and said, "It looks to be an old barn; we can set up our base camp here. It's close to the portal if we need a quick exit. Let's clean out these back two rooms; the roof looks intact over them."

As the protectors began to clear the rooms, Spider sent a message to Kent letting him know that everyone had arrived safely on Hyrila.

Vega was leaning out of one of the windows, searching the area around through a long-range viewer. "The scenery isn't lush and green like Catella described. The whole area is dry and brown. I can make out a large structure over the next rise, probably the multilevel laboratory building."

Ursa stepped up beside Vega. "If that is the laboratory, then the city will be beyond it. Spider's scanner doesn't reach that far without sending up a bot. Until we know more about this place and the technology, he doesn't want to take the chance of it being noticed."

"Phoenix and I are going to scout out the building Vega saw," Spider said. "If it looks safe, I'll launch a bot and get a detailed readout of the building and the number of workers and animals inside. Once I have that information, I'll send the bot toward the city, and Phoenix and I will return. I can manage the bot from base, and based on the information it sends, we can decide what to do next. Make sure each team understands the cover story Kent developed. It may or may not be of help. Kent was working with outdated information. We won't be gone long, because I want to do recon on the lab and city today."

As they waited for Spider and Phoenix to return, Minor looked up from reading Beta's cover story and asked, "Do you think anyone will believe we are looking to purchase animals trained for rescue operations?"

"It's as believable as us being habitat security inspectors," Vega answered.

Arris said, "Cabe helped Kent come up with our covers because of the animal sent to Catella. Animals are still being used; listen, you can even hear them."

"I can't wait to inspect that growling one's habitat," Vega grumbled, causing Ursa to laugh.

"Spider and Phoenix are back," Arris announced.

"Did you sense them coming?" Vega asked.

"No, I can see them from the window."

Spider cleared off an old bench and set the display on it so everyone could see the layout of the multilevel building from the bot's search.

"As you can see, there are three levels to the building. The floor underground looks to consist of labs or operating rooms. There was no sign of activity on this floor. The ground floor looks more open, like it's used for training and working with the animals. The top floor is divided up into offices. From the body signatures inside the building, most activity seems to take place on the top floor; all but two of the twenty signatures were there. The ground floor is interesting, as there seem to be small cages that open into a main room and an adjoining room that looks to be living space. These small cages could hold animals like the one sent to NAHQ. There is one person in the main room with three small animals.

"Look closely at the lower floor. At one end, there is a small room with one person lying on the floor or a cot. It's hard to tell which." Spider pointed to the area. "I think we have identified where the Nebula investigator is being held, and from the heat signature, it's clear he is still alive. The ground floor shows signs of someone living there, perhaps confined with the small animals. I would guess that that's the person who sent the call for help. This could be Catella's friend Kohlo." Spider paused and studied the monitor.

"What about the large pens near the back of the compound?" Arris asked, pointing at the monitor.

"Since the animals are enclosed, I don't think we need to worry about them," Spider answered.

His words didn't ease her apprehension.

"As soon as the bot completes its circle of the city, I'll bring up the readout. Once we are familiar with the layout, we'll head toward the city. I want to get there and scout around before dark. Everyone, eat some food and get some rest. Once we leave, we may not return until we've completed our mission."

After Spider finished going over the readout of the large city that the bot had sent, Ursa told the others, "Repack your bags. We'll take them with us in case we don't return to base."

Spider closed the monitor and secured it in the pouch, which he slung over his shoulder. When everyone was ready to leave, he said, "Neither Phoenix nor I saw any sign of guards or security cameras when we did recon on the lab. We'll take the same route to the lab and then decide the fastest way to the city."

Spider led the way from the crumbling building, and the protectors followed single file. When Spider signaled for them to stop, they had reached the edge of the enormous three-story building. He took the scanner and slowly moved it around.

"The body signatures are the same as before. We can skirt around the front of the building and then continue to the city."

Arris pointed at the scanner. "The signature that you think is the Nebula investigator hasn't changed position. Maybe we should check on him. He could be hurt. Why else would he not have moved?"

"It shouldn't take long to skirt around to the back corner of the building, where the room is located. Perhaps there is a door we can use to gain entry. But if it is the investigator, why haven't you picked up his signal chip?" Phoenix asked as he studied the readout.

Spider tapped on the scanner as he thought about Arris's suggestion. "Sirus and Vega will come along with me and

Phoenix to check out who is in the room." After a pause, he added, "You too, Arris. You may be able to sense whether it is the investigator or someone else. Ursa, you and Minor will stand guard. Phoenix will keep his monitor active, so if you see any movement coming our way, signal him."

Spider led the way with the others following behind. They made no sound as they crept to the edge of the building and then around to the back. The windows on the ground floor were placed high up and didn't allow them to see inside. Spider signaled a halt when they reached the back of the building.

"We need to cross to the other end," he said, "but that will take us in front of the entrance to the ground floor. Arris, go ahead and see if you can sense anyone near the entrance."

Arris moved to the edge of the building and stood still. From her position in the back of the building, the sounds she could hear from the animals housed in the cages were louder and caused her to lose her concentration for a minute. She steadied her senses and did not hear any sound or sense anyone. She looked back at Spider and signaled for the rest of them to come ahead.

Spider stepped around Arris and motioned for the others to follow. When the small group was halfway across the ground floor, strange noises began, like someone fast clicking with his or her tongue. The noises continued to grow louder.

Arris grabbed Spider's arm. "Someone's coming."

"Get against the wall until we know what's happening," Spider said. "Be ready to move."

As the group backed against the wall with weapons ready, a whispering voice echoed out from a window overhead.

"Who's out there?" When no one responded, the voice asked, "Catella, is that you?"

As everyone breathed out in relief, Spider raised up and whispered, "Catella received your message and sent us. Is there a way inside?"

"No. I've been locked inside for a couple of years. No one is allowed to open the door," the voice answered.

"Is the door alarmed or just locked?" Spider asked.

"No alarms," the voice responded.

It took Spider a couple of tries before he had the oversized lock opened. Quickly, the group entered the building and closed the door behind them. It was dark inside; the only light filtered in from the high windows.

"Come this way," the voice ordered.

The small group followed the voice into a room with cages running along one side. A long work table filled the middle of the room, and on the table, sitting up on their hind legs, were three small animals that were an exact match to Echo.

"They must have picked up our scent and sounded an alert," Arris said.

The voice belonged to a small person who turned around and squinted his eyes to better see them. He looked startled at the sight of Spider. Then his eyes grew large at the sight of Vega and even larger when he saw Sirus.

The small being stuttered, "Catella received my message. I can't believe you are here. When I overheard there was a person from Nebula locked up downstairs, it gave me hope that someone would come for him."

"Are you Kohlo?" Arris asked the small, bent man.

He looked at Arris and smirked. "Many years ago I was called by that name. It was a name of honor. But no one has called me that for a long time." His narrow shoulders slumped, making him look even smaller.

"Can you tell us what happened to cause you to send a message asking for help?" Arris asked.

"Susum. That's what happened. No one would listen when I tried to warn them that he was up to no good. Then it was too late. He had too many under his spell, and he got rid of anyone who opposed him and what he was doing." Kohlo grimaced, and his bony body shook as he began to pace around the room, causing the three small animals to begin scurrying around and emitting a different noise.

Spider reached out and stopped Kohlo to stop the animals from signaling their presence. "We don't have a lot of time. How do we get downstairs? I need to check on the investigator from Nebula."

"If Susum finds out you are here, you will be hunted down by the beasts caged out back and killed," Kohlo warned, pointing a crooked finger toward the door.

Spider nodded. "I understand, but it is a risk we must take."

"Go back outside. On the corner is a door that leads downstairs. I doubt it's locked, but the room where your investigator is will be secured," Kohlo explained.

"Sirus and Arris, come with me. Phoenix and Vega, stay here with Kohlo." Spider turned and headed outside.

The door leading downstairs wasn't locked, and it only took one nudge from Sirus to open the door to where the Nebula investigator was imprisoned. Spider hurried over to the check on him.

"Can you sit up?" he asked.

The investigator opened his swollen eyes and recognized Spider. He slowly shook his head no.

Spider reached under him and helped him sit up. After a quick examination, he said, "He is severely dehydrated and has been starved. He wouldn't have lasted another day. Sirus, carry him upstairs, and we'll get him something to drink."

While everyone waited for the investigator to recover after being given one of Spider's energy drinks, Kohlo filled them in on what had happened on Hyrila.

"Susum came here from another planet to lead a team of scientists working on mind control. It was originally designed to be used to combat fears, to help a person overcome a specific fear of something. But then it changed to mind control over others. I wasn't part of the group, but I heard gossip. Anyone who didn't go along with the new program began to disappear. Then the fractured animals out back started to be used as punishment for the protestors. I tried to make others aware by sending messages to the leaders on Hytura and Hydea, but Susum learned of my efforts and imprisoned me here. If it weren't for my work with these little guys, I'm sure he would have fed me to the beasts penned in the back." Kohlo fondly petted the three small animals. "You see, they will only respond to me."

"Why don't the people in the city do something?" Vega gruffed, upset by what he had heard.

Kohlo flung his bony arms around and explained, "They are all under his control. That's why. Susum found a way to exert mass mind control, and he is controlling all of them."

Sirus bent over, examining the investigator, and then turned to Spider. "He has been severely beaten and isn't able to walk. He has multiple broken bones and I suspect internal injuries. He needs immediate medical treatment."

"His signal chip must have been crushed during the beating, and why I never picked up a signal," Spider said. "We need to move quickly. Kohlo, you can't stay here; you must to come with us."

"I can't leave my pets. No one will take care of them," Kohlo protested.

"We can take them with us, but we need to go now," Spider replied.

Kohlo scurried to the row of cages and returned with a one large enough to hold the three small animals. He set the cage on the table, opened it, and whistled a signal. The three animals ran inside. He closed the cage and picked up a sack, which he then filled with the same pellets that he'd shipped with Echo.

"We're ready."

Sirus carried the investigator, who was almost asleep. To ease his pain, Spider had given him an injection from the assortment of pins he always carried with him. Vega carried the cage with the three animals. Arris helped Kohlo walk; after having been locked in the lab for two years, the small scientist wasn't all that mobile.

"Are you sure we should break up the team?" Ursa said, worried, as they made their way to the city.

"I didn't have much of a choice," Spider replied. "Sirus is the only one able to get the investigator through the portal. He may have to carry him back to NAHQ, depending on what Catella decides. Vega has to protect Kohlo and his pets at base camp. I'm not sure if Susum will hunt for Kohlo when he learns both he and the investigator are missing. According to Kohlo, the animals penned in back are starved and used for sport. They have been trained to hunt down and kill whoever they are set after."

Spider and Ursa led the way, followed by Phoenix, Arris, and Minor. Spider was determined to finish their mission by finding out everything he could about Susum and the current situation on Hyrila.

CHAPTER 4

THE DISCOVERY

When they came to the outskirts of the city, Spider halted his fast pace. He told the others, "We'll rest here while I review the readout and determine where we are and where to go next."

He removed the monitor from its pouch and opened it. The protectors sat down, opened their packs, and removed drinks to quench their thirst. The walk to the city had been fast, dusty, and hot. The sun was on its downward path, and night was not far off.

"It shouldn't take you long to reach this circle in the center of the city where the buildings form a ring. Most of the incoming streets end at the circle. These buildings are the highest in the city and are where any commerce or trading information would be found. There is a space dock not far from the city, but there are only two ships in port. Ahead, there looks to be some vacant buildings. I'll set up in one of them and monitor everyone from there. Phoenix will stay behind in case I need to send someone to help. Ursa and Minor, you will use your cover story to gather information.

Arris, you will go with Ursa and Minor, but stay back and see if you can sense how this mind control is happening. If you run into trouble, signal. We'll meet back after dark to review the information you find and then decide our next step."

After Spider gave out orders, he headed for a vacant building that looked to have been used for storage at one time. He had updated the protectors' wrist comms with directions for how to reach the circle of buildings and then return to his hideout.

The protectors met very few people on the streets as they made their way to the center circle. The people they met walked in a stilted manner or like they would stumble at any time. There were faded signs showing transportation schedules. All transportation must be public, since there were no small, individual vehicles parked on the streets, but the public transportation system didn't look to be in use. The buildings they passed were unkempt and had begun to deteriorate from lack of care. Litter had blown around the buildings, giving the city a dirty look.

The people looked as unkempt as the city. Most of their heads hung down as they made their way down the street, lost in their own worlds. Ursa glanced at Arris when they walked past a man slowly ambling down the road. Arris understood Ursa's questioning look, which meant do you sense anything? Arris shook her head. The man gave no mental awareness as he passed three strangers on the road.

At the city center, there were more people moving around. Some were carrying bags or other items, but all went their own way, either not noticing or not caring that there were others around them. No greetings were spoken, and they did not nod to one another. It was like everyone had their own schedule or task to complete. The tallest of the buildings on the circle had double doors. That was the building the various individuals were entering and exiting. Ursa headed toward the double doors with Minor close behind.

Arris hung back, waiting until Ursa and Minor were inside, and then she slipped in. She looked around and noticed that Ursa was standing in front of a reception desk talking to a man in what resembled a blue uniform. The coat looked misbuttoned, and the belt sagged around his thin waist. Minor stood to the side, his eyes doing a slow scan the area. When Ursa and Minor followed the man toward a row of offices, Arris moved against the back wall to observe any activity taking place. She hoped she could find out how so many people could walk around in a trancelike state. Her senses were actively trying to pick up any feelings or emotions from those around her.

As Arris stood against the wall, she noticed a faint humming sound. No one else would have noticed it, but because of her excellent hearing ability, she did. Arris glanced around. The lobby was spacious, with glass-fronted offices down each side. Directly across from where she stood, moving steps ran up and down, allowing people to reach the upper floors. There were four upper floors that opened onto the lobby, and each floor had a deck with a railing where someone could stand and look down at the lobby. The lobby was unadorned; there were no decorations or plants to make it a pleasing place to visit. Arris knew the building was higher than the four floors she could see, but she could not see a way to go any higher than the fourth floor.

The few people milling about the lobby seemed to have blank minds or were numb, without any feelings that Arris could detect. Some of them should feel anxious, excited, happy, or mad, but Arris picked up nothing like that. She started to change positions, as she had lost sight of Ursa and Minor when they'd left with the uniformed man and she wanted to keep a visual on them. As she stepped away from the wall, however, a jolt rocked her senses, and her ears seemed to vibrate. She felt as if she had been hit by a lightning bolt. She knew the sound she heard was internally sensed and not externally heard.

Arris stumbled back against the wall, trying to regain her senses. As she fought for control, she realized that someone was trying to break into her mind. On Daedro, when she had met her Aunt Celeste, her aunt had had the ability to practically read Arris's mind, and many times, Arris had had to blank her thoughts to keep them from Celeste. Celeste had been curious and had wanted to learn more about her niece, but there were some details that Arris had wanted to keep private. This mind invasion Arris was feeling now was far more intense and probing.

Arris knew who was trying to break into her thoughts. It was Susum. Kohlo had told them about his extraordinary ability to take over another person's mind and make him or her say or do whatever he wanted. As Arris blanked her mind, she heard, *I know you're there. Who are you?* When she didn't respond, she heard again, *I can feel you. You are special. Why have you come here?*

Arris was beginning to shake with the effort of not responding and keeping her mind blank; her brow became wet with perspiration. Arris knew that she had just met someone with sensory powers she had never encountered before, and she had to get out of the building before Susum found her. She lowered her head and slowly started to make her way to the double doors. She quickly glanced around but did not see Ursa or Minor.

She glanced up and was jolted. Standing on the deck of the fourth floor was a being unlike anyone she had seen before. Living at NAHQ and having traveled to various planets, she had met some very interesting and different-looking individuals, but none gave her the fear she felt when she saw Susum.

Arris knew her one chance to avoid being detected was to blend to make her escape. Arris emptied her thoughts and slowly absorbed her surroundings. She breathed in and out, trying to keep control. She watched Susum walk to the edge of the railing and look down into the lobby, trying to find her. What galaxy or planet he came from, Arris had no clue. He seemed massive in size and wore a long, beige robe that hung to the floor. The hands that clutched the railing were huge and covered with brown hair that resembled fur. Long nails curved from the ends of his fingers. His head matched his size and was covered with brown fur that continued down his neck until the robe hid it. His mouth was twisted, revealing pointed, yellowed teeth. But the black eyes, which held menace beyond anything Arris had experienced, were the scariest of all.

Arris reached the double doors without Susum detecting her. Just as she stepped outside, a person knocked into her.

"Where did you come from?" the startled man asked, causing Arris to unblend and expose herself. Arris stared into piercing green eyes and could sense the man's surprise as he gripped her shoulders. This man was not under any kind of mind control, and from his anxious look, Arris knew he too was trying to get away without Susum detecting him. The man let go of Arris's shoulders, turned, and hurried down the street. It took a minute for Arris to gather her wits, and not wanting the man to disappear without talking to her, Arris chased after him.

Arris didn't want to run after the man who had bumped into her; if Susum had security posted around the building, she would be noticed. She was sure that this main building was his headquarters, which was perhaps why there was no way to reach the upper floors. Arris lowered her head and walked as fast as she dared. When she reached the end of the building, she could continue her circle around the city's main block, but she felt the man would have taken one of the streets that ended at the circle to make his retreat. Arris looked around and selected the street to her left. It looked deserted, and with the sun starting to set, one side of the street was in shadows. Arris stepped to her left.

She crossed the circle and reached the darkened street. She was about to signal Spider when she saw movement up ahead. Arris hurried forward so as not to lose sight of the man, all the while thinking she should contact Spider. She was still recovering from her mental battle with Susum. Suddenly, everything went black as a large sack was dropped over her head, and before she could react, her arms were bound by a rope. Someone picked her up, put her over a shoulder, and continued down the dark street. Arris tried to wiggle and kick her way free, but other than causing the person carrying her to stumble, she made no progress toward her freedom.

A door was pushed open and then closed. The scent coming through the bag changed as she was carried into a musty building. She was dumped on the floor but didn't try to get loose or stand up until she regained her bearings. With her arms bound at her sides, she had no way to signal Spider for help. She heard voices coming from the next room; they were muffled by the walls, and those talking were trying to keep their conversation at a whisper level. But Arris still heard what was being said.

"She was following Vergil. That's why I took her," one voice explained.

"Don't blame Chares. I bumped into her trying to get away from Susum. He appeared from the fourth floor and was examining the lobby. I was afraid he would recognize me." Arris was sure this speaker was Vergil.

"Now what do we do with her?" This voice was female and sounded older and tired.

"We can't turn her loose; she could be a spy for Susum." It was Chares who answered.

As Arris listened, she didn't pick up that she was in danger but rather in a difficult situation. This group of people she was hearing must not be under Susum's control. She came to a decision and yelled to be heard.

"Why don't you come and ask me?"

Everyone in the next room went silent. Arris could hear movement and then footsteps as the group came into the room where she sat on the floor. She felt the rope being untied, and then the sack was lifted from her head. Arris gazed at the man called Vergil, who had bumped into her, and then looked at Chares and the older woman. As they returned her stare, each of them looked confused.

Arris decided it was up to her to get out of this predicament. "My name is Arris," she explained. "I am from Nebula and came to this planet after receiving a call for help."

It was clear from their faces that no one believed her story.

"There is a scientist called Kohlo," she continued. "He sent a secret message to Nebula Headquarters for help."

"There is no way anyone can get a message off planet," the older woman said. "Susum has everyone under his control, and anyone arriving or trying to leave is captured and taken to him. Most never return. You must be working for him." She turned to the others. "We need to get rid of her."

Arris had no way to prove who she was or where she was from. Because of the secret nature of their arrival, Spider and the protectors carried no documentation. As she tried to think of a way to prove who she was, an alarm sounded.

"Some has broken in. We need to get away," the woman almost screamed, and terror filled her eyes.

Arris leaped up to protect the woman and drew her hidden weapon. She would have no trouble going against anyone Susum sent. Vergil and Chares picked up guns that looked to be pieced together from other weapons.

"Don't waste you bullets. Make sure your shots count," Vergil warned as he and Chares, along with Arris, formed a ring around the frightened woman.

Just then, the doors to the building were blown open, and Spider dropped from the ceiling. The woman screamed and fainted. Chares grabbed the woman before she hit the floor. Spider had his long dagger drawn, and Phoenix rushed through the smoking door with weapon in hand.

"Don't shoot!" Arris yelled. "We are not in danger." Arris bent down and took the woman's hand. "We came to help. You are safe."

Phoenix put his gun down and said, "We need to leave. That blast will have been noticed—if anyone around here notices anything."

"This way," Vergil said.

Chares picked up the woman and followed Vergil into the next room, where he exited through a small door into the dark. Spider, Phoenix, and Arris brought up the rear, keeping watch to make sure the group wasn't being followed.

They crossed several streets, heading away from the city center, before Vergil made his way around to the back of a deserted warehouse. He didn't open the back door of the building but rather reached down and pulled up a scuffed wooden panel to reveal narrow steps leading downward. He held the panel up to allow Chares to help the woman down the steps. Then Vergil motioned for Arris, Spider, and Phoenix to follow. Spider nodded his approval before the group entered the basement.

Arris was surprised by what she saw. The basement was an underground operations center, filled with tables that had various pieces of equipment sitting on top. Monitors were wired to the equipment, and there were several men sitting in from of them. The men all startled when they saw that strangers had entered the room.

"Get Marly some water," Vergil ordered. "Everyone, we have visitors, gather round while we hear why they are here."

The men stopped what they were doing, stood up, and walked to the front of the tables. They formed a line on each side of Vergil, who rested against one of the tables. The group gave Spider their undivided attention, anxious to find out where these strangers had come from.

Spider explained the secret message that Kohlo had been able to send to NAHQ and his connection to Catella. He told them about the Nebula investigator who had been sent being taken prisoner and almost killed and explained that their reason for staying was to assess the situation and report back to Catella.

"Now will you tell us how this Susum was able to gain control of almost everyone?" he asked.

"For the past two to three years," Vergil began, "Susum has had control of most of the population. He knows what is going on where and by whom. Anyone who has tried to stop him has been killed or has found a place to hide. About a year ago, those of us who were hiding and who his mind control didn't affect began to work together. We have to be careful who we trust, or we'll be turned in. The only way we can get our city back is to find out how he is controlling everyone and stop it. Susum was able to take over by having select groups meet for various reasons. It was a very devious scam. He was able to hypnotize everyone in the meetings and keep them under his command. We just can't figure out how. One of the scientists working in the labs told us that the hybrid animals respond to hidden signals or sounds, and that could be how. But we haven't been able to hear any broadcasts by Susum. That is what this equipment is being used for."

Arris immediately realized the reason for the faint humming sound she'd heard in the lobby. She spoke up.

"Susum is using sound waves, but they are very faint and being heard unconsciously by those under his spell."

Arris looked around and explained, "You need to look for a very-low-voltage hum. The humming could be made up of instructions or orders or could just serve to keep everyone tuned into the sound. That could be the reason everyone looks like they are in a trance; their subconsciouses have taken over."

Vergil looked stunned. He turned to the team of men and ordered, "Reset the scanners to as low a voltage possible and then work up from there decimal by decimal."

The men rushed to their equipment and started resetting the dials.

While the scramble to reset the equipment was going on, Arris asked Spider, "How did you know to come? I didn't signal."

"When I noticed the signal from your tracking device move away from city central, I became concerned. I repositioned the bot to follow you and knew you were captured when another form combined with yours," Spider explained.

Arris nodded and said, "I'm glad you had my back. I wasn't sure I could convince my captors that I was from Nebula."

CHAPTER 5

HIDDEN SIGNALS

As the men began to reset the equipment to scan for the hidden signal Susum was using to control those under his spell, Vergil walked up to Spider and asked, "How can Nebula help us? I haven't heard about Nebula in years and didn't think they became involved in intraplanetary disputes. Something about their mission being to resolve wars." He folded his arms as he waited for Spider to answer.

Spider looked at Arris and Phoenix before he said, "You're correct. Nebula's mission is to assist in resolving conflicts if possible. Many situations become escalated because of differences of opinion, and once heated, they many times lead to war. We have liaisons who will act as intermediators and bring the conflicting parties together without the threat of violence. Many innocent lives have been spared because of this. The galaxies and planets that have joined Nebula have seen positive results."

Marly was listening to the conversation and came over. "There is no conflict here. Susum has eliminated anyone who dared to oppose him, and no one has done one thing about it." Her voice was bitter, and the look on her face was that someone who craved revenge.

"Marly's husband and son were killed by Susum," Vergil explained.

"They were told their only chance was to escape the beasts. No one escapes the evil that Susum keeps locked up. Others actually cheered when they were caught and slaughtered. Can Nebula bring back all those who've been killed?" Marly's voice shook, and her shoulders slumped in grief.

Arris was rocked by the utter despair she felt from the woman. She looked at Spider and in a firm voice said, "We can't go back and not help these people. They've suffered enough from this evil."

Phoenix looked like he wanted to protest, but Arris stopped him.

"I've felt and seen Susum, and I've never sensed anything like him before. I'm not sure where he came from, but we can't leave without trying to help these people end his control."

Spider checked his wrist comm and said, "I need to get back and find out why Ursa or Minor haven't checked in." Spider turned to Marly. "I'll do what I can to help, but if we are found interfering outside of Nebula's mission, it could cause issues for Catella and the council."

He reached inside a pocket and removed a small communicator, which he handed to Vergil.

"Keep this with you. If you need help, use this button to signal, and I'll open a comm link. If I find out more about Susum from my team, I'll contact you. Let's meet up tomorrow and determine what we can do to help."

Vergil put the communicator in his pocket and held out his hand to Spider. "Thanks. You have given us our first hope in years," he said as he and Spider shook hands.

Spider checked the scanner as he led the way through the dark streets. The three did not meet anyone as they made their way back to the hideout. No sounds could be heard, but a few lights flickered from various buildings. Once inside the hideout, Spider turned on a small light he had placed on an overhead beam.

He looked around and said, "Ursa and Minor haven't returned. No one has been in here since Phoenix and I left."

Spider used his wrist comm to send another signal and waited for Ursa or Minor to reply. No response was returned.

"Their individual signals show they are still inside the building," he said.

Arris knew he was concerned and said, "Susum may have blocked communications coming in or going out of the building. I'm sure this building is the place from which he is sending the control message."

"They should have returned long ago and would have left before the building was shut down for the night," Phoenix said. "One of them would have sent a message if they were staying the night."

"You said they left the lobby with a uniformed man and went into one of the offices?" Spider asked Arris.

"Yes. But when I went to find out which office, Susum appeared. If they went or were taken someplace else, I don't know where. There are stairs that reach the upper four floors, but the building has two or three higher levels. I'm sure this is where Susum has his headquarters."

"I'll monitor their signals throughout the night and make sure they don't move," Spider said. "Tomorrow we will go back to the building and find them. Get some rest; we'll leave as soon as it's light."

Ursa shook her head, trying to get rid of the cobwebs behind her eyes. She felt like she was waking up from a deep sleep, escaping some dream where she had been captured. She listened but could not hear a sound. Minor. Where was he? She tried to remember, but her thoughts were fuzzy. Had she been gassed? And was she tied up? Ursa tried to sit up straighter, but her arms were bound behind her back. She tried to move her legs, but they were secured to the legs of a chair. Ursa wasn't afraid but rather upset that she had been captured and couldn't remember the how or who. The man in the uniform. He had answered her questions about purchasing rescue animals. Rescue animals. She remembered that was her and Minor's cover story. The man had sat down behind the desk, spoken to someone, and then said to follow him, that he had what they were looking for.

Ursa slowly opened her eyes and was surprised at the bright light shining down on her. She blinked twice and then turned her head to see that she was in a small room. The chair she was tied to was pushed up to a metal table made for two people. The space across from her was empty. Where was Minor? Ursa worried for her teammate.

Minor had awakened shortly before Ursa and was fully aware of his situation. He was not as affected by the gas as Ursa. He discovered that he was bound to a chair seated behind a small metal table and that he was the only person in the narrow room. He tried to move his hands to reach the communicator hidden underneath his sleeve. The straps that held his arms behind his back were tight, but Minor felt a small give when he moved his wrists. Time to get to work. He needed to get free and find Ursa. Minor recalled following the uniformed man into a room, where they were told to wait, and then hearing Ursa's warning cry of "Gas!" Before they could free the small respirators they each had hidden in a pocket, the gas had overcome them.

Minor heard the key being inserted into the door and stopped twisting his wrists. The straps had loosened enough that he was sure he could slide one hand out. The same uniformed man opened the door and stepped aside. Minor glared at the man, who didn't seem to notice the unspoken threat. The man held the door open for the strangest person Minor had ever seen. The person was even larger than Sirus and was wearing a robe-like garment that covered most of his body. The hands held together in front were large and covered with brown hair. The person came into the room and pushed back the chair across from Minor. With effort, the person sat down in the chair. Minor waited for the chair's legs to give way, but they held. The person leaned forward to study him. Minor wanted to move back but didn't. Instead, he studied the person back. Brown hair covered his head, and his eyes were such a deep black that they almost looked purple. Minor didn't know the species of this person but knew that it was Susum who was inspecting him like some kind of bug. He recalled everything Kohlo had told them about this creature.

"Well, well, what have we here?" Susum said. "From your features, I suspect you could be a Theran. Maybe not." Susum shrugged as if it didn't matter where Minor originated from. "The main question is, why you are here? The story your companion gave was a silly hoax. So, now you can explain to me the purpose of your visit."

Minor decided not to answer but sat up straight in the chair and stared straight ahead. When his head felt like someone was trying to drill a hole in it, he knew Susum was trying to gain control of his mind and hypnotize him. In protector training, the students had been subjected to various methods of mind control. What worked best for him against this type of invasion was for him to go someplace else in his mind. Minor decided to visit a colony of ants. They were busy little creatures, always doing or going somewhere. Minor made himself into an ant and joined in their happy parade. In his mind, he sang a marching song. He sang and sang and marched and marched. Minor was brought back from the parade of marching ants when Susum growled, slammed his plate-sized hands on the table, and stood up. Minor kept his expression neutral as he watched Susum stomp from the room. The uniformed man closed the door without acknowledging the scene that had just played out.

Minor knew time was running out, especially with Susum's outburst. He twisted his wrists, collapsed one hand, and wiggled free from the bands. He bent down and untied his legs and hurried to the door to listen. He heard a door close and knew that Ursa was in the next room and so was Susum. Minor bent down and inspected the lock. He quickly removed a small file from his pocket. He adjusted the handle and inserted the file into the lock, moving it around and turning the handle to allow the file to mold to the shape inside the lock. When the file wouldn't move any more and locked into shape, Minor used it like a key to unlock the door. He then placed the file in his pocket, hoping the same key would open the door where Ursa was being held.

Minor slowly opened the door and peered out. He saw no one around and slipped out into the hall. He crept to the next door and could hear Susum talking to Ursa. Minor would have to wait until Susum left before he could free Ursa. He slipped back into his room but kept the door opened a crack to watch for Susum to leave. He pushed up his sleeve to reveal his wrist comm and signal Spider, but the comm had no light to indicate that it was active. Somehow, their communication link to Spider had been shut off.

When Susum sat down across the table from Ursa, she had almost recovered from the effects of the gas. She immediately realized who was sitting across the table and what he was capable of doing.

Susum stared at Ursa and then finally said, "Your friend didn't fare so well when we talked. Perhaps you will cooperate and answer my questions."

Ursa stiffened at hearing about Minor and leaned into the table. "You'd better not hurt him," she almost growled.

Susum clapped his huge hands. "How brave. Just like a mother bear defending her cubs."

Ursa leaned back in her chair to put some space between them.

"If you want your companion to be left alone," he told her, "just answer my questions." When Ursa didn't respond, he continued. "I want to know who you three are and where you come from. Where is the one who has the ability to read minds?"

Ursa was relieved but didn't show it. Arris had gotten away, and Susum wasn't aware that Spider and Phoenix were in the city. He must not have learned of the investigator being rescued or of Kohlo's escape.

"We just came to purchase recuse animals," Ursa answered. "I'm not sure who you are referring to that can read minds."

Susum's face darkened, and he leaned close and snarled. "You can stop playing your games. If you want to see your companion—alive, that is—answer my questions."

Ursa blanched as she heard someone scream but then realized it was Susum projecting the scream into her thoughts.

"He will scream more if you don't cooperate," Susum threatened.

Ursa nodded. She needed to keep Minor alive as long as possible so that Spider could rescue them.

"We came from Nebula to look for a missing man." Ursa would only give as few facts as possible, but she knew that they must be partially truthful for Susum to believe her.

"Continue," Susum said.

"That's it. We came to this building to see if we could find him here," Ursa said.

"I don't believe you. No one arrives or leaves without my knowledge. You didn't come through the docks, so you must have gained entrance another way. Who are you working with?" Susum drummed his fingertips as he waited for Ursa to answer.

"Spider," Ursa said.

Susum slammed the table with his plate-sized hands and growled, "Enough. I've had enough ants and now spiders." Susum stormed from the room.

After he'd gone and the door shut and locked behind him, Ursa wondered if she had heard correctly. Ants and spiders?

Ursa heard the lock click again and groaned, thinking Susum had come back. She watched as the door opened on its own, but no one entered the room. Slowly the door shut, and then she felt someone untying the straps that held her wrists. Minor had blended and somehow gotten free.

"Minor," she whispered, but Minor silenced her with two taps on her arm, a signal not to speak in case they were being monitored. Ursa nodded as her arms were freed. She pushed back, untied her feet, and stood up.

Minor led her to the door and tapped to signal that she should wait. The door opened, and Minor slipped out. A minute later, he opened the door and took Ursa's arm. He led her around a wall and stopped. From here, they could see the moving stairs running down, and across the hall, the stairs ran upward. After being gassed, Ursa realized, they must have been moved to the second floor and tied up in neighboring rooms. Daylight filtered into the lobby on the ground floor, and people were entering the building and using the moving stairs to reach the offices where they worked. As the foot traffic increased, Minor and Ursa made their way to the stairs. As they walked, Minor unblended. There was too much motion for him to stay hidden. The two walked slowly and kept their heads lowered as they rode the stairs descending to the lobby.

There was a different uniformed man at the reception desk when they walked past. The man didn't take notice of them. They came to the double doors, and it was all they could do not to sprint outside to freedom. Minor felt the hidden weapons he carried. Evidently, no one had searched them or taken anything from them after they'd been gassed and tied up. Susum must have been confident that once captured, they could not escape.

After they were outside, Ursa breathed in deeply and said under her breath, "I can't believe we survived"—she squeezed Minor's arm—"thanks to you."

They had barely made it across the street to head back to Spider's hideout when Phoenix stepped out.

"We've been worried. Why didn't you signal?"

"Long story," Minor said. "Let's get out of sight before we're missed and someone starts looking for us."

CHAPTER 6

ANTICONTROL PLOT

As they walked, Phoenix signaled Spider that Ursa and Minor were safe and they were on the way back to the hideout. They kept their pace slow and heads lowered so as not to raise suspicion. There were more people on the streets heading for the city center and circle of buildings.

"What do all these people do all day?" Minor wondered as they walked past a man heading toward the center.

"I'm sure the city is still active in trading and other commerce. Susum can't shut everything down and not raise suspicion among the people of the other planets," Phoenix answered before changing topics. "Arris ran into a man named Vergil who is working with a group of people to overthrow Susum. Spider and Vergil are meeting this morning in the hideout. Spider is anxious to hear if you've found out anything about how Susum is maintaining control."

"We didn't learn much," Ursa said, "but Susum knows we're here and wants to find Arris. He asked who we were working for, and when I said Spider, he became upset and left. His answer was strange. He yelled that he didn't want to know any more about ants or spiders."

Minor laughed out loud, and Ursa and Phoenix knew that somehow, Minor was the source of Susum's anger.

When they entered the hideout, Spider was sitting talking to Vergil. He stopped and introduced Ursa and Minor to him.

Vergil nodded and said, "I'm very glad you made it out alive. No one usually does once Susum takes them."

"I understand that after meeting him," Ursa said. "Minor was the one who was able to get us out." She turned to Spider. "Susum knows about Arris and is looking for her. On the way here, we noticed that there is more foot traffic heading to city center than there was yesterday. Susum may be planning something."

"I need to contact someone," Vergil said. "She may know. She has a contact in the building Susum hides out in. Maybe he's heard something." Vergil stood up and walked outside.

Spider turned to Arris. "You should leave the city before Susum finds you. When it's dark, you can go help Vega guard Kohlo and his pets."

Before Arris could protest, Vergil hurried into the room looking excited. "They found the signal Susum is broadcasting on. This is the first real break we've had. Now we need to find out if we can interrupt or override it somehow."

"You must proceed carefully," Spider cautioned. "You don't know what Susum may do if the signal stops working. He could have something programmed that could harm everyone if they can't hear the signal."

"Like a built-in self-destruct?" Minor gasped.

"What should we do?" Vergil asked with a look of horror.

"Can you capture someone under Susum's control and isolate that person in a room where he or she can't hear the subliminal message?" Arris suggested. "Watch the person's reaction as the connection to the signal is lost. I should be there. Maybe I can pick up on the person's feelings when he or she is released from the signal. If I sense an impulse for self-harm, we can stop the person from doing it."

Vergil still looked shocked. He turned to Spider and said, "I see why you said this team from Nebula is the best-qualified team you've ever worked with. In less than a day, they've accomplished more than we have in over a year."

Spider looked at Arris and said, "I would feel more comfortable if you were away from the city, but it's your decision if you want to stay."

"I can be of more help here," Arris answered.

Spider turned to Vergil. "Take someone today that you know is under Susum's control. You need to be careful and not cause this person any anxiety; Susum may become aware of it if you do. He is more powerful than anyone I've encountered before. I'll bring Arris when you're ready to isolate the person. We need to see the person's reaction before we can plan to bring down the signal."

"I'll contact you when were ready," Vergil said, and he left the hideout to set their plan in motion.

While they waited, Arris told Spider, "I'm positive Susum's headquarters is in the upper floors of the building we were in. I didn't see any way to go higher than the fourth floor, but there could be hidden stairs in the back."

"Susum is large and not agile. I don't see him climbing many stairs. I bet there is an elevator to take him up and down the floors," Minor added.

"While I was waiting to go in and search for Ursa and Minor," Phoenix said. "I noticed the upper floors all have windows. Maybe we could get in through one of them and investigate."

"It is worth looking into. After dark, we can go find out," Spider replied.

Vega returned to the old barn being used as base camp and told Kohlo, "I didn't see any activity around the lab building. If Susum has learned about you and our investigator escaping, he hasn't ordered anyone to search."

Kohlo sat perched on an old feeding trough. "I'm not sure if that is good or bad. Susum is extremely evil, and when he learns of my escape, he will retaliate. It's his way." He reached out and fed each of his pets one of the pellets. "That should do you for a while," he told the animals, which were skittering around the crumbling building, enjoying their freedom.

"What are the animals that are penned in the back of the compound? Are they hybrids of some sort?" Vega asked.

"Most definitely hybrids, although I haven't seen what is back there in years. When the hybrids are set free to hunt, my pets react to the signal. They know what those signals mean and run and hide in their cages when the beasts have been set loose," Kohlo explained.

Vega was curious. "Can't those signals be interrupted, like to confuse the animals, make them do something besides hunt and kill?"

Kohlo sat up and placed a hand on his forehead in thought. "Interesting suggestion. I know the frequencies they use; I've heard them enough. There is one frequency that tells them to hunt, one to kill, and one to return to their cages. I don't think the trainers use more that those three. The hybrids are not stable, and I overheard that only three are still alive. Some died from the cloning not working, and others became rabid and had to be put down. The reason for the separate pens is that they fight with each other over food because the trainers keep them half starved."

Vega walked to the window and looked out. "I wonder what is happening in the city. It's been two days since we returned here; Spider told me not to signal unless we were threatened."

"It would be good to know. I would like to return to my lab." Kohlo sighed.

Vega looked stunned. "Why do you want to go back there? It's been your prison for years."

Kohlo looked over at Vega and shrugged. "It's the only home I know. I am happy there with my pets."

Suddenly, the three little animals raised up on their hind legs and began to make clicking noises.

Kohlo stood up and said, "Someone is coming."

Vega removed his gun from its holster. "Get into the back room. Silence your pets."

Vega crouched down and waited by the door as Kohlo signaled his pets to follow him into the back room.

Vega could not hear anyone or anything approaching and slowly raised up to look out the window. He almost fell backwards when he came face to face with Sirus, who was looking in the window.

Vega gasped. "You could have signaled."

Sirus recovered from his shock and explained, "I didn't know the situation here. I wanted to make sure before I revealed myself."

When Kohlo stepped from the back room carrying his three pets, "Oh, that's how you knew I was coming," Sirus said.

The three little animals scurried from Kohlo's hold and ran to greet Sirus, each making a noise that sounded like a whistle.

Vega asked how the investigator was doing, and Sirus replied, "Catella asked that I bring him to NAHQ. The medical staff and equipment there is superior to that on Bankos. While there, I updated Catella on the situation and then came straight back. What's our status here?"

Vega told Sirus that there was no update from Spider or additional activity at the labs. He and Kohlo were waiting for an update.

As the three small animals cuddled in Sirus's arms, he asked Kohlo, "What is so special about these guys?"

Kohlo explained that he'd trained them to react to specific sounds or situations and that they could be used as sentries to guard someone. He was interrupted by a loud growl that echoed from the cages and shuddered.

"Susum uses those beasts for sport and to maintain control. Anyone who dares to go against him is hunted down and killed," he said.

"Eventually, anyone who uses this type of terror to control will be taken down themselves, but not without cost," Sirus said then added that he was tired. It was becoming dark, and he needed to get some sleep, as he had not stopped to rest since he had carried the injured investigator into the portal.

While waiting for dark to investigate Susum's headquarters, Spider sent the bot to circle the city buildings. As he watched the readout from the bot on the monitor, he commented, "There is a constant stream of people in and out of the main building. They don't seem to stay inside for long before I see them exit. After dark, I will climb to one of the windows. I sent the bot in for a closer look, and the top-floor windows are all open, like they are being used for ventilation."

Phoenix walked over and looked at the monitor. "If the top floor is where the equipment is located to send the control sound, it would need extra venting. To send the signal as far as the city limits and without interruption would take a number of devices running full time and using a lot of power."

"If you wanted to take down a large number of machines at one time, how would you do it?" Spider asked. Phoenix's knowledge of systems and how they operated was second only to that of Kent, which was the reason Kent had requested Phoenix's help on occasion.

"If I could inspect the system setup, I would be able to answer this better, but if taking down the signal doesn't affect those under its spell, I would cut the power to the equipment. If they're all in the same building and on the top floor, there would be a single power source. Cut the power, and the machines will crash." For Phoenix, the answer was simple—no power, no hidden message.

"If Vergil is successful tonight, you and I will breach the building after we take Arris to him," Spider said.

"What about me and Minor?" Ursa asked.

"I'll need one of you to stay here and one to stay with Arris," Spider answered.

Spider's comm beeped, and he opened a connection. "Were you successful?"

"Yes" Vergil answered. "We have sedated a man and will keep him asleep until you get here. I'll send you directions, but we are not far from the basement where we met."

It was dark outside as Spider led the protectors from the hideout—minus Minor, who was staying behind to monitor everyone's status and in case Vega signaled for help. Spider followed the directions Vergil had sent, and when they reached the building, he tapped on a side door. Vergil opened the door.

"Arris and Ursa will stay here until Phoenix and I return," Spider whispered. "I'm going to get a better look at what's on the top floor of Susum's headquarters. We think it's where he is sending the control message from. After we know the effect on the man you captured and what's on the top floor, we can decide what to do next."

Vergil stood aside to allow Arris and Ursa to enter and watched Spider and Phoenix disappear into the dark. He said, "The man is downstairs asleep. We've shielded a room and made sure no signals can make it in. If you're ready, we'll take the man to the room and wake him."

Arris nodded her head in response and followed Vergil down a hallway and into the shielded room. A single light hung from overhead, and the walls, windows, and ceiling were covered by metal plates. Vergil must have had a lot of help to carry and place the shielding. Chairs were placed around the edge of the room.

Vergil motioned for Arris and Ursa to take a seat, but Ursa refused. "I'll wait outside and watch the house. Inside the room, none of our communicators will work. It's safer this way."

Arris watched as a man was brought into the room being held up between two men. One of the men Arris recognized as Chares. Chares moved a chair into the middle of the room and helped to seat the man in the chair. Marly was the last to enter the room, and she shut the door. She took the chair next to Arris. Chares gave the man in the chair a drink and helped him to drain the cup.

Marly told Arris, "He may take a few minutes to wake."

As the man came awake, everyone anxiously watched for his reaction to being shut off from the constant noise. He slowly straightened up and looked up at Chares, who was standing next to him.

"Where am I?" he mumbled.

Chares reached out and placed his hand on the man's shoulder. "You're safe, brother."

Chares's brother started moving his head back and forth, and his eyes had a frightened look. "No. I-I-I can't hear," he stuttered.

Arris could sense the brother's concern and went to him. She knelt down and took his hands.

"What can't you hear?" she asked.

When the brother continued shaking his head, she repeated her question and squeezed his hands to make him look at her. The eyes that looked back at her were glazed with confusion, and he kept mumbling that he couldn't hear.

Arris looked at Vergil and said, "I don't sense anything but confusion. I'm not sure how to bring him back out of Susum's spell." Then she had an idea and turned back to the man. "What do you need to hear?" She yelled to penetrate his dazed state.

"Orders. My orders?" The man anxiously looked at Arris.

"Your orders are to wake up. Now." Arris shook the man's shoulders. "Wake up."

Arris sensed a change in the man. He was becoming calmer. Finally, the man looked around and demanded in a dazed voiced, "Chares, what is going on?"

Chares looked as if he could dance as he pulled his brother into his arms. "Stefan. Oh, Stefan. You're free." Chares had tears running down his face.

It took a few minutes to convince Stefan that what had taken place really had happened and that he had been in a trance for two years. But when he saw the shielded room and others told him what had been happening, he finally accepted the truth.

Arris told the group, "You can't bring them out from under the signal without a way to bring them back. I'm not sure how you can do this all at one time. Susum used small groups to put them under his spell and then used the hidden signal to keep them under his control. Perhaps you could get everyone in one place and then take down the signal and replace it with orders to wake up. You will need someone they know and trust to tell them what has happened. Do you have anyone like that?"

"Yes. We have someone they all trust." He smiled at Marly as he answered.

Everyone was seated in the main room talking when Ursa stepped in and said, Spider and Phoenix are back. They walked into the room, and Ursa followed them inside, anxious to learn what they had discovered.

Spider looked surprised when he was introduced to Stefan and told what had happened in the shielded room.

"Good," he said. "Now we know we can break the spell; we just need to figure out the details. Phoenix was correct. The upper floor is filled with equipment, and all are connected to a single source of power. It will be simple to cut the power and take down the signal."

"How did you get into the room upstairs?" Chares asked.

"From the outside wall. They don't call him Spider for no reason," Ursa said and grinned when she saw the astonished look on everyone's face.

CHAPTER 7

THE HUNT

The following morning, the reason for the heavy traffic to Susum's headquarters became evident. Susum's voice boomed from the old speakers placed throughout the city that had originally been set up to make service announcements for the people. Vergil had arrived at the hideout to meet with Spider shortly before the first message blared down the streets. They were trying to determine how to take down the equipment on the top floor of Susum's headquarters but stopped talking at the sound of Susum's voice.

"To those of you who came from Nebula to cause trouble, you must turn yourselves in. If you do not, you will suffer the consequences. The scientist Kohlo has been deemed a traitor and will be killed on sight. Orders have been given that if anyone detects a stranger, they are to report it immediately, and you will be apprehended by my security team—alive or dead, the choice is yours. The one with mind powers must come forward to meet with me. You have one hour to comply, or else you will face the beasts."

Vergil stood up and cringed. "You should leave. If he sets those monsters loose, you won't stand a chance."

Spider stayed seated and shrugged. "I don't like being threatened."

"And protectors don't run away," Ursa added, and the other protectors sitting in the hideout voiced their agreement.

Again, the same threatening message resounded from the speakers, Susum's promise to turn the beasts loose giving evidence of his cruelty.

Spider told Vergil, "You need to make sure your people get someplace safe. Continue to work out the details on how to take down the equipment that sends Susum's control message." Spider paused. "Thanks to Susum for demonstrating that you can use these outside speakers to broadcast the wake up order and tell everyone to go to a specific place, where Marly can explain to them what has been happening in the city for the past two years. Have others on your team positioned on the streets to assist everyone to the meeting place. It will be hard for them to understand that they have lost two years of their lives under Susum's mind control. Signal me when you have finalized your plans. And don't worry about Susum's security team; we will take care of them."

On seeing the grim look on Spider's face, Vergil nervously asked, "What will you do?"

Spider looked at Vergil and confirmed, "What we do best when threatened by someone like Susum."

Vergil nodded to the protectors and wished them luck. Then he left the hideout.

After Vergil left, Arris asked, "How does Susum know we came from Nebula?"

"He was probably able to get that information from the investigator, but I'm sure Catella only gave him the minimum facts for the investigation. Susum only knows of you, Ursa, and Minor and thinks he doesn't need to worry about the three of you. He has no idea there are more from Nebula in the city and does not know the number of citizens not under his control that are opposed to him," Spider explained.

"What's our next step?" Phoenix asked. "We can't stay here. I'm sure Susum will have security teams searching all the vacant buildings."

Before Spider could answer, static crackled from the outside speaker system, and then Susum's voice sneered, "Hidden one, I am looking for you. What am I thinking? If you come forward, I won't hurt your friends that got away."

It was clear from Susum's taunting that he had started to play a mind game with Arris, and if she were to respond in any way, he would find her.

Arris cringed at hearing the message aimed at her. She looked at Spider. "What should I do?" Suddenly, she felt a sharp, piercing pain behind her eyes. She held her head in her hands until the pain stopped. Then she looked up at Spider and shakily said, "He knows I'm still in the city and may be able to find where we're hiding."

"Minor, signal Vega that I'm sending Arris to base camp and he should watch for her," Spider quickly ordered. "If Susum can't find Arris in the city, he may think we've left." He turned to Arris. "Leave now and stay out of sight, or your location will be turned in to Susum. Your wrist comm has the route back to base camp, but take a detour if it means that you stay hidden."

216

Arris picked up her tote and, as the others cautioned her to be careful, slipped outside. She went around to the back of the building and ran for the cover of nearby bushes.

After reading the message from Minor, Vega told Sirus and Kohlo that Arris was on her way back to base camp. To keep the communication as short as possible, Minor hadn't sent that Arris must stay hidden to avoid being seen. Anxious for her to arrive and fill them in on all that had happened in the city, Vega and Sirus took turns at the window watching the open field in the direction of the laboratory building, not realizing that Arris would not be returning that way.

A sound echoed outside, and Kohlo's three animals jumped to attention and began chattering, making a different noise from the one they'd made when Sirus had arrived. When the sound began to fade in and out over and over again, the three pets shrieked, ran to their cage, and scurried inside.

Kohlo looked frightened and warned, "That's the signal for the beasts to hunt. They make it louder and louder to rile them up before they set them loose. When the beasts' cages open, they will send the kill signal. We should run, but I don't know of any place that would be safe."

As he talked, the three small animals continued to shriek from inside their cage.

Sirus and Vega looked at each other, both realizing who the prey was. It was Arris. It was no coincidence; she was coming, and the beasts were being set lose. Sirus and Vega removed the weapons they carried with them from their holsters and set them on the windowsill. Each carried two small pistols, knives that folded out to the length of a sword, and several flash and smoke bombs.

Kohlo came over and inspected their arsenal. "I doubt if all your weapons combined can take down even one of them."

"It will have to do." Sirus grimaced as he checked the loads on the pistols. The pistols were small, but thanks to Sirus, they were as powerful as many larger guns.

Vega looked at Kohlo. "You mentioned you know the signal for the beasts to return to their cages. Can your three pets make that sound?" Vega had to yell to be heard over the pet's screeching.

"They know the sound. I can't say whether I'll be able to get them to repeat it as a signal for the beasts." Kohlo responded.

"You have to try. If not, Arris could be killed." Vega sounded as worried as he looked.

Kohlo agreed to try. He hurried to the cage and began to soothe his pets. It was like there was a special link between Kohlo and the three small animals. As Kohlo began to make clicking sounds with his mouth, followed by hand signals, the pets calmed down. When Kohlo changed clicking sounds along with hand signals, the three pets' fur stood up straight, and they scurried around in circles. Kohlo was persistent as he worked with his pets. He knew that what he was asking them to do would put them in danger, but they were all in danger anyway, especially Arris. No one escaped the beasts when they were turned loose to hunt and kill.

"It's the kill signal. The beasts are loose," Kohlo exclaimed when a new sound reverberated against the walls.

Sirus extended the knife full length and held it in one hand. "I'm going out to see them so we can decide how to eliminate them for good," he said to Vega.

"Wait for me." Vega pocketed his weapons and followed Sirus from the barn.

They could hear them before they could see them. Loud growls that sounded like they came from a bear were repeated. Low, menacing howls came next, the signal that something was searching for a scent. But the strange birdlike screeching that came next, so unnerving that it sent shivers down Vega's spine, was the worst of the three.

Vega and Sirus hid amid a stand of trees that stood on a mounded hill, and they waited for their first sight of the menacing trio of death. The first to appear was a huge hybrid wolf with legs so tall that it made them wonder how it stayed upright. It would have been like running on stilts, which they had done in the gym on Nebula for balance training. Drool hung from its mouth as it sniffed the air for prey. Even climbing to the top of the trees they hid behind would not keep them away from the wolf's snarling jaws.

Off to the side, the source of the screeching appeared. A birdlike creature stopped when it crested the hill, keeping its distance from the hybrid wolf. It stopped screeching and extended long wings with feathers that were the shape of knives. Sharpened claws protruded from its huge, knobby feet, but strangest of all was its tail of brightly colored feathers, which fanned out. Inside each feather was a swirl, and in the center of the swirl was an eye looking around for prey.

Next, the huge, hairy head of the third beast appeared, followed by shoulders as wide as the barn door. Finally, the full figure of the mangy, dark-brown bear came into view. It was walking upright on its back legs. Its lumbering gait was slow, but the size of the bear, from the muscled hind legs to the massive head, was astonishing. The arms that swung to the side could crush anything that got in their way. At the top of the hill, the huge beast stopped to catch its breath, snorting steam from its nostrils.

The fierce creatures stayed away from each other but turned to one another and snarled, growled, or screeched a warning aimed at the others. They were starving and would not share even one bite when they captured their prey. Each beast stood at attention in its own manner, searching for the two-legged creatures they were to find and kill.

Sirus crouched behind the trees to think. He had never seen any beasts like these before. They had been designed as killing machines, and the reason why escaped him. Why would anyone want to create such threatening creatures? Sirus had hunted and been hunted on his home planet. The hunt was a ritual the men participated in to gain status. Sirus had gone with his brother after his brother had signed up for the planet's brigade. Before his brother's deployment, they had gone with other men to hunt the creatures on his planet. Much of the planet was still uninhabitable, except for the areas that had been cleared of jungle and the creatures that lived there. Therefore, they needed the brigade to protect the settlements.

Sirus knew that the first thing to do was to assess the enemy's strengths and weakness. The wolf was fierce; his strength was limited to his huge jaws and elongated fangs, and his weakness was in his legs. The bird was dangerous, beak, claws, and feathers; its only weakness would be its skinny neck, which did not have protection. The bear was strong with long-reaching arms; it would take an army tank to bring it down. Sirus could see no weaknesses until he remembered the slow, lumbering gait.

Sirus turned to Vega and shared his assessment.

"How do you want to do this—let them come to us or try to separate them and take them one at a time?" Vega asked.

Before Sirus could answer, the wolf let loose a low howl, a signal that it had found a scent. Vega stood up, took out his long-range viewer, and searched the open field for Arris.

"I still can't see Arris!" he exclaimed.

Sirus turned and looked at the wooded area beyond the barn and noticed movement. "Look over there." He pointed, and Vega quickly swung the viewer in that direction.

"Oh no. Arris is running along the tree line. She doesn't know about the beasts!" Vega was frantic. The three monsters had spotted Arris, and all had turned in her direction.

CHAPTER 8

THE HUNTED

"If we run around the barn, maybe we can intercept the beasts before they reach Arris. Can you signal her and tell her to get back into the trees?" Sirus yelled as he took off running, taking a slanting route that would go behind the crumbling barn and come out across from the direction Arris was running.

Vega raced after Sirus, pushing up his sleeve to reach his wrist comm as he ran. He pressed on the button to open a link with Arris, but he didn't receive a response from her. Vega kept pace with Sirus and was grateful for the death drills that had pushed him to his limit. It would take every ounce of speed he had to get to Arris. Vega almost stumbled as he tried to contact Arris again, and again he got no response.

As Sirus and Vega ran from behind the barn, they could see the wolf and bird gaining ground on Arris. The lumbering bear had covered only half the distance. Vega knew if he yelled, Arris wouldn't be able to hear him, so he again pushed on the button to open a link.

Arris continued to run at the edge of the tree line, unaware of the fast-approaching danger. She turned from the trees to head for the barn and saw Sirus and Vega running toward her. Arris waved her arm to show she had spotted them. Sirus raised the long knife over his head; it was a sign that meant prepare for battle. Arris didn't understand what Sirus was trying to warn her about; she laughed, thinking Sirus and Vega were playing a game with her.

First the wolf appeared, followed closely by the bird. When Arris saw the strange-looking creatures, she stopped so fast that she stumbled and almost fell to the ground. She knew these were the beasts that Susum had said they would face. She looked behind her and realized that she would never make it back to the trees before she was overtaken. When the wolf opened its huge mouth, exposing its razor-sharp fangs, Arris froze where she stood. Childhood memories and nightmares of big, snarling dogs flooded her brain, causing her to become immobile.

"Run!" Vega yelled at the top of his lungs. Why had Arris stopped? Why hadn't she readied her gun? Didn't she realize that neither he nor Sirus could reach her in time? She just stood there, frozen, as the wolf and bird closed in on her, snarling and screeching, each eager to reach the prey first and run away with its kill.

In the back of his mind, Vega heard noises—three distinct sounds. Hoo, ooo, woo. The sounds repeated over and over.

The bear stopped first and made a low moaning sound, shaking its massive head. The bird began to run in circles, its head bobbing up and down on its skinny neck. The wolf started to wobble on its stilt-like legs and howled like it was in pain. These beasts recognized the return signal, but because they had been starved and had already spotted Arris, they were fighting against it. During their training, they had been severely punished when they had not responded to the command signals. Now they were willing to risk being punished to eat.

Sirus glanced backward toward the barn. Standing statue-like on the top of the crumbling wall were Kohlo's three pets, each one taking a turn as they imitated the return-to-cage command for the three beasts. Kohlo stood below, encouraging the trio to keep mimicking the signal sounds.

Sirus knew this was their only chance to save Arris, and he raced toward the vicious bird. He glanced at Vega and pointed toward the wolf. Vega nodded and ran at top speed to engage the rabid creature on stilt-like legs.

The bird noticed Sirus approaching and screeched. Trying to ignore the command to return to its cage, the bird unfurled its large wings as it ran in circles, hoping to cut Sirus with its knife-sharp feathers. Sirus could tell the constant sounds were beginning to fade as the bravely singing trio begin to tire. It was now or never. As the bird turned in a circle, Sirus ran at top speed toward it. Timing his jump just right, he landed on the bizarre bird's back. He steadied his feet, and with one swing from his sword, he removed the bird's head from its neck. The bird's legs collapsed, and Sirus jumped to the ground. He quickly backed away as the bladed wings flopped up and down on the ground. Sirus shuttered as he watched the eyes in the tail feathers closed in unison as the vicious creature died.

In her peripheral vision, Arris saw Sirus jump onto the strange bird's back and slice through its neck. Vega appeared to be racing to intercept the wolf as Arris struggled to gain control over her fear. If she didn't help Vega, he would be killed when the vicious beast caught his scent.

With shaking hands, Arris took out her gun, aimed it at the wolf's head, and fired. The first shots missed. She tried to stop her arms from shaking and took aim at the wolf's head again, trying not to see the huge, slobbering jaws and pointed fangs. Arris steadied herself into a firing position.

The wolf sensed danger and turned. It saw Vega coming. The wolf wobbled on his stilt-like legs and leaned his head to the side. He snapped his huge mouth, intending to grab Vega with his fangs, but as Vega came close, he slid down on the ground where the wolf could not reach him because of the height of its legs. The wolf's mouth closed on air. Vega continued to slide under the wolf and reached out with his knife, cutting the back of the wolf's front legs. The knife severed tendons on both legs, causing the wolf to collapse in pain on its front knees.

Vega continued to slide on the ground past the wolf as Arris started shooting. She emptied her gun into the wolf's head, splintering bone and brain. After the gun was empty, Arris still continued to fire at the wolf.

Vega rushed to Arris and shook her. "Arris, you can stop shooting. The creature is dead." He removed the gun from her stiff fingers and pushed her in the direction of the old barn.

As Vega and Arris neared the barn, Kohlo's pets collapsed, exhausted from making the constant sound.

Kohlo lifted them down and carried them inside the barn to give them each a pellet to help them recover.

Without the return signal to confuse him, the lumbering bear started toward the barn.

Arris gasped and pointed at the bear. "What is that?"

Sirus ran up and joined Arris and Vega outside the barn. "Any suggestions on how to stop it?" He paused to catch his breath after his race to reach them before the bear.

"He's not all that fast, but he would eventually run us down if we tried to escape," Vega replied.

"I'm not sure how effective our guns will be. His hide looks like armor." Sirus studied the slow, lumbering menace. "Arris, help Kohlo get his pets out the back and to that copse of trees. It should give you a little protection, as the bear is too wide to get between them."

Arris carried the cage holding the three exhausted animals, and Kohlo carried their bag of pellets. They reached the band of trees where Sirus and Vega had first seen the frightening beasts. Kohlo's three pets had not made a sound, still recovering from their tireless singing.

"Your pets saved our lives," Arris said. "The distraction they caused for those beasts led to their downfall."

Kohlo smiled. He made a clicking noise to his pets and reached inside the cage to pet each one. "They said they are glad they could help," he said.

Sirus looked around and told Vega, "Get the bear's attention and have him follow you inside."

Vega stared at Sirus, not sure what he was planning. "The barn's not big enough for me and that monster," he said.

"Once he's inside, run to the back and climb out a window. It will follow, thinking you're trapped inside," Sirus explained.

"OK," Vega agreed. He stepped to the front of the crumbling barn and began waving and yelling at the approaching menace slowly lumbering toward the barn on its hind legs.

As the bear came near, Vega began to step backward while loudly calling the beast various names to keep his attention. The bear's shoulders touched both sides of the opening that had once held double doors. Its head reached the rafters that held up the missing roof. Vega turned and ran into the back room. He hoisted himself up and out the window just as the bear growled and swung his massive arms at the rafters, causing boards to crash to the floor.

As the enraged bear was breaking down the roof to reach Vega, Sirus leaned over from the corner of the roof where he had been hiding and dropped two smoke bombs at the bear's feet. The bombs exploded, sending eye-stinging smoke billowing up into the bear's face. The burning sensation and the blisters that formed on the bear's eyes caused it to bellow in rage. The double dose that Sirus had released had done what he had hoped and blinded the brute.

Sirus jumped from the side of the barn's roof and onto the bear's huge shoulders. He had his knife held between his teeth. He didn't have one second to waste against this monster. Sirus reached around the bear's neck and buried the blade deep, cutting a major artery. Sirus then pulled the blade from the bear's neck, jumped down, and raced from the barn as the enraged bear began to flail his arms around, trying to stop the pain in his eyes and neck.

Sirus ran to the copse of trees to join Vega, Arris, Kohlo, and Kohlo's pets. They watched as the enraged bear continued to tear down the old barn.

"It won't take long for it to bleed out," Sirus told the others.

Kohlo looked at Sirus and Vega and shook his head. "It's a miracle. Those beasts have finally been killed. You don't know what this means to us who watched our friends die because of them." Kohlo wiped a tear away.

Sirus replied, "It was a pleasure?"

Vega laughed. "Some pleasure. I can think of a lot more pleasant things." Then he turned to Arris and asked, "What happened to you out there? You just froze."

Before Arris could answer, Kohlo took her hand and said, "A large dog must have scared her quite badly when she was young, and she has never dealt with the fear it caused. It's over, my dear. You have faced your fear and come through it."

Arris smiled at Kohlo and asked, "How did you know?"

"I've seen the same reaction in others many times," he said quietly, "especially when they saw the beasts." Kohlo's pets must have understood his sadness because they began making a cooing sound.

"Well, that explains it. Why didn't you say something?" Vega asked.

But Arris had no answer. It was something she had never wanted to think about, let alone tell someone else.

"We should go back to the city. Spider may need our help," Sirus said.

Kohlo started to protest, but Vega told him, "You can't stay here unprotected or go back to the lab until it is safe."

"There are some places in the city where you and your pets will be safe," Arris added.

Everyone agreed. Without the beasts to worry about, they could make their way to the city without the fear of being eaten. Besides, Arris had another fear she had to face—a fear named Susum.

On the way back to the city, Arris told the others about meeting Vergil, about Chares's brother being freed from Susum's spell, about the plan to take down Susum's hidden message, and about his threat to have his security team kill them all.

Vega replied, "A security team will be a piece of cake after those beasts."

CHAPTER 9

THE PLAN

The street corner was dark. Spider stopped, looked around, and said, "We should be safe here. I noticed this vacant building when I climbed Susum's headquarters. It looks to have been abandoned for some time, and Susum's security detail won't expect us to be hiding directly across from their headquarters. Besides, from here, we can see what his security is like and keep tabs on what is going on in the city. Once we are settled, I'll open a link to Vergil and let him know we are safe."

After Arris had left, Spider, Phoenix, Ursa, and Minor had hid in the woods directly behind the building they had been using until dark. If the building had been inspected by a security guard, it would have looked as unused as when they had found it. They had watched and waited during the day but had never seen any activity around the building or in the streets that they could see from where they hid. The deadline Susum had given them to surrender had come and gone, but he had made no further announcements. Everyone had wondered whether with

Arris out of the city, Susum would think they had run away in fear of him.

For safety, Spider had told everyone to turn off their communicators and go silent. Spider had had the bot return to the hideout and had turned it off before they'd left. He still didn't know if the security team could monitor and track their communicators and didn't know the depth of their technology. Now that Susum was aware their presence, he may have increased his security protocols. With all of the people under his spell, security had become lax, or else they would not have been able to free the inspector and Kohlo so easily.

Their only cause for concern had been when they'd heard the strange signals coming from the lab. They had been sure it was the beasts being set loose, but after the first signals, they had heard no further signals. Plus, keeping watch from the trees, they had seen no sign of any predator animals. They had discussed whether the sounds had been a tactic to scare them into turning themselves in.

Now, at night, the city looked abandoned. No one was on the streets, nor did any of the streetlights work. Only a few faint lights appeared in the buildings. Spider kept to the darkest part of the streets as he led the others to their new hiding place.

Once inside, he told Minor, "Secure the door so no one can get in without alerting us. We'll make camp on the third floor. It will give us the best view of the city center. We can watch all the activity going in or out of Susum's headquarters. I'm sure that is where his security team is located. Once we learn the layout of the building, we can begin to investigate the security team."

After everyone had unpacked the few items they would need for the night, Spider said, "We'll take turns standing guard so we can get some rest. We need to be ready when Vergil is prepared to take down the equipment sending the hidden signal. Phoenix will take first watch, then Ursa, and then Minor. We'll watch the center today and see what we can find out."

"That was Spider," Vergil told the others hiding in the basement. "He said they've found a safe place to hide but didn't say where. When we have finalized the plan to take down the signal, he'll come to us and go over it."

"What if we take down the signal and can't wake everyone up?" one of the men who monitored the equipment asked. He was worried because his wife was one of the people under Susum's control.

"We were able to bring Stefan back without any problems. We have to go off of that fact, as we don't have time to bring someone else out. Besides, one missing man won't raise any alarms, but if multiple people start to disappear, it will be noticed," Vergil answered.

Marly, who was seated in the room, asked, "Have there been any reports that the beasts have been sighted? I know their return-to-cage signal was never broadcast."

"I was told that the labs were evacuated when the beasts were freed," Chares said, "so maybe there isn't anyone to monitor them and see if they completed the kill. We think they were set loose to find Arris, who helped bring Stefan back."

Marly shook her head. "The poor girl."

Everyone hiding in the basement went silent. Each of them had lost family or friends to these monsters.

"Let's get back to work," Vergil said. "First item: We need a team to cut the power that runs the equipment. Second item: We need a message ready to broadcast that tells everyone to wake up and go to the city center. The voice should sound as much like Susum's as possible. Third item: We all need to be out on the streets helping the people get to the center. Once we have everyone there, Marly will take the stage."

"What if we run into trouble with security or those who have gone along with Susum and are not under his spell?" a man asked from the back.

"We don't have enough members or firepower to go against the guards," another man added.

Vergil answered. "Spider said that we wouldn't have to worry about Susum's security team. He and those with him will handle them. I've met the ones who came from Nebula, and I wouldn't want to go up against Spider or any of them."

Chares laughed and added, "I'd put my money on Ursa before any of Susum's scum."

His statement caused the others to laugh, lightening the somber mood in the room.

"Can we be ready in two nights?" Vergil asked.

Those heading up the different tasks talked with their teams, and one by one, they answered, "Yes."

"We'll strike just before dawn, and when everyone wakes and can't hear their orders, we will give them new ones," Vergil said. This was the time to act, now that they had help from Nebula.

"I've spotted twenty different men in similar attire. If they are uniforms, they are not actual uniforms but rather pieced-together outfits. Most of the pants are the same brown, but the shirts and coats vary," Minor told the team on the third floor.

"Have you noticed where they are coming from or going?" Phoenix asked.

"I haven't seen any of them coming out except through the main doors," Minor answered. "If they have access from behind the building, they are not using it during the day. The guards patrol the city center; they walk around the circle and back into the building."

"Tonight, we need to do recon on the back of the building. I'm meeting with Vergil later, and his team is planning to be ready tomorrow night. We don't want any surprises from Susum's guards and don't want any of Vergil's team getting hurt," Spider told the others.

"They've suffered enough," Ursa agreed. "Minor, what weapons do these guards carry?"

"I've only seen small holstered guns, but I'm sure they must have more firepower available," Minor replied.

"For Susum to have gained control, the guards would have needed more than small guns to keep everyone who didn't go along with their master in line. Now that they think all opposition has been eliminated, they probably don't feel the need to carry them," Ursa guessed.

"Make sure your weapons are loaded and ready for tomorrow night. Carry everything—both guns, reloads, and smoke and flash bombs," Phoenix said.

Minor answered, "Count on it."

When Sirus, Vega, Arris, and Kohlo finally reached the large laboratory, Arris suggested, "We should stay here for the night. Kohlo is having trouble walking and needs to rest."

"I wouldn't object to stopping for the night." Vega sighed and wiped his brow. "Battling beasts tends to take it out of you."

Sirus laughed, and inside the cage he carried, three small laughs mimicked him. Kohlo's pets had taken to Sirus. When running loose, their favorite climb was to the top of his shoulders. Sirus only objected when one of the pets tried to climb to the top of his head.

Everyone was hot, tired, and dusty but jubilant about their defeat of Susum's monsters. They walked around to the back of the building.

"There is no one here," Arris said. "The building is empty."

"Maybe everyone left before the beasts were set loose in case the beasts were still hungry and came for them," Vega suggested.

"That is a possibility. How the guards could maintain control of the beasts using various signals always worried many of the scientists," Kohlo replied.

When they came to the door of the room where Kohlo had been held prisoner, the three animals began to make a strange noise. Vega stopped and looked around.

"What's happening?" he asked.

Kohlo bent down to the cage and began making his own sounds. Finally, he stood up and explained, "My three pets do not want to go back into our home. They have tasted freedom and do not want to be locked away again."

"You can't blame them," Sirus said. "I couldn't be locked up either."

"Is there someplace else you can stay with them?" Arris asked.

Kohlo chuckled. "This building has many rooms no one has seen in years. I can move our stuff to one of these rooms. I'll let my pets know that they will keep their freedom."

As Arris helped Kohlo pack the items he would need for the night, Vega and Sirus walked to the back to inspect the enclosures that had held the beasts.

"These pens are filthy, and they stink." Vega was having trouble not gagging at the horrible stench.

"It was callous to keep them locked up in here and starve them. They are better off dead," Sirus said. "This whole area should be burned to the ground. There are more pens around the side, enough to hold a dozen hybrid animals. It's disgusting. No wonder Catella left this place."

When Sirus and Vega returned, Arris told them, "The offices upstairs look like they have been stripped clean of any documents. When I told Kohlo, he said that Susum could be trying to sell the plans for how to create hybrids. They had enough success with the program that it could be sold to anyone wanting to create their own monsters."

"That is concerning. We need to let Spider know as soon as we can contact him. We still can't reach him on our comms," Sirus said.

The following day, as they were preparing to leave for the city, Kohlo said, "I will not be coming. I will be of no use in the city and will slow you down."

"What if someone comes? Susum gave orders that you were to be shot on sight." Arris worried.

"My pets will warn me, and we can hide. There are hidden rooms in this building. I'll ready a few, and if someone other than you comes here, we will hide." Kohlo had made up his mind.

Arris looked at Sirus and Vega, wanting their opinion, and both agreed that Kohlo would be safer here than in the city, especially with the order to shoot him on sight.

After saying good-bye to Kohlo and his pets, Sirus, Vega, and Arris started for the city. It would be dark by the time they arrived to begin their search for Spider and the other protectors.

CHAPTER 10

THE TAKEDOWN

The following morning, Spider told the protectors about his meeting with Vergil and the others working to take down Susum.

"Tonight is a go. Be ready to leave as soon as it's dark, and position yourself behind the building. You can watch for Susum's guards to run out as soon as they hear the explosion. From what I was told of their plans, it will be a big one. Vergil wants to make sure Susum will not be able to power the entire building, let alone the top floor where the machines are."

"If the building goes dark, nothing inside will work unless there are backup generators," Phoenix said.

Spider turned to Ursa and Minor and asked, "What did you discover last night? Were you able to get inside?"

"We were able to get to the building without being seen," Ursa replied, "but the building was locked down. We couldn't find a way inside. There is a large ramp in the back of the building that runs downward and ends in locked metal doors. The doorway is large enough to drive vehicles through, so there could be tanks or other large weapons we don't know about."

Spider thought for a minute. "Phoenix, get explosives ready that we can place beside the doors. If the guards do have military vehicles, we will blow them up before they reach the street."

"As far as extra firepower," Ursa continued, "we don't know what we could be facing."

"Then we prepare for the worst," Spider said. "Minor, keep watch today and let me know if you see any activity from the guards that is out of their normal routine. Ursa, help Phoenix ready the explosives. As soon as it's dark, we need to leave, get the explosives placed by the door, and then find positions for ourselves."

"Let's stay out of sight until dark and then make our way into the city," Sirus said to Vega and Arris. "We don't know the situation or where Spider and the others are, so we'll not make ourselves known until we find them."

Vega tried to reach Phoenix on his wrist comm, but there was no response. He shook his head and said, "I'm glad we don't have long to wait. I'm getting concerned that we can't contact Spider or Phoenix."

Arris set her tote on the ground and removed a drink. She looked from the trees where they were hiding and pointed. "There's the building where we hid, but no one's there now. I'm sure Spider found another hideout, and they could be with Vergil and his team."

"Let's get some rest until dark," Sirus said. He sat down and leaned back against a tree; even with his eyes closed, he was fully aware of his surroundings.

Arris and Vega did the same.

Phoenix whispered when he crept up. "The explosives are set. If the guards try to drive anything out of the building, they'll get a surprise."

Spider's voice was low. "Find the spot Minor designated to watch from. We should be able to see Vergil's team when they place the bomb and see the guards come out of the building afterward. Give them one warning to surrender before you fire."

Ursa, Minor, and Phoenix nodded that they understood the instructions and crept away in the dark to wait.

This close to Susum's headquarters, Spider kept to silent mode, unsure whether the guards had monitors placed around the building. He wondered about Arris and Vega. Had Susum released the monsters, or had that been an idle threat? He would have liked Sirus back with the team. Sirus was a master with firearms, and if the guards did have larger weapons, Sirus would figure a way to take them out.

Spider knew Vergil's men were coming; he could smell a difference in the scent that stirred in the air. The two men placing the bomb had been workers in the city and knew where the underground tunnel that ran beneath the circle of buildings was. Inside the tunnel were all of the power cables that fed the buildings. The plan was to take out only the cable feeding the building Susum was using as his headquarters after it branched off. It would require skill to place the bomb in the exact place needed to cut the power to his headquarters and not affect the rest of the buildings. The men had a built a timer and would only have a few minutes to get to safety. Not being able to test their plan, everyone understood they were taking chances.

Spider heard a slight scraping sound and knew that the men had removed the hatch to climb down into the tunnel. He was sure the others heard the sound, and it wouldn't be long before the bomb exploded and the fight to free the people would begin.

Spider was expecting it but still jumped. It was one of the biggest blasts he had heard. It wasn't the size of the blast—the bomb wasn't all that large—but the after effects were spectacular. The explosion blew the cover to the tunnel into the air, and it crashed against the windows of the building, causing glass to shatter and rain down. It created a forward rush of air that erupted at the building's entrance. The walkway in front of the building buckled, and pieces of the walkway flew against the doors, sealing the entrance shut. The whole area around the building rocked from the blast, knocking down street lights, tumbling over containers that had at one time held plants, and causing trash containers to roll crazily down the street. Smoke billowed upward from the many openings in the street created by the blast. It looked like a war zone, and Spider had fought in many. As Spider stood up and readied his weapon, he realized, this too was another war zone.

As the building rocked and swayed, Minor, Phoenix, and Ursa ran up. "It's not safe to stay so close to the buildings. There are pieces of glass and metal flying around. If we get hit by them, we'll get hurt," Phoenix yelled above the noise.

The four huddled together in the street outside of the ramp that ran downward into the building. Just then, sirens began screaming loudly, adding to the racket, and the metal doors started to slide open.

"Get ready," Spider said as over a dozen guards, all carrying guns, hurried out the doors.

Spider, Ursa, Phoenix, and Minor stepped forward to meet them.

"Drop your guns and surrender," Spider yelled, and the protectors laid a row of warning shots in front of the guards.

The guards were stunned at seeing Spider and the protectors, not having realized the reason for the blast. One of the guards yelled out orders, and the guards quickly retreated into the building.

"Do we follow them inside?" Ursa yelled.

Before Spider could answer, the guards reappeared, and each held a protective shield. The shields covered the guards' heads and reached to the ground. In the center of each shield was an opening that was large enough for a gun to extend through. They came out in rows of three, with one guard shooting ahead and the guards on either side shooting to the left or to the right.

"Take cover!" Spider yelled when the protectors' bullets did not penetrate the shields.

A few of the guards took a step backward when hit with the bullets, but they regained their footing and started forward again. Bullets whizzed past the protectors and hit the ground and buildings as they ran for cover.

The protectors and Spider crouched behind a low wall and returned fire.

"Save your bullets," Spider eventually said as he assessed their situation.

"The guards are better armed than we thought. The guns they are carrying are larger than those they carried on patrol," Minor shouted.

"We can't stay here. The guards will reach us soon," Ursa said.

"Phoenix, set off the explosives," Spider ordered. "It will scatter the guards and buy us some time."

Phoenix pushed the detonator and crouched down with the others to avoid being hit by any debris created by the explosion. Two blasts sounded one right after the other. Screams were heard; the guards were not protected from behind. Some of the guards' uniforms had caught fire, and they dropped their shields to try to keep from being burned.

Spider and the protectors stood up and began to shoot, but their bullets fell short of their targets. Their guns were not powerful enough for the distance. As the guards regrouped, Spider ran from their hiding place and across the street that circled the buildings. He stopped next to the building where they had been hiding. Ursa, Phoenix, and Minor ran up and stood with their backs against the building.

Before they had a chance to catch their breath, Vergil and Chares raced from across the street and joined them. Each carried the same pieced-together guns as before.

"The guards must be stopped before everyone wakes up," Vergil said, sounding panicked. "We must broadcast new orders and tell everyone where to go."

"The guards will shoot anyone in the street," Chares added. "Some of them came to the planet with Susum and are as cruel as he is. They would cheer for the beasts when they were set loose."

"We have to make a stand and not let the guards into the street. Do you have any barriers or something we could block their way with?" Spider asked Vergil.

Vergil thought and then replied, "There are some disabled transport buses, but we don't have a way to get them here in time. Many have their wheels removed and can't be pushed."

"We can't meet the guards head on without some kind of protection!" Phoenix exclaimed.

Chares groaned. "It's becoming light. We are in trouble."

"Where are the others?" Spider asked. He was worried about Vergil's team.

"They are still hiding in the basement, afraid to come out because of the guards."

Minor pointed. "The guards are coming. Same formation of three."

"Go back and guard the basement," Spider told Vergil and Chares. "I'll signal you when it's safe."

As Vergil and Chares ran down the street, Ursa asked, "What's our plan?"

Spider and the protectors watched as the guards came out in their teams of three and lined up in the street, waiting for daylight to begin their attack.

"What if we aim for the ground at their feet? It could cause them to stumble, and we may even hit a foot," Phoenix said, trying to figure out a way to even the odds.

Before Spider could respond, three shapes wearing face protection appeared behind the guards in the breaking daylight. They made no sound as they ran up and dropped smoke bombs directly behind the guards. Before the guards realized what was happening, eye-blistering smoke billowed upward, held close to the guards' faces by the shields they carried. After dropping their bombs, the three shapes ran away.

"Get ready. As soon as the smoke clears, rush the guards. Don't shoot unless you have to," Spider ordered.

When the smoke cleared, all of the guards were on the ground with tears streaming down their faces. They screamed as they tried to wipe the smoke from their eyes now blind with blisters. Spider, Ursa, Phoenix, and Minor rushed across the street and kicked the guards' weapons away. Sirus and Vega ran over and began to pick up the guns.

"Their shields didn't protect them from smoke bombs," Sirus said, grinning as he looked at Spider.

"We are glad to see you!" Ursa exclaimed as she threw the shields into a pile.

"Where's Arris?" Phoenix asked Vega.

"She's ..." Vega had started to say right behind me, but when he turned, Arris wasn't there.

Vega rushed over to Arris, who was crouching down, holding her head between her hands.

CHAPTER 11

MIND BATTLE

Spider opened his communicator to signal Vergil that the guards were no longer a threat. It was full daylight, and the people under Susum's spell would be waking up. The new orders must be broadcast before the people started to panic.

Sirus and Phoenix had the guards sitting against the building and were waiting for instructions from Vergil on what to do with them. Not one of the guards had put up any kind of protest at being told what to do. Not having their guns or being able to see made them very agreeable.

The overhead speakers began broadcasting a message, and the recorded voiced resembled the deep tones of Susum. "Wake up and come to the city center." The message was repeated over and over. In the streets, the members of Vergil's team began to appear, each member standing on one side of the street to help guide the people when they came from their homes.

Vergil walked up with Marly. They stopped by Sirus and looked at the incapacitated guards.

Sirus turned to Vergil and asked, "What do you want to do with them?"

Vergil seemed stunned. Now that their plan had really worked, other matters needed to be considered, like what to do with the guards that had helped keep the people under Susum's control.

Before Vergil could answer, Marly did. "I think we should feed them to the beasts. We can cheer like they did when we lost our families and friends." Her voice shook with emotion as she stared down at the weeping guards.

Upon hearing Marly's words, the guards began pleading for their lives.

"That sounds like a good idea, but there is one small problem," Sirus said.

Marly and Vergil looked at Sirus expectantly and then Marly gasped.

"The beasts are loose!" she cried, and she grabbed Vergil's arm, looking like she might collapse.

"No, no," Sirus said quickly. "The beasts are dead, thanks to Vega, Arris, and me."

Vergil and Marly looked confused, and Marly stuttered, "Y-y-you killed them?"

"Well, they weren't breathing when we left them lying on the ground," Sirus answered.

Marly rushed forward and hugged Sirus. "Thank you." She wept.

Sirus told Vergil, "The pens are vacant and would be a good place to lock these creatures up until you decide their fate."

"Good idea," Vergil said. "Can you hold them here until we have the people out from under Susum's control? Then I'll have my men take them to the pens."

Vergil and Marly left to go help wake the people up and take them to the place where Marly would explain what had happened to them.

Spider hurried up to Vega and asked, "What's wrong with Arris?"

Arris was still crouched down holding her head in her hands. Spider realized it was Susum. He had invaded her mind. He knelt down and held her shoulders. "You are stronger than he is, Arris. You must fight back."

The look on Arris's face changed from fear to determination. She straightened her shoulders and spoke. "All of your guards have been defeated, and the people have been freed from your control. We are coming for you next."

Arris tried to stand up, and Vega steadied her.

"You can't run and hide any longer." Arris was quiet for a moment and then said, "We are coming for you. You are a coward if you run. Come and face the people you've tortured."

Arris shuddered.

"You can't threaten me," she said. "Come find me; I'll be waiting." Then she almost collapsed in Vega's arms. She looked over at Spider. "Susum is a coward and plans to run. He is—or, was—in the building, but I've lost contact with him. He threatened to hunt me down and said I'll be sorry."

Spider took Arris's hands and said, "Let him try. You won't be alone." He turned to Vega. "Take Minor and Ursa and sweep the building for Susum. We have the back covered, and the front doors are blocked. He has no way to escape." He then led Arris over to where Sirus and Phoenix watched the guards. "Stay here until I return. I want to check with Vergil and see if there are other ways out of the building."

Later that day, Spider and the protectors sat in the building where they had watched the guards. Vergil and Marly had joined them.

Marly told them, "There is no way we can thank you enough. Without your help, we would never have been able to get free of Susum. I intend to open talks with Hytura and Hydea and make sure that what happened here becomes known. I'll have Susum branded a wanted criminal, and if he's found in Hydris, I'll make sure he stands trial."

"I don't think he is on Hyrila any longer. One of the spaceships that was in port is missing. Susum must have had a secret passage to escape and reach the port. There was no sign of him when Vega did a sweep of the building. One of the scientists said that Susum had had all the hybrid data combined and given to him. Then all the data in the labs was destroyed," Vergil reported.

"I'm sure Susum has had exit plans ready since he took over. When we get back to Nebula, I'll have Catella bring what he has done before the council and place him on NAHQ's watch list, especially if he is trying to sell the information on creating hybrids. When he shows up, I'll go have a chat with him," Spider assured Vergil.

Arris spoke up. "There is a scientist still in the labs with his pets. Kohlo is the one who was able to get a message to Catella asking for help. Without his and his pets' help, we would not have been able to defeat those beasts. Make sure he is taken care of and has a home for himself and his pets."

Marly nodded. "I'll see to that myself."

"We leave tomorrow," Spider said. "Remember your promise to contact Nebula and join the coalition."

"I won't forget, and I'll have contacts for the other planets. I want to make sure what happened on Hyrila never happens in this galaxy again," Marly answered.

Spider and the protectors left early the following morning. They wanted to reach the portal site before dark. It would be a fast trek with only one stop. Everyone wanted to say good-bye to Kohlo and his pets before they left the planet and returned to Nebula. They were anxious to update Catella and place Susum on a Nebula watch list.

The End

BOOK 6

FALLEN HEROES

CHAPTER 7

THE NEWS

The protectors finished their latest workout in the simulators, which now included driving and flying training that covered everything from the latest warship technology to on-road vehicles that could have one to six wheels and even adapt to go underwater. Sirus wanted each of them proficient in case they found themselves in situations that would require these skills. Arris loved flying and excelled in those routines, but on-road vehicles where you were close to other vehicles trying to outrun or run over you or force you to run into something was a different matter. Arris always seemed to come in last—that is, if she made it through the routine at all.

Minor excelled at driving all the vehicles and could even beat Vega in the cycle routines. Minor still talked about the shooter scooters they'd seen in action on Daedro. The protectors enjoyed the change in routine, a break from Sirus's physical death drills. Once every few sessions, Sirus would include a shooting session to make sure they all kept their skills at marksman level, the highest they could achieve.

As they were leaving the simulator area, Arris looked at her wrist communicator and said, "Kent wants to meet in comm room 32 after lunch. I haven't seen him in over a week; he must be busy working on something."

Vega leaned over and read the message. "Do you and Kent have a secret and that's the reason he wants to meet with just you?" he taunted.

Arris pulled her arm away and said, "Even if we did, I wouldn't tell you."

"And why is that?" Vega demanded.

Arris shrugged. "Then it wouldn't be a secret."

"Be that way," Vega huffed and quickened his step to catch up with Sirus and Phoenix. Minor had left earlier, saying he had to see someone, but he wouldn't tell Vega who, which also annoyed Vega.

Ursa took Vega's place by Arris as they walked toward their rooms to clean up for lunch. "Guys," she said. "Either they are too nosy or they don't pay attention."

Arris laughed and agreed but secretly wondered who wouldn't pay attention to Ursa.

When lunch was over, Arris made her way to comm room 32 after being reminded several times by Vega to not miss the secret meeting. Arris sat down in the empty room to wait for Kent. She looked around, trying to remember how many times she had sat in the room planning missions or debriefing afterward. She was lost in thought when Kent hurried in, looking like he hadn't seen his room to sleep and clean up in days. His clothes were rumpled, and his blond hair could use a trim or a ribbon to keep it out of his eyes.

"Sorry I'm late, but I had to finish something." Kent sat down without telling her what needed finishing.

Arris waited for Kent to catch his breath. He placed a device in front of him and opened it.

"Since I told you about Katy writing to you and knowing that you felt bad about not being able to keep in touch," he explained, "I wanted to show you what I've found."

Arris leaned over the table. "How?"

Kent pushed a button on the device, and a hologram opened between them. "When I closed the compound on Earth, I left the bot in orbit, just in case someone else came snooping around. After I told you that Katy had written, I programmed the bot to search for any information about her and her family. I was able to track down the base they'd moved to and found an announcement about Katy's graduation and enlistment in the army like her father."

Arris watched a holo of the Earth circle between them. She absently said, "Katy was an only child and adored her father. It makes sense that she would follow in his footsteps."

"I was able to retrieve this picture," Kent said as the holo of Earth changed into a hazy image of four young women all dressed in army fatigues.

Arris leaned close and pointed. "That's Katy. Her smile is still the same. She always had a smile on her face and would help anyone in class. That's probably why she became my friend—because I didn't have one." Arris's eyes grew misty at seeing the image of the young woman Katy had grown into.

"That explains why this team volunteered to go into a hostile region to teach the local girls basic reading and writing," Kent pondered.

Arris looked at Kent, knowing there was more that he didn't want to tell her.

Kent sighed and continued, "I was able to read a correspondence between Katy's father and a sergeant who was sent to the same region to locate a missing team. Apparently, Katy's team arrived safely on location, but after they began to make visits to the villages in the region, they disappeared. This region is a rugged desert area and is sparsely inhabited. These remote villages lack the required technology to track the team's movements. All contact with Katy's team has stopped, even though they were equipped with their own communication equipment."

Arris frowned as she worried about the safety of Katy and the other soldiers pictured in the holo.

Kent continued, "The project to begin educating the girls in the villages was approved at the government level by both countries, but there have been protests by local tribal leaders, who do not want to allow the girls to receive the same education that the boys receive. It's OK for boys to attend classes, but not girls."

"Can you find the last location where contact was made with Katy's team?" Arris asked.

"It will take some time," Kent replied, "and I'm working on something else. I'll try to find out and let you know as soon as I can." Kent looked at Arris and knew from the determination on her face that she was planning something.

After Kent hurried out of the room, Arris sat there for a minute thinking about Katy and worrying about her and the others' safety in a hostile situation. She stood up to go find Catella and remembered that Kent had never said what he was working on that was so important.

Kent ran down the steps that led to the immense control center for NAHQ and almost stumbled in his hurry. He had to try one more setting to see if he could identify the origin of the pulsating portal. According to Calais, the portal would disappear and reappear at random intervals, and Calais could not determine the exact times to set up the equipment to track where the portal was coming from.

Calais had reached out to Kent for help a few weeks ago, and both had been trying to understand the anomaly and why it had started to appear on the moon of Bankos. According to all known documents, the moon of Bankos had never been inhabited or used for any portal activities. If an enemy of the galaxy was trying to gain entrance without being noticed, this could be taken as an act of war.

Kent and Calais had been friends since childhood, both having been identified as readers and sent to reader training on Celtus, the largest planet in the Riddan Galaxy. Celtus was advanced in intergalactic understanding and was the center of knowledge for Riddan. After completing basic reader training, Calais had been sent to Bankos, where he'd trained to become the galactic reader for the Riddan Galaxy. Kent had been sent to train on Earth, replace the current reader, and work under the guidance of Catella. Both Kent and Calais had become experts in monitoring and understanding all the galaxies that NAHQ tracked.

Kent sat down in front of the monitor and keyed in the new search criteria. It was difficult not being at the exact location where the portal was opening, and the data he entered was another educated guess. He needed to speak with Calais; he had an idea, but it would require them to go to the moon of Bankos.

Kent felt about Calais the way Arris did about Katy, the difference being that when the two readers had been sent to different galaxies, they had stayed in contact. One of the perks of being a reader was that you were aware of the many different ways to stay in touch. A game the two had played many times was to hide a message for the other and then wait until it was found. They had often laughed at how short a time or how long it had taken the other to discover the hidden message.

Kent understood Arris's concern for her childhood friend. He knew that if Calais went missing and was in danger, Kent would use all his knowledge and means to find him. After Kent uploaded the new data, he turned to another machine that was controlling the bot circling Earth. He began a new search to find the last known location from Katy's team.

Arris sat and unconsciously tapped on the table, causing Vega to frown at her. They were watching a demonstration of the proper way to disassemble and reassemble the latest laser-guided finder that could be used in locating underground hideouts or missing items that had been buried or hidden. The new device was small enough to be attached to the belts of their uniforms. They were sitting in the back of the room, which was located next to the workout area.

Vega leaned over and whispered, "What's with you?"

Arris shook her head and ceased her tapping. "I'll tell you after."

Her answer seemed to appease Vega, for now. Arris knew she should explain to Vega, because as annoying as he could be, he was always watching out for her.

After the demonstration was over, Arris and Vega walked toward the transport to return to their rooms. As they passed an empty common area, Arris said, "Let's sit here, and I'll explain what's going on."

After they had sat down, Vega nodded for Arris to begin.

"A while ago, Kent and I were talking about friends from our childhoods, and I mentioned a girl I had been friends with who had moved away and promised to write to me. I mentioned that I felt bad that I'd never heard from Katy—that's my friend's name."

Arris paused, waiting for Vega to comment. Surprisingly he stayed silent.

She continued, "He told me that Katy had written to me a couple of times, but I had never been given her letters. Catella had felt that it could put both me and Katy in danger. Kent felt bad about keeping the letters from me and initiated a bot search for Katy. What he found is distressing." Arris bit at her lip, not sure how much to share with Vega.

"I think there's more you're not saying," Vega prompted, leaning forward in his chair.

Arris nodded. "Katy joined the army and was sent on a mission. Now she has gone missing. Kent is trying to find out her last known location. I went and told Catella of the situation and asked if there was a way we could help Katy and the others on her team. He said that when Kent finished his search, he would review the findings. I'm just so anxious to hear, knowing that my friend is missing and could be in great danger."

259

"Now I understand why you've been so fidgety. I don't see how you can help your friend back on Earth, especially after she's been missing for days. But if you do go, I'm available." Vega looked sincere.

Arris didn't doubt Vega's sincerity but did doubt his motivations, especially if there was a Starbucks nearby. "Thanks, but I have to wait for Kent to find further data before I can meet with Catella."

Two days later, as Arris was getting ready to climb in bed, the intercom in her room beeped. Kent's voice came from above.

"I've finished the search for Katy and sent all the data to Catella. He'll meet with you after he reviews it."

"Thanks, Kent," Arris said, and Kent hastily wished her good luck before the intercom went silent.

Arris wasn't sure she could sleep, anxious to hear what Kent had learned and find out if there was any way to help her friend. She grinned recalling Kent's short response; he must still be busy with that something he was working on.

CHAPTER 2

THE PLAN

Kent had one more instruction to leave for Phoenix before he portaled to Bankos to meet with Calais. After he had sent Catella the latest findings on Arris's friend Katy, he had asked for a few days leave. Kent very seldom took time off from his work at NAHQ, and Catella was more than willing to allow him a few days away from his job. Phoenix would assist in the comm center while Kent was away.

Catella was aware of the portal anomaly that Calais had found and of Kent's involvement. He had monitored Kent as Kent had trained and then taken over as reader in the compound on Earth and was aware of Kent and Calais's hide-and-seek game. He had been amused at the two young readers' ingenuity and was glad of their friendship. Both readers had excelled in growth and knowledge as galaxy monitors. Their devotion to their jobs helped keep NAHQ and the Riddan Galaxy safe.

Kent checked his bag one more time, not wanting to forget the items he would need to discover the portal's source. Calais had been able to secure a transport ship they could fly to the portal's site on the moon and had agreed with Kent's idea of sending the discovery equipment when the portal was the strongest. The pulsating made it difficult to track, and the equipment, once inserted into the portal, would send information back to them until it exited at the portal's source. Check, check, and recheck. Satisfied, Kent hurried to catch a carrier to take him to the portal room on NAHQ. Next stop: the moon of Bankos.

Arris didn't hear from Catella for two days. It was hard for her to wait and not request a meeting. Arris knew that Catella was extremely busy, but he would always make time for her. That was the reason she didn't want to take advantage of his friendship. That morning she finally received a notice that Catella wanted to meet with her later in the day, Arris sighed with relief that she would finally learn what Kent had found. She hadn't received any further updates from Kent. She knew he was working on something important, so she had not bugged him either.

Arris lightly knocked on the door that led into Catella's spacious office and heard Catella say, "Come in Arris." She knew that he was expecting her, but unless he had security monitors hidden to see who was at the door, how had he known it was her and not one of the hundreds of other residents of NAHQ?

Arris opened the door and stepped inside to see Catella seated at his desk and Spider standing behind him, both looking at a monitor sitting on top of his desk.

"Give us one minute. Go ahead and take a seat at the table," Catella told her without looking up.

After Catella and Spider finished their discussion of what they were looking at, both walked over and sat down at the table with her. Spider entered his passcode into a device mounted on the table, and a holo of Earth opened. Arris watched as the holo circled above, and in her head, she said the names of the oceans and continents. She was happy that she had not forgotten them. Catella's voice brought her back from her reminiscence.

"After I reviewed the data Kent sent, I asked Spider to find out if there was a way to help your friend. You must understand that the area where your friend and her companions disappeared is very remote and unfriendly to anyone who is not wanted. The Earth's inhabitants are still many years away from becoming a people that can look beyond differences and work together for the good of all. You cannot change a civilization overnight; it takes time and small steps."

Catella paused, and Arris wasn't sure what to say.

"The mission your friend is on seems to be viewed by some of the local leaders as something that threatens their control or power, and therefore they do not want your friend there. From the position where her group was last in contact, Spider has identified a possible entry point, but it will only stay viable as an exit for a couple of days. This is where we are concerned. If we do send an investigator, we may not be able to find your friend before the investigator must return. Doing so also conflicts with Nebula's mission." Catella looked at Spider and nodded.

Spider typed something into the device, and the holo rotated and zoomed in on a specific area.

"This is the last known location of the team. It is a remote outpost but is not that far from a larger village. The picture from the bot isn't very clear, but we can see a building, a few tents, and a corral for animals. There doesn't look to be any motorized vehicles at the outpost. This shadow here looks like a well for obtaining drinking water. The portal exit is outside the larger village, and finding your friend would require securing transport or hiking to the remote outpost." Spider zoomed in on the village.

Arris gasped and leaned forward. "Is that an army tank, and do those trucks have guns mounted on the back?"

"Yes," Spider replied. "It is a very militant area, which is cause for concern when sending an investigator."

Arris knew that Nebula investigators were never armed but sent only to collect data and facts about a situation. Sending an unarmed investigator in to this area would put that person at great risk.

She looked over at Spider and said, "Send me. I am familiar with Earth and could remain hidden, especially if I'm dressed like the villagers. Katy is a friend, and Earth is the only home I know, so I will be acting on my own. It will leave Nebula in the clear."

"No," Catella said loudly as he stood up and stared at Arris. "I will not risk your life, especially without further details."

Arris had never really opposed Catella until now, but Katy's life could depend on it. She stood up, looked back at Catella, and stated, "I am a Nebula protector. I am trained to survive in harsh conditions. I am trained in weaponry. I am trained to be able to blend in with locals. I am trained in communication. You know this because you trained me.

I should go, not an investigator." Arris folded her arms as she sat back down and glimpsed a smile on Spider's face before it vanished.

Catella looked almost shocked, and there was very little that could shock him. He spluttered as if about to say something but instead closed his mouth. Finally, he said, "I can see how important this is to you. A friend's life is not something to be ignored. If Spider can work out the details to my satisfaction, you and Spider will portal to Earth and find your friend—hopefully alive—in the short time the portal is available."

Arris felt that she could leap over the table and hug Catella, but instead, she stood up and said, "Thank you. I'll be ready to leave as soon as Spider finalizes the mission details."

Arris almost skipped out of the room.

Calais was waiting when Kent stepped from the portal onto Bankos. Both readers were excited. Their feelings mirrored those of their younger years when they would set out on treasure hunts, hoping to find undiscovered bounty in some galaxy. Their hunts had never extended farther than the barracks where they were living, but their imaginations had traveled far.

Calais picked up the bag that held the items that Kent had decided were required to monitor the portal. From the information sent back before the portal closed, the two readers would be able to determine the location of the galaxy and planet from where the portal originated and maybe its source.

Calais told Kent, "It isn't far to the space shuttle. I thought we could walk."

Kent shouldered his tote, which contained a change of clothes and a few supplies, and said, "I don't mind the exercise. I've barely left the comm room in weeks. It feels good to be outside again."

As the two friends walked to where the shuttle waited, they took the opportunity to catch up with each other.

Calais asked, "So, are you still glad you transferred to NAHQ? Ever wish you could do something different?"

Kent was surprised by the question and replied, "I couldn't be happier. Sometimes it's crazy busy, but I like the challenge."

"You don't get bored?"

Kent stopped and looked at Calais. "Hey. What's up?"

Calais shook his head. "Sometimes I find myself staring off into space and wondering if there isn't more out there. It's not that I don't like being reader, and I know what we do is important, but I have been getting this feeling quite often lately."

Kent didn't ask Calais to explain because they had reached the space shuttle. Calais walked up the ramp and entered a code into a panel on the side of the ship. A sealed door slid aside, and the two walked in.

"Put you bag over there. The ship isn't large, just an interplanetary shuttle. I have the use of it for as long as I need it. Then it goes into storage. It's obsolete, and everyone wants the newer models," Calais said.

Calais sat down in the pilot's seat and rechecked the settings. He had previously entered all the data required to fly them to the moon and return to Bankos.

Kent sat down in the copilot's seat. "When we send the discovery instrument into the portal, we could do a fly around the galaxy." He grinned at his friend.

Calais laughed. "I like that idea, but I'm not sure how far this tub will go before it gives out."

The shuttle was old and slow, but Kent didn't mind. He was enjoying being away from NAHQ and on a mission, even if it was not a real one. The area was dark when they finally landed.

"The lights from the shuttle should be enough for us to pitch sleeping tents. I've brought a small stove to cook on and food for a couple of days. The portal is so sporadic that it could take that long to get a stable opening," Calais explained.

After they ate, the settle back to relax in fold-out chairs.

Calais said, "The moon of Bankos is the outermost formation in Riddan. Beyond is space; the next galaxy is light years away."

Kent thought he could hear a longing to explore in the tone of Calais's voice. He wasn't sure if he should be concerned about his friend or not, but something was definitely bothering Calais.

The following morning, Calais and Kent hiked to the area where the portal would appear at various times. They placed markers around the area where the openings would occur.

"Let's stay behind the markers until we are sure the portal is stable; then we can measure it. If it looks like a strong portal, we should have time to reach it and send the tracking device in. You have constructed a well-made device that should withstand the trip," Calais said, examining the piece of equipment Kent had assembled that morning.

"I had help from Phoenix in creating it. He is quite good at determining what is needed for a specific solution," Kent explained.

The two didn't have long to wait before a pulsating light begin to appear within the area ringed by the markers. Excitedly, Calais and Kent watched the light brighten and a portal begin to appear. Calais was holding a monitor that would determine the portal's stability.

"Get ready. Let's go," Calais almost yelled in his excitement when the monitor beeped, signaling that the portal was stable.

Kent and Calais carried the monitoring device between them as they hurried to the steady beam of light that signified the portal was open.

"On three," Kent said as they swung the device back and forth to gain momentum before they sent it off on its discovery mission.

When Kent said three, they released the contraption into the portal, but it only went half as far as they thought it would go. One corner of the device had caught on Calais's shirt sleeve and started pulling him into the portal behind it.

A mad scramble ensued as Calais tried to loosen his shirt before he was sucked into the portal. Kent was sure he'd yelled as he'd reached for Calais's waist but wasn't sure what he'd yelled. The portal began to pulsate, like it was sucking air and then blowing it back out. Calais fell forward and was pulled by his arm further into the portal. Kent stumbled while reaching for Calais and was only able to grab hold of one of his legs. Kent bear-hugged Calais's leg and tried to stand up and back out of the portal.

The sucking became more intense. Kent hung on to Calais, who was attached by his arm to the device. They resembled a freight train, with the tracking device chugging forward like an engine, Calais becoming the middle car, and Kent the caboose. Kent could feel the rush of space around him as they flew forward. He felt like he had been shot from a cannon and held tighter to Calais. The portal dimmed and closed, and then all was quiet on the moon of Bankos.

CHAPTER 3

BACK ON EARTH AGAIN

It was pitch black when Arris and Spider arrived on Earth. After receiving a signal from Spider once they'd exited, Phoenix shut down the portal. An expert in the Nebula comm room would constantly monitor the portal for Spider's signal to return, and then the portal would be reopened.

Dust rolled upward from Arris's shoes as she stepped forward carrying a small tote. Arris stifled a cough, not wanting to alert anyone of their presence. Spider's voice came in her ear telling her to put on her night vision goggles. After Arris had secured the goggles, she could see Spider looking at the small communication device he carried. Both Spider and Arris had ear pieces through which they could hear any sounds the comm picked up. Spider had programmed the comm to interpret the local dialects. This way, they could understand any conversations taking place around them.

"We are just outside of the larger village. According to the signatures readout, there is a group of men gathered not far from here sitting around a fire. I'm going to get close and see what I can learn. Take cover next to those boulders and wait for me. I won't be gone long."

Spider had whispered, but Arris had clearly heard every word. She crept toward the boulders and then looked up at the night sky, marveling at all the stars above. Growing up in a city, she had not been able to see this many stars because of all the smog. Arris shifted her position sitting against the boulders. Waiting definitely wasn't one of her strong points. She was anxious to find Katy and see if she was all right. It had been over a week since she had learned that Katy was missing. Arris knew the longer it took to find Katy, the worse her situation could be. Lost in worrying thoughts as she was, Spider's sudden appearance startled her.

He crouched down beside Arris. "From what I could tell, Katy and the others are being held prisoner in the outpost about two miles from here. These men have something planned, and the prisoners are part of it. We need to get to the prisoners and get them out of there before whatever they are planning happens. It won't take us long to make it to the remote village. There is a narrow road, and from my scan, it looks deserted. We can be there long before sunrise."

Spider secured the comm under his jacket and put on his night vision goggles. He then stood up, picked up the small tote he'd brought, and nodded to Arris a silent question: was she ready? Arris stood up and nodded back. She was more than ready. Arris ran after Spider down the dark, narrow road.

Running was easy in her Nebula uniform, which was expertly made for covert situations like this one. In their totes, Arris and Spider had robes that would allow them to blend in with the locals, but they decided not to wear them unless they needed to. Arris had weapons secured in the pockets of her uniform and knew that Spider carried an arsenal of weapons he could use in any situation they may find themselves in.

Spider slowed and motioned to Arris to get off the road. A couple of lights twinkled up ahead.

"This is the only cover near the outpost," Spider explained. "I need to scan the area and find where the prisoners are being held. Then we can decide what to do."

Spider removed the scanner, made some adjustments, and began to slowly move it around.

"There are four signatures inside the building, and it looks like two guards are sitting on the ground outside the door. We need to circle around and come up from behind, but that will put us near the animal pens. I think they are camels, but I'm not sure. The readout shows large forms resting on the ground. If they smell or notice us, they may alert the guards of our presence."

"It's a risk we need to take. We can't stroll down the road, even if no one is awake. That is a bigger risk," Arris whispered.

"Slow and quiet," Spider said.

He stepped out from their hiding place and crept toward the back of the encampment. Arris made no sound as she circled around the camp but was extra careful as she passed the camels in the pen. One of the large animals raised its head and chewed on hay as it watched them, but it didn't sound an alarm at seeing strangers.

They stopped at the back of the building where the prisoners were being held. Spider motioned with his hands to tell Arris that there were two guards and that they would approach from the side that was closest to a small ridge that ran behind the camp. Arris signaled that she understood and would go first; she would blend and creep up beside the guards. Spider agreed, and they began their approach.

The two guards looked like they were sleeping but would probably wake at the slightest noise. Arris took a minute to steady her breathing and slowly began to fade against the building. As soon as she was blended, she quietly stepped around the building and behind the men. She would take out the farthest guard and Spider the closer one.

Dressed all in black and soundless as his namesake, Spider was on top of the guard, silencing him with one blow to the neck. At the same time, Arris took out her guard with a tap on his head from the butt of her gun. Quickly, they tied and gagged the guards before they woke up. Spider dragged the two guards around to the back of the building.

Arris was examining the simple lock on the door of the building when Spider came up. He took a small tool from his pack and in seconds had the lock open.

"Do you hear anything?" Spider asked.

Arris nodded her head and replied, "Light gasping and breathing."

Opening the door, Spider slipped inside. It was a storage building with a dirt floor and no furniture inside. Against the back wall, four figures were huddled together in various stages of consciousness. They were covered with a couple of blankets that had once been used for the camels. Filthy didn't even come close to describing the scene Arris saw. She hurried over and began to examine the prisoners one by one.

"They are alive but barely." The disgust in her voice was evident, and she didn't whisper. She found Katy and tried to revive her. Katy slowly came conscious and tried to focus on Arris with glazed eyes.

Spider set his tote beside the four soldiers and removed a couple of drinks. "Share these between the four. I only brought the two for us."

Arris nodded and opened one of the bottles. Two of the soldiers stirred and tried to sit up, but they were too weak. Arris held Katy's head and almost poured half of the bottle down her throat. Katy began to recover.

"You're safe," Arris said. "Rest until we get you out of here." Arris then moved to the next soldier and repeated the drill until the other three had each been given half a bottle of Spider's elixir. She placed the empty bottles in Spider's tote. Slowly the soldiers began to stir, and Arris repeated, "Stay still. You're safe. We'll get you out of here."

Spider finished what he was doing on the comm and came over to look at the prisoners. "Do you think they can walk?" he asked.

"We can try," Arris replied, "but they have been starved of food and water since they were captured. Where should we take them?"

"Not far but far enough away that they can be picked up. There is a flat area beyond the road that has probably been used to land helicopters. Those are the coordinates I sent. Help is on the way, but we need to move before the others sleeping in the tents wake up."

Spider helped the closest soldier stand up. She frowned and tried to focus her eyes on Spider. As the soldier wobbled on her legs, Spider lifted the next soldier. He placed his arm around her waist to steady her and then took the wobbling soldier in his other arm and made for the door. Over his shoulder, he said, "Arris, bring the other two."

Katy was standing but not very steady. Arris lifted the last soldier up off the dirty floor and could smell the stink from the conditions they had been living in—no food, no water, no bathroom. She placed the soldier's arm around her neck and held her around the waist. She then took Katy's arm with her free hand and started after Spider.

It was dangerous to move outside. Both Spider's and Arris's arms were full with injured soldiers and not guns as they crept from the building. Once it was daylight, it would be easy to follow the tracks they were leaving. The stumbling soldiers left a clear trail as they dragged their feet.

The slow escape seemed to take longer than the run to reach the outpost, but soon, a small clearing appeared. The area looked big enough that two or three helicopters could land at the same time. Arris could clearly see this through her night vision goggles and wondered why this remote outpost would require a helicopter landing site.

The soldier she was holding groaned and slumped against her. Arris let go of Katy's hand and caught the other soldier before she hit the ground. Arris lifted the starved soldier and carried her to where Spider had stopped. Both of the soldiers he'd been carrying were lying on the ground and groaning in pain.

"Lay her down here. I'm going to give them something for pain. It should help until they can get medical treatment." Spider removed his case of pins from his bag.

Arris noticed Katy had come up.

"Are they going to be OK?" she asked.

Arris turned and looked at Katy in her ragged, dirty uniform. She was starved and filthy, but in her eyes was a look of care and concern. This was the Katy that Arris remembered.

Arris and Katy watched as Spider touched each of the soldiers with one of his pins. One by one, the soldiers fell into a quiet slumber, the first they'd had in over a week. Spider looked at Arris and silently asked about Katy.

Arris took Katy's hands and said, "We can give you something for pain too."

Katy shook her head and stared at Arris. "Do I know you? You seem familiar?" Katy's words were slurred from weakness.

Arris helped Katy sit down next to her companions. She faced her friend and then made a decision. She said, "A long time ago in grade school, you were my best friend, and you still are."

Katy seemed confused. Finally, she sighed, "Mary Jane, is that really you?"

Arris had to smile. Mary Jane. She hadn't heard that name in years. Tears glistened in her eyes and she nodded.

Katy reached up and touched Arris's cheek. "You've changed, but your eyes haven't."

"I could say the same about you."

Arris laughed and hugged Katy, causing Katy to groan. "Sorry," Arris said.

"I think the outpost is waking," Spider said. "I'm not sure how long we have before they realize the prisoners are gone."

"Should we make a stand? It doesn't look like there are that many sleeping in the tents. We could hold them off until the rescue team arrives." Arris was concerned. They were so close to getting away with the rescue.

"Keep everyone hidden," Spider ordered. "I want to do some recon." He ran into the dark.

"How did you find us?" Katy asked as they waited for Spider to return.

Arris watched the sky for the first signs of light. "I heard that you had disappeared and asked if I could help." Arris wasn't sure how much to tell Katy.

"Are you part of an ops team?" Katy asked.

"Yes. Deep-space ops. I really can't explain more," Arris answered.

Katy groaned again.

"We can give you something for the pain," Arris said again.

Katy looked over at her teammates all in a deep slumber. "Will they remember anything?"

"Maybe not. Sometimes an aftereffect of the medicine is a couple of days' memory loss."

"Then no. I don't want to forget you," Katy said as she looked at Arris.

"Katy, you can't tell anyone about who rescued you. We could get in trouble if the wrong people heard about it," Arris warned.

"Dad tried to find you. He read about your mother and was told by the police who investigated the accident that you went to live with you aunt." Katy sighed, closed her eyes, and muttered again, "I don't want to forget you."

The first rays of dawn were appearing above the ridge behind the building where Katy and the others had been held. Arris put her hand on her chest, wondering if she should remove her weapons and get ready for a shootout with the men in the outpost. She wouldn't be sorry to defend the soldiers after the way they had been treated. Katy and the others could not be taken prisoner again, because they would not survive.

Arris felt the necklace that she now wore. Her aunt Celeste had given it to her. It was part of the royal jewels that had been once been worn by her ancestors. It was a small stone that glittered in various colors. When Arris had seen the colorful stones that had been crafted into jewelry, she had laughed. They'd reminded her of the mood rings that were popular on Earth when she was a girl. Arris reached around and removed the necklace and put it around Katy's neck.

"Wear this to remember me. Remember the mood rings we wore? This is sort of like them," she told Katy.

Katy looked at the necklace. "It's pretty. Thank you. I won't say anything about our rescue, and I'll always have this to remember you." Katy tucked the necklace under her uniform.

Arris removed her goggles and secured them to her belt. Day was breaking and she felt something was going to happen and soon.

Just then, Spider appeared and said, "I know what they are going to use the prisoners for—a trap. They planned to free them and ambush the rescue team when help arrived."

Arris gasped. "Is that what we did, walk right into their trap?"

"Not quite," Spider said as he was looking at the outpost through his distance viewer. "It's going to be close, though."

Katy had fallen into an exhausted sleep next to her companions. Arris started to say something but stopped and listened.

"I can hear helicopters in the distance," she said. "Are they coming for the soldiers?"

Spider nodded. "I signaled for a pickup and for someone to send word to Katy's father that she is alive." Spider looked down at the sleeping soldiers. "We need to move before we are seen. Let's go back to the boulders we hid behind to watch and make sure the rescue goes OK."

Arris didn't want to leave Katy and the others but could hear the helicopters getting close. There would be too much to explain if they were seen by the rescue team. She turned and ran behind Spider to the boulders. They watched three helicopters appear. At the same time, men ran from the tents.

Robed men with turbans on their heads began yelling and pointing at the arriving helicopters. Two men ran to the building where the prisoners had been held and ran back screaming that the prisoners and guards were gone. The comm Spider carried easily interpreted what was being yelled loud enough to be heard over the noise from the rescue helicopters.

The robed men seemed unsure of what to do but stopped their frantic performance when a figure ran from a tent holding a large satellite phone. The figure began screaming orders and pointing to the ridge beyond the building. "'Set the missiles' or 'get the missiles'" was repeated in Arris's earpiece. Arris watched as half of the men raced for the ridge and began to climb to the top.

To add to the confusion, the camels in the back pen became agitated at the chopping sound of the helicopters and the screaming of the men. They started bellowing out their own deafening sounds. The din from the frightened camels sounded like a pack of irate bears with bronchitis. The camels started running from side to side until the rails of the pen gave way. Then they made a mass exit for freedom.

The three army choppers hovered above the sleeping soldiers. Two uniformed men slid down on ropes and began to inspect the four prisoners. Arris pulled out her distance viewer to get a closer look. Katy had awakened from the noise and was speaking to one of the soldiers. The other three prisoners slumbered away, oblivious to what was happening around them. One of the rescuers signaled for the medical chopper with a huge red cross painted on the side to land, and as it did so, it caused dust to swirl around.

"This should be interesting," Spider said, bringing Arris's attention back to the ridge.

The men had made it to the top and were loosening camouflage netting, letting it float to the ground. One of the nets landed on a camel, covering it from head to tail and making it look like an escaping tank on four knobby legs.

The camouflage nets had been hiding five missile launchers, all painted a brownish color to blend in with the desert ridge.

Arris gasped when she realized the rescue choppers were the targets and the launchers were aimed at the landing site—the same landing site they had used to bring in the launchers to set up the ambush. They were going to shoot down the helicopters and kill the prisoners and the rescue team. It was a nasty, deceitful plan, using the prisoners as bait.

Arris grabbed at Spider's arm and gasped. "We have to do something. Those missiles will take out the choppers and kill everyone. It's too late for them to get away; there isn't enough time." Arris was shaking with rage, realizing that she had unknowingly been part of the devious plan.

Spider didn't seem upset. "Watch. It should get interesting. Medical vehicles are off limits to fire on, or are supposed to be."

Arris wanted to scream at Spider's calm acceptance of the situation. She swung her attention to the landing pad and saw men carefully lifting the unaware prisoners onto stretchers to carry them to the chopper. Arris knew these men were aware of the dangerous situation they were in, but they went determinedly ahead with the rescue. Two of the choppers had moved back with their guns aimed at the ridge. Arris could tell the guns mounted on the choppers would not reach the rocket launchers.

The screaming and yelling intensified as the men in the village lifted their rifles in the air and danced in joy at the success of their ambush. Their long robes were circling around their legs. One by one, the triggers on the launchers were pulled, and the man behind each launcher elatedly raised his arm, signifying his part in the ambush done.

For one long minute, nothing happened.

The yelling of the men, the chopping of the helicopters, and the bellowing of the camels filled the air. Then a louder noise erupted. The five launchers exploded, spewing fire and debris all over the building, the tents, and the men below.

The impact created by blasts caused a landslide, and the dirt ridge began to slide forward, carrying what was left of the launchers onto the ground below. The building and tents immediately caught fire, and the men who had escaped being hit by shrapnel were batting at flames that now consumed their long robes. Their joyful yelling turned to screams of pain as men pulled off their burning clothes and rolled in the dirt billowing up from the collapse of the ridge to put out the fire.

Arris had never seen anything quite like the scene playing out before her. She realized now why Spider had been so calm. He had learned enough about the ambush to examine what was hidden behind the camouflage on the ridge that he had seen through his scan of the area and must have sabotaged the launchers when he was doing recon after rescuing the prisoners.

Arris watched as three stretchers were loaded onto the medical helicopter. Before Katy was lifted into the chopper, she turned and looked around. When Katy's eyes swept the area where Arris was hiding, Arris tapped a button on her distance viewer and sent out three quick flashes. Katy smiled and put a hand to her neck as she was helped into the chopper.

The medical helicopter lifted off, and all three choppers disappeared from view. Suddenly, armed trucks came racing down the dirt road from the village. Every truck was filled with men excited to witness the carnage their ambush had caused. What they found when they arrived was not what they expected.

"How do we explain this to Catella?" Arris said, chuckling, from their hiding place.

"We stopped a major conflict from happening, and the only conflict that may happen now will be between these fanatics and the terrorists who sold them the defective launchers. Catella will be pleased with the results, and no one will be the wiser. We'd better make a run for it. I sent Phoenix a signal to open the portal. It should be open by the time we get there. Think you can keep up with me?" Spider grinned at Arris.

"Try to lose me," Arris said to Spider's back as she chased after him.

While the two waited for the portal to stabilize, Arris told Spider, "Thank you."

"It was my pleasure," he replied, and they stepped into the portal together.

CHAPTER 4

KENT'S PUZZLE

First came the monitoring device, then came Calais, and last came Kent. All in a row, they tumbled from the portal onto a rock-hard surface. Kent heard Calais moan as he hit solid ground. Kent's arrival was cushioned by Calais, but he still landed hard. Kent didn't move for a minute, surprised that he was still alive after the wild portal ride he had just experienced. This was the first time he had passed through a portal lying flat on his stomach and hanging onto someone's leg. Calais moaned again as Kent slowly pushed off of Calais's back and tried to sit up.

Kent's head was spinning from the terrifying ride and crash landing. He shook his head to clear the ringing in his ears, but he could still hear high squealing noises. Calais moved his arms and tried to push himself up. Then he collapsed back down on the hard ground, making a rumbling noise as the breath he had been holding escaped his lungs.

Kent, worried for his friend, leaned over and asked, "Calais, can you hear me? Are you OK?"

Calais moved his head and lifted a hand with a thumb sticking up—a good sign.

"Hey, pal, I don't know where we are, but we are not alone," Kent said as he slowly looked around, trying to locate where the squealing sounds were coming from.

The area where they had landed was in shadow, but Kent could make out a couple devices that somewhat resembled the computers in the communication room at NAHQ pushed off to one side. Movement caught Kent's eye as three small figures ran squealing from the shadows and escaped into the light. The bright light made Kent squint his eyes, and that's when he realized they had landed in a very large cave or an area that had been carved out.

Calais managed to sit up and mumbled, "What happened?"

"We just went for a very scary portal ride," Kent responded, causing Calais to hold his head and groan once more at the memory of what had just happened.

Calais shifted over and inspected the device that had pulled him into the portal, causing the terrifying chain reaction. "The monitoring device looks to be in good shape. Maybe we can tell where we are from the tracking information and send for help."

Kent and Calais sat in the middle of the cave trying to make sense of the readout from the time they'd lifted off from the moon of Bankos to the time they landed wherever in the universe they were now. The numbers didn't make any sense to either of the readers. These were numbers beyond anything they had seen before. Maybe the wild ride and crash landing had scrambled the data that had been recorded. They both stopped trying to decipher the readout when they heard the sound of rapidly approaching footsteps.

Suddenly there were a number of very tall beings, each one holding a very sharp, pointed pole, filling the entrance to the cave. Their clothes ranged from ragged uniforms to a variation of animal pelts. From behind the legs of the taller beings, three shorter beings were pointing at Kent and Calais and chattering away in high, squealing voices. Kent knew these three smaller creatures were the ones that had run from the cave and returned with their elders.

From the frowns on the faces of these beings, Kent knew that their arrival had not been expected and was not welcomed. The tall creatures formed a circle around Kent and Calais, and one of the creatures stepped forward to prod Kent with its sharp, pointed pole. It motioned for them to stand up. Kent raised up on shaky legs and bent down to help Calais up. As Calais stood, he moaned and held his head, which now sported a very large bump in the front. Wobbling as if they were drunk, Calais and Kent slowly stumbled from the cave and into the blinding sunlight. But which sun was it, Kent wondered, and what species were these strange-looking beings?

The cave entrance was not high in the mountainside, and the steps leading to the ground were not steep. For this, Kent was thankful. He held tight to Calais's arm to keep him from falling over. Surrounded by the menacing creatures, they slowly made their way toward some structures below the cave that looked like they were attached to the side of the mountain. In the mountain itself, Kent could make out what resembled doors.

These strange beings were not ugly or deformed in any way but exactly the opposite. Kent studied them as they walked. Their long legs moved smoothly without any sign of a hitch. The older ones were tall, perhaps a head taller than him or Calais. Their skin was a smooth, creamy color without any signs of hair. Their heads were more oblong than round, and they had large, dark eyes. They looked like intelligent creatures, but what were they doing living in dugouts under a mountain? The ground continued to slope downward to a valley that was so long Kent could not see where it ended.

The creatures spoke no words but made their intentions clear with the long poles they carried. As they passed by the doorways carved into the mountainside, the doors were opened, and more of the creatures crowded into the openings to get a look at the unwanted visitors. Maybe they communicated telepathically and didn't need to speak words aloud. They came to the final structure in the row, and a makeshift door was opened. Kent and Calais were pushed inside a crudely formed room. The door was shut and bolted with a pole that looked like the ones the creatures carried. Their heads almost touched the ceiling. The walls were made of poles like the ones they carried, and floor was bare stone. Both readers were still shaken, and Calais was unsteady on his legs, so they collapsed on the floor.

Once they were as comfortable as they could get on the stone floor, Calais whispered, "Where are we?"

"I don't have a clue," Kent replied. "I didn't have time to recheck the tracker's readout before our hosts appeared, but nothing I read made any sense."

"Some hosts," Calais muttered. "They were not very welcoming."

They stopped talking when they heard the pole being lifted from the door. The door opened, and a different being looked inside. At least this one wasn't carrying one of the pointed spears, and it looked smaller in size with less pronounced and softer facial features. It wore clothes that looked to be made from varying pieces of hides that had been crudely stitched together. Seeing Kent and Calais sitting against the back wall, the being nodded, and two of the small creatures that had been in the cave appeared from behind. One was carrying an urn-like vessel, and the other a platter filled with what looked like fruits. The small being carrying the platter motioned for them to eat and placed the platter on the floor. The other one placed the urn beside the platter, and the three backed outside. Again, the door was bolted.

Kent moved over to examine what had been delivered. "They don't seem to want to starve us," he said as he examined the different fruits.

"Maybe they want to fatten us up to eat us," Calais grumbled. "Why did you have to suggest that we send a monitoring device into the portal?"

Kent smiled; Calais was feeling better. "It was your sleeve that got caught," Kent reminded his friend.

Calais looked over at Kent and asked, "Why didn't you let go of me?"

"No way would I have let you come alone." From the look shared by the two friends, both knew that if the situation had been reversed, Calais would not have let go of Kent's leg either.

Kent stood up and picked up the urn left by the door. He sipped at the liquid inside and said, "It must be this planet's water source. A little tart but good." He took a longer drink and then handed the urn to Calais.

Kent picked up the platter, sat down by Calais, and placed the platter between them. As the two ate, they discussed the strange situation they were in.

"I wish we could communicate with them. Maybe we could find out where we are," Calais said between bites as juice dripped down his chin.

Kent pushed up his sleeve and inspected his wrist comm. It had made the trip without suffering damage. Satisfied, he pulled his sleeve back down to hide the device.

"If we can get one of them to talk to us," he said, "I can get a recording of their voice patterns and maybe find an interpreter for their language. The smaller ones were definitely going on about us, but with all the commotion, I didn't think to record them."

"Until they learn to trust us, we won't be getting out of here. If we sign 'thanks for the drink and food' when they come back, maybe we can open a dialog with them," Calais suggested.

"It's the beginning of a plan. We need to get back inside the cave if we are to have any chance of getting home," Kent said, trying to see the positive side of their situation. He laughed. "I didn't think solving the puzzle of the portal would turn out like this. I was planning on being back to NAHQ in a couple of days."

"Some adventure it turned into. We don't have a clue where we are or how to get back," Calais replied, and then he yawned. "I think I'll close my eyes for a few and clear my head. I have a feeling were going to need all our wits about us to get out of this situation."

Calais went to sleep, but Kent could not. He couldn't turn off his mind and kept thinking, trying to figure out where they were. The beings were not like any he had seen before, and he lived at NAHQ, where there was a multitude of different beings from different planets and cultures. What puzzled Kent was why they seemed so backward in their existence. Their clothing looked hand sewn from various animal pelts, and the urn and plate looked like they had been formed from the same stone as the wall he rested against. Sleep finally claimed Kent, and he closed his eyes.

It was the noise of the pole being lifted from the door that eventually woke Kent. Groggily, he pushed himself up from the floor. It took a minute for him to remember where he was. He nudged the still sleeping Calais.

"Wake up. Our hosts have returned."

Slowly, Calais opened his eyes and looked around. The bump on the front his head had begun to turn a purplish color. Calais's brown hair had fallen forward while he was sleeping and covered some of the bruising. Calais pushed up to sit against Kent as they watched the door being opened. The bright sunlight had disappeared, and the view outside was a muted shade of orange.

It was the same being that had brought them water and food, but this time, it was alone. The being bent over as it entered the room and stopped before Kent and Calais sitting on the floor. It studied them for a minute and then bent down and reached out to push Calais's hair back from his brow. It inspected the bump and then placed a hand on the bulge and felt around. Calais frowned and muttered,

"Ouch," when the being pushed on the bruise. Calais's complaint caused the being to smile at him, and a twinkle filled its eyes.

This being was a prettier version of the others who had locked them in the room. Its large eyes were a deeper purple than Calais's bump. The hands looked soft and well cared for. It stood up and gave a slight nod of its head. From its inspection of Calais, it seemed satisfied that he would recover from his injury. As the being made to leave, Kent picked up the plate and held it out.

"Thank you," Kent said slowly and made a bowing motion. He then touched his mouth and asked, "Do you speak?"

This caused the being to frown and move to the door.

Kent was afraid it was leaving and said, "I'm sorry. I didn't mean to frighten you."

The being pulled the door closed, pointed at it, and then uttered words. The words were soft toned and smooth sounding. Kent quickly moved a hand over to secretly engage his wrist comm. The being didn't seem to be annoyed at speaking if the door was closed. It mimed that they should be quiet if the door was open, holding a finger to its mouth. Kent nodded that he understood. The being smiled again, its features soft as it studied the two readers' appearance.

Kent needed to keep it talking now that the wrist comm would capture anything that was said. He pointed to himself and said, "Kent." Then he pointed to Calais and said his name. Kent waited for the being to respond.

It pointed to Kent and said, "Keent." Then pointed to Calais. What came out sounded more like "Caaas." It smiled and shook its head.

"Ca-la-is," Calais said and then repeated it slowly.

The being listened and then said, "Ca-la-is." It smiled, and its eyes twinkled.

Calais smiled back and said, "Very good."

Kent took the opportunity to point and asked, "What is your name?"

From the look it gave him, Kent knew it understood, but it hesitated. "Sonna," it finally said, pointing to itself.

Both Kent and Calais repeated, "Sonna."

"That's a beautiful name," Calais told Sonna.

"Can you tell us where we are?" Kent motioned outside and then made a circle with his hand.

Sonna shook its head no, which seemed a strange answer. Kent was sure Sonna understood his question. When he started to ask another question, Sonna made the quiet sound and opened the door and left. Sonna shut the door but did not place the pole in the holders to keep them locked inside. Both Kent and Calais realized what had happened.

"Think this is a test, or is it letting us escape?" Calais asked.

Kent pushed his sleeve up and engaged his wrist comm. "Sonna didn't speak enough words for the interpreter to decipher the language, but Sonna knew what we were asking. It's strange that she doesn't know the name of this planet."

"She?" Calais repeated.

"From looking at the ones that captured us and at Sonna," Kent said, "I think she is the female of the species and the others are the males. When the three younger ones ran away, they returned with the protectors or elders."

"When the door was open, it looked like the sun was setting. Do you think we could wait for dark and then push open the door? Maybe we can get a position from the night sky." Calais suggested.

"Just don't talk if we open the door until we know the reason to keep quiet," Kent cautioned.

The sky turned dark, and various stars began to twinkle above. Kent and Calais studied the night sky, but did not recognize any patterns in the stars above, even though both knew all the galaxies and their unique formations from years of monitoring the realms of space.

A quiet crunching of footsteps signaled that someone was coming. The night view was blocked when someone stepped into the open doorway. It was Sonna, and she looked alarmed as she scanned the darkened room. When Calais whispered, "Here we are." It looked like Sonna wanted to thump Calais's bump and hard.

Sonna scowled and motioned for them to get up and follow her from the room.

CHAPTER 5

SURPRISING STUFF

The night was dark as Kent and Calais followed Sonna back the way they had previously walked. In the distance, strange noises could be heard. Growls or roars or howls—Kent wasn't sure exactly which but was glad they sounded far away. Sonna didn't say a word as she led them to one of the doors built into the side of the mountain. She stopped and glanced around before softly knocking at the door. The door opened, and Sonna almost shoved Kent and Calais inside. She stepped in behind them, and then a being shut and bolted the door from the inside.

It wasn't a room they found themselves in but rather something like a wide hallway. One of the younger creatures that were in the cave spoke to Sonna and pointed at Kent and Calais. Sonna smiled and patted the youngster on the shoulder, and the two started down the hall together. Without being told, Kent and Calais followed behind Sonna and the younger being. Kent was anxious to learn more about this race—who they were and where they came from. He had a feeling that they were not native to this planet.

After walking a short distance, Sonna stopped at another barred doorway and waited for Kent and Calais. She again knocked on the door and spoke words, which Kent was recording on his wrist comm. When the door opened to allow them inside, both Kent and Calais gasped at what they saw.

The area was cavernous and brightly lit from the ceiling. The area was filled with tables and benches that looked to have been hand carved from boulders and some type of wood. Pleasant smells filled the air, and a hush fell over the room as all verbal communication stopped. Creatures stepped forward from around the room and formed a half circle around Sonna and the youngster. Kent and Calais stepped beside Sonna and looked back at the growing group. Sonna said something to the crowd and pointed at the two intruders. No one answered, but they did not look hostile, only curious. There had to be a hundred or more of these beings that resembled Sonna and the youngster.

Kent felt that they were waiting for him to do or say something. He took one step forward and held out his arms, nodding to the crowd before him.

"Thank you for allowing us to enter your dwelling," he said and then bowed and stepped back.

Words were exchanged among the crowd, and then there were nods of approval.

"So far so good," Calais mumbled.

The youngster took Kent's hand, led him to one of the tables, and motioned for him to sit. Sonna escorted Calais to the table. Once they were seated, the others began to sit at the tables. After everyone was seated, food was carried out and passed around. They were all given small mats that they placed before them, and when the food reached them, they put their food on the mats and began to eat.

Kent recognized the youngster as the one who had brought them food and motioned for them to eat. Kent decided to try to communicate. He picked up a piece of food, held it to his mouth, and said, "Eat." Then he ate the piece of food. He looked at the youngster and motioned for him to do the same. Mimicking Kent, the youngster took a piece of food and moved it to his mouth and said what sounded like "amagah."

Kent tried to pronounce the word back and must have screwed it up badly, because the youngster laughed out loud and shook his head in despair. Kent joined in the laughter. Hearing laughter from the youngster and Kent, the room went quiet again. Sonna, sitting next to the youngster, looked stunned. The youngster turned to Sonna and quickly said something and started laughing again. Sonna looked as if she were going to cry but instead joined in laughing with Kent and the youngster.

"I don't know why you're laughing, since you are the butt of the joke," Calais told Kent.

Kent wiped at his eyes and said, "I realize that." Then he picked up another piece of food and again mispronounced the word and shoved the food in his mouth. He started exaggeratedly chewing the food, and his actions sent the youngster on another laughing jag. One by one, others in the large room began to laugh until the room was filled with the happy sound.

After the youngster stopped laughing, Kent decided to learn his name and went through the motions of saying Kent and pointing to himself, saying Calais and pointing to his friend, and then pointing to Sonna and pronouncing her name correctly. The youngster followed Kent's example, pointing to Kent and repeating his name. It took him a couple of tries to say Calais, and he laughed again when he pointed to Sonna and said her name. Finally, he stood up across the table from Kent, pointed to himself, and said, "Nerie."

The rest of the meal was a happy time, and both Kent and Calais felt that they had passed some test and had been welcomed into the tribe. Nerie did not leave Kent's side the rest of the evening, and Calais seemed to be happy staying close to Sonna.

When they were led from the large room by Sonna, Kent thought they would be taken back outside and locked in the small room. That was not the case. Several tunnels led away from the main room, and all were lit by the same glowing orbs set into the ceiling. They came to the end of the tunnel that they were going down, and Sonna stopped and pulled aside a long cloth that looked much like some of the clothes the beings wore. Inside the room, across from each other, sat two narrow beds, and the mattresses looked like they were formed from dried plants surrounded by some type of covering. A small table and a bench stood between the beds.

Sonna motioned for them to sleep, but Kent stopped her and had her say the word for sleep. She said the word, and he repeated "sleep" to her in his own language—another word paring for the wrist comm to record. Kent had used the evening to record as many words and their translations as possible. Alone in the room tonight, he would try to find a match for the language and perhaps learn about their hosts.

Sonna motioned that she would return in the morning and said her word for goodnight, which was more aimed at Calais than Kent. Nerie had disappeared earlier to go to his room but had told Kent goodnight and motioned that he would see him when he woke. Kent felt confident that what they had learned tonight could be used to find their way back home.

Kent and Calais stayed awake late into the night working to find a translator for the language Sonna and Nerie spoke. After they had finished eating, Kent had had Nerie introduce him to some of the men in the room. From greetings to good-byes, Kent had carefully repeated and captured the words. It turned out that the wrist comm had no specific translator for the new words, so Kent spent hours matching known words to the new ones they had captured to create a new translator.

Kent told Calais, "We've come across and entirely new species and language. I've been able to build a program to translate by combining a few different ones. The language closest to this language is from the Theta Galaxy. I wonder if these people are from an ancient race that helped to populate the galaxies eons ago."

"I'm glad you wore your wrist comm. I didn't bring any tools with me, since it was supposed to be a fun trip to the moon and back." Calais yawned. "We'd better get a few hours' sleep before Sonna comes back."

Kent pulled his sleeve over his wrist comm and laid back in bed. "Maybe we can find someone who knows where we are or at least what galaxy we're in."

It seemed that they had just gone to sleep when Sonna pulled back the curtain to their room and announced, "Good day."

Nerie followed her into the room and went to Kent's bed and bounced him.

Kent grabbed Nerie, said, "That's not fair," and wrestled with him.

Sonna stepped over to Calais and again examined his big purple bump. She lightly pressed on the bump and grinned, waiting for Calais to protest.

Nerie escaped Kent's hold and jumped back. "Time to eat," he said, making the motion of putting food in his mouth and chewing exaggeratedly. Laughing at his own joke, he skipped to the door and motioned for Kent to follow.

The expression on Sonna's face showed her pleasure in his happiness. Sonna turned to Kent and Calais and tried to explain. "It has been a long time since laughter has been heard." She pantomimed, trying to relay her meaning, but Kent understood her words. It was another riddle to solve—what had happened to these people?

After they ate another meal of vegetables that resembled the previous night's meal, Sonna stood up and said, "Come with me."

"Where are we going?" Kent asked. He spoke slowly and in Sonna's language, which startled her. From the previous night's effort, Kent and Calais had learned many words and their meanings. They had quizzed each other like when they were in reader school, making sure they would be able to communicate with Sonna and Nerie today.

Sonna nodded that she understood and replied, "To meet Thale. He is old."

Kent knew the translator had not correctly translated the word for old and thought that Thale could be the tribe elder. Kent now wore an earbud through which he could hear what his wrist comm could translate.

When they exited the huge dining room, Nerie told Kent he would meet him later and skipped away. Apparently, the meeting with Thale would not include children. Sonna led the way down another hall across from the one that led to their bedroom. Again, Kent marveled at the light coming from the ceiling. He tapped Sonna's shoulder to stop her and pointed above.

"What makes the light?" he asked.

Sonna nodded and made a digging motion. "We find in mountain."

Kent nodded and continued to follow Sonna, trying to figure out how to get his hands on one of the glowing pieces. He wanted to examine it and see if he and Calais could find its origin. If they could identify the mineral, it could help them find out where they were.

At the end of the hall, Sonna stopped beside a doorway covered with the hanging material this species used for doors. Sonna announced herself, pushed aside the material, and stepped inside, dropping the material to cover the entrance behind her. Kent could hear words, but they were too far away and hushed for his wrist comm to pick up. Sonna pushed the curtain aside and motioned for Kent and Calais to enter.

Kent gasped when he entered the room. It looked more like a library than the sleeping quarters he'd expected. The walls around the room were filled with plant leaves that had been dried and cut into squares. The squares contained writing and what looked like a numbering system. One wall held individual letters and numbers, probably the basis of their language and math. Kent was awed by the wonder of it. Once he could figure out the alphabetic and numeric systems for these beings, he would be able to translate all the scripts that filled the walls. No one uttered a sound as Kent studied each of the walls.

Kent turned to Sonna and stammered, "This is amazing."

Sonna laughed and motioned to an ancient being seated at what resembled a desk with writing utensils. "Thale has captured our history. He is the only one left of the originals."

Thale looked at Kent and Calais, and the two readers studied the frail-looking being. Thale's voice was soft and hesitant when he spoke.

"Where have you come from?"

Kent stepped closer and explained, "A galaxy we call Riddan with planets and moons and a large star that they all orbit." Kent used his hands as he tried to explain. Thale looked confused, so Kent continued. "Can you tell me the name of this planet or galaxy?"

Kent began to worry that Thale did not understand his translated sentence, but Thale lifted a bony arm and pointed to one side of the room. On one of the papers was a crudely drawn map that showed a sun and several planets. One of the planets had a smaller circle around it depicting the orbit of a moon. Sonna hurried over to the drawing and took it down. Then she carefully laid it in front of Thale.

Thale pointed to the planet with the one moon and said, "This is us, but I do not know where we are or any names. This planet seems to be young, and I have never found any other beings."

After the short explanation, Thale leaned back in his chair, looking exhausted from the effort of talking.

Sonna hurried to Thale and said, "He must rest. Your being here has caused much excitement. I am going to take him to his room."

"Can we stay and learn from Thale's drawings?" Kent asked. "I'm sure I can read all this if given time."

Before Sonna could answer, Thale lifted an arm for her to stop. He looked at Kent and nodded his approval to Kent's request.

CHAPTER 6

HISTORY REVEALED

It didn't take long for Kent and Calais to figure out the drawings that made up the language. Thale had explained each letter with an illustration below it. The language was simple, requiring only twenty individual characters. The numeric system was like most others the readers had studied. One or two, off or on, even or odd—mathematics were the same across the universe. Kent kept steadily inputting information into his wrist comm, capturing what had taken Thale years to write down. Once back in their room, he and Calais could reread every detail.

Once they mastered the writing, Kent and Calais carefully read each page that filled the room, starting on the wall next to the alphabet and working their way around the room. It was harrowing to read the story of the Umbries and learn their history. As Kent figured, this race was eons old, and the sun of their home planet had gone nova, destroying their entire planetary system. That, at least, was what Thale thought had happened. Their leaders had not heeded warnings and prepared for their survival. They had been advanced enough that the entire race could have been saved. Evacuation portals had been opened, but only a few had escaped before the portals collapsed from the sun's explosion. Thale had no idea if other Umbries had been able to reach other galaxies.

Thale had still been consider a child when the group he was with had exited the portal on this planet and not at their intended destination, much like what had happened with Kent and Calais. They'd landed in a hostile environment, and none of the elders had been prepared to survive without their technology. The few devices that had arrived had been damaged and of no use. The Umbries had then been hunted by beasts that roamed the planet, and only when the group had made it to the mountains and hid in the caves had they been able to survive. By that time, most of the adults and many children had been lost as prey to the creatures who hunted them.

It was sad to read how the Umbries had starved before finding what plants could be eaten; how they'd learned to defend against the predators; and how they'd learned to avoid being found when outside the caves, which was the reason no one was allowed to talk when outside. The monsters that roamed below and soared above had excellent hearing and hunted both day and night.

After finding refuge in the mountain caves, the Umbries had been able to survive in these harsh conditions. Slowly, they had rebuilt their lives inside the caves. From their digging, they had discovered the stones they now used for lighting. The winged creatures didn't fly in the dark, so if they worked by the light of the moon and made no noise, they could gather nearby plants to eat and use for clothing. They had been surviving in these conditions well over two hundred years, if Thale's calculations were correct. Thale had tried to document the movement of the planet and its moon around the sun via a crude method he had developed using stones and shadows to determine the length of time that made up one day.

Both Kent and Calais were startled when Sonna appeared behind them. She laughed when they jumped and told them, "It is time for evening food."

Kent was stunned. Had they been so engrossed in what they were learning that the entire day had passed? It was Calais's rumbling stomach that confirmed it.

Seated at their table in his assigned seat, Kent looked around as he waited for his turn to take food, which he now understood was difficult to get. He was looking for Thale but didn't see the old man.

Sonna must have understood the reason for his search, because she reached across the table to take his arm and said, "Thale does not come here. He is too weak and eats in his room. He was very impressed with your abilities to learn our language. Perhaps tomorrow he will be able to meet with you longer."

"I would like that very much," Kent replied, anxious to get to bed and review everything he had captured on his wrist comm.

Sonna hesitated before telling him, "Thale has said that our rescue would come from the portal. Perhaps that is the reason Nerie and his friends were messing with the machine to open a portal. Nerie is very smart and must have figured out how to work the machine."

The following day, after morning meal was over, Sonna told Kent that Thale would like to talk with him. Kent was excited and asked if Calais could come along. Sonna looked confused and told him that Calais had asked her to show him around outside.

"Isn't that dangerous?" Kent asked, looking over at Calais, who had not said a word.

"We will be careful," Sonna answered. "You may go see Thale when you are ready. He is in his work area."

As Sonna and Calais walked away, Kent watched Nerie join up with the other two boys and walk down a hall. *They must attend some sort of school,* he thought. Kent noticed others in the room leave in groups. Everyone seemed to be engaged in some activity to support their livelihood.

Kent stood up to go meet with Thale, anxious to talk with the elder. He had questions from his previous night's review that he hoped the old man could answer. From the few days he had spent learning the language, Kent was now able to communicate with very little help from the translator. Calais was becoming proficient in communication from spending time with Sonna. Kent missed not having Calais attend the meeting but could tell that Calais was happy being with Sonna.

Kent spent the following days after morning meal with Thale. He spent as much time telling Thale everything he knew about the universe as Thale did about the home remembered. When Kent asked about returning to the cave to retrieve his device, he also asked about the other machines stored there.

Thale admitted that long ago, he had been able to get them working and had tried to contact his race, but he'd never received a response. The boys must have become curious, as they can be, and somehow opened the portal that he and Calais had found. When Kent asked about the reading from the tracking device, Thale could not help him understand the numbers because he had nothing to check any of the findings against.

Thale seemed to get tired sooner as the days wore on, and he admitted to Kent that his time would soon end. He was the last of the learned, or the ones that had come via the portal. He had spent his last years trying to capture everything he knew to pass down, although outside of Sonna, not many of the others were interested. He admitted that surviving each day had taken on more importance than maintaining the knowledge of the past.

Kent had been so engrossed in learning all that he could from Thale that he was taken by surprise that night when Calais told him it had been fifteen days since they had portaled from the moon of Bankos. Calais didn't seem to miss Bankos or his life there and spent his days with Sonna, Nerie, and Nerie's two friends.

"I need to get back to NAHQ. I hadn't realized we've been gone so long. I'm sure that Catella has started looking for us by now." Kent was worried about having been away so long. "Thale admitted that he'd had the equipment in the cave working at one time and had tried to contact others of his race. We need to go to the cave and see if we can trace a path to return. I'm sure we can figure out their equipment."

"Tomorrow, Sonna and I are going on an excursion. The diet they're all eating is causing them to become weak, and that's the reason there is no population growth. Nerie and his two buddies are the only young ones that have been born in years. Sonna said there are birds that fly during the day and have nests in the mountains. I want to try to catch one and see if these birds are a food source. There are lush forests in the valley below, but if they try to go there, the beasts kill them. I want to get a look at these creatures and determine how we can fight them. I showed the men how to sharpen their spears so they can pierce the skin of the beasts. The poles aren't strong enough and break. I made bows and arrows for Nerie and his pals and want to try them out. Do you want to come along?"

Kent had never heard Calais this excited, even when they'd been young and had gone on their own excursions.

"I need to go to the cave and inspect our tracker and the machines the Umbries brought with them. Maybe I can figure out a way to open the portal again." With his knowledge of the Umbries' language, Kent was sure he could get the machines working and reopen the portal to the moon of Bankos. "Besides, I'm sure that Catella has started searching for us," Kent repeated, concerned because he'd been gone so long, leaving NAHQ without his support.

"Let me know if you figure something out," Calais said as he turned over in bed.

He quickly fell asleep, leaving Kent to wonder about his friend. He still wasn't sure what to make of this new Calais.

Kent spend the following day in the cave alone. Calais and Sonna had left immediately after first meal. Calais's excited chatter followed him from the room. Kent worried that Calais wouldn't take the hostile situation outside seriously enough. But Calais would never put Sonna or Nerie in harm's way. He was sure of that, and that eased his worry.

It didn't take long before Kent determined how to reset the machines to open the portal. The main problem was that Nerie and his friends had almost drained what was left of the power by messing around with the machine. These machines had stayed active for over two hundred years drawing on a power source that ran them without being renewed. The Umbries' technology amazed him. Kent wasn't sure of the source that powered the machines but could read the levels and knew that with one more drop of the gauge, the power would be gone. That didn't leave any opportunity for experimenting. Thale said the machines worked, and Kent would rely on his word.

Kent inspected the tracker that Phoenix had helped him build. It had a few dents and dings, but the internal parts looked intact. The numbers on the readout amazed him, and he still had no idea where in the realm of space he and Calais had ended up. Kent felt that the planet they were on was newly created relative to the age of the universe, which could mean it was a few billion years old, and that the galaxy was in its infancy stage. That was why the landscape and creatures who roamed it looked like they were what he would call prehistoric—or in their early stages of development.

Kent was trying to determine a way to send a signal bleep to the location on the moon where everything had started. If he could reverse the tracking coordinates, would there be enough energy to push the signal through? Kent knew the coordinates of the moon, but there was no way he would know if the contact bleep was delivered. He was deep in thought when he heard Nerie call to Sonna and Calais. It surprised him, because during the day, he usually never heard a single noise. *The mighty hunter has returned,* Kent thought, grinning at the idea of Calais as a might hunter. Neither he nor Calais had ever hunted anything remotely dangerous, except on one of the training consoles.

The following days were filled with trips to search the valley below for food sources. Calais and Sonna were now accompanied by some of the men, who now carried better weapons to fend off the predators below. On their trips to the mountain tops, they captured bird eggs with nets tied to the ends of long poles, and the eggs had become a part of the daily meals. Sonna took Calais to where the daily supply of water came from, and they caught fish with the nets. Calais showed the Umbries that were in charge of the meals how to prepare and cook the fish. They now had a variety of nourishing ingredients to choose from when preparing daily meals.

At night, Kent constantly reminded Calais that he could use his help in the cave with the machines. Two days ago, Kent had used what power was left in their tracking device to dispatch a signal bleep to the moon. If anyone was at their campsite on the moon, they would notice the signal light on the equipment. This was what Kent hoped, and he began checking the tracker daily to see if a signal was returned.

Kent was in the cave checking for a return signal when he heard Sonna loudly calling Nerie's name. She sounded panicked. He hurried outside to see what was happening. Sonna was standing at the edge of the path that ran along the front of the buildings. Kent hurried down the steps and ran to her.

"What's is it?" Kent asked as Calais ran from the room where they once had been held with a spear in his hand. The room was now filled with improved weapons for the daily trips to the forest below to gather food.

"Nerie's gone, along with Jai and Elan. They told their instructor yesterday that they were going scouting with me today, but that was not so. The instructor saw me inside and asked about the boys. They must have followed some of the men outside, but I can't find them." Again, Sonna called out for Nerie.

Calais looked down and inspected the path running into the valley below. "Nerie was interested in what we've done to secure the valley from predators and kept asking questions. I think the boys have gone to the valley. Look, there are fresh footprints going down the path." He turned to Kent and Sonna. "Get a spear from the room and follow me." Calais then took off down the path with spear in hand.

Sonna ran to the room and brought out two long spears with rock-sharpened ends. She tossed one to Kent and raced after Calais. Kent caught the spear and looked at it, unsure of what to do until Sonna disappeared down the path. Kent ran after her. Nerie and his friends were in trouble, and this was not the time to hesitate.

It was only seconds, but it seemed to him as if he were running in slow motion as he made his way to the valley below. He had never gone with Calais or Sonna on their trips, instead spending his time with Thale or in the cave trying to contact NAHQ. Everything he noticed was strange to him, and he wished he had taken the time to explore with Calais.

Calais and Sonna had stopped at a point where the mountain dropped off into the valley. It was a small ridge, but it allowed them to see much of the valley floor. Calais motioned to Kent to be quiet. In the stillness, they could hear a small whimpering sound. Calais turned and listened in different directions before motioning for them to follow him. With spears held in front of them for protection, the three stepped forward into the forest.

After they took only a few steps into the trees, a low menacing growl came. Calais stopped, crouched down, and crept forward. Sonna and Kent followed his lead. With each step they took, the low growl became louder. The beast was tracking its prey, getting ready for its kill of the day. As the growl grew louder, so did the whimpering, and the three knew the beast had cornered the boys. Kent could feel the hairs on his neck bristle at the danger that lay ahead.

A strong musty smell alerted Kent to the nearness of the beast. The animal was so intent on its prey that it didn't notice them until Calais loudly yelled and jumped between it and the three boys huddled together behind a tree. The animal jumped backward, startled by the arrival of Calais. Sonna rushed up beside Calais and held her spear forward, aiming it at the snarling animal.

The word *cat* didn't describe what Kent was looking at. Long fangs extended from its mouth, and its head was covered in a brownish fur. Even from a crouched position, the cat was as tall as his waist. Claws that could rip apart even the toughest of hides extend from its paws. The animal was tensed, ready to jump at Calais, when Kent stepped out with his spear pointed in its direction. With eyes so intense, the animal assessed the situation. This animal survived by knowing when to attack and when to retreat. At the sight of the spears, the animal slunk back into the dense growth, giving a final growl.

"Stay on guard," Calais ordered. "Sonna, get the boys and stay behind me and Kent. Then slowly back out the way we came. This beast isn't going to give up easily."

As they slowly backed away, six armed men hurried up and surrounded them to protect them as they made their way out of the forest and back up the mountain.

When they reached the path that ran along the mountainside, Kent said he wanted to shut down the equipment in the cave before going inside. Calais and two of the men waited for him in case the hungry cat had followed. Sonna hurried the three boys to the open doorway, where others were anxiously waiting.

Shortly thereafter, Kent rushed back out of the cave, anxious to tell Calais that the tracker was blinking, signifying that their signal had been received on the moon of Bankos.

CHAPTER 7

ARRIS FINDS OUT

The day after Arris returned to NAHQ from rescuing Katy, she was sent on a mission. A mining treaty had been written, and the new ambassador to the Cettus Galaxy had requested the protectors' assistance until each of the planets involved in the treaty had signed the pact. The ambassador felt that once the pact was signed by the planets of Tusilan and Nocerno, the situation would be stable, and they would not require Nebula protection. Since Arris and Vega had been on one of the planets previously, they were sent along with Beta team. Phoenix was still filling in for Kent. Ursa, as team leader, assigned duties and shifts until they returned to NAHQ. It was an uneventful mission for the Nebula protectors. Vega pointed out that it was nice not being shot at on mission.

At breakfast after they returned from their two week assignment, Arris asked why Phoenix was still working in communications. Ursa answered that she thought Arris had known that Kent and Calais had gone missing and that Phoenix was at their base camp on the moon of Bankos trying to figure out what had happened. The rest of the team had been aware of the situation, but Arris had not been briefed about it because she had been on Earth. Arris felt as if her heart had skipped a beat when she heard the news about Kent.

"Both Kent and Calais had requested time off," Vega explained, "and it wasn't until they didn't returned to their jobs or make contact that anyone realized they were missing. Catella dispatched Phoenix to their last known location on the moon of Bankos, and Phoenix has been trying to figure out a way to contact them."

When Arris said she needed to get to Bankos to help Phoenix, Vega asked, "What are you going to do? Calais and Kent are experienced in portals and know how to take care of themselves."

Arris didn't have an answer but knew she just couldn't sit around. So, she rushed off to find Catella. Arris hurried into Catella's office almost before he had answered her knock with "come in." Spider was there already.

Arris couldn't wait and asked, "Is there any news on Kent? I just now heard that he is missing."

Catella and Spider were seated at the table and had stopped talking at her entrance. Catella understood how close Arris and Kent were and said, "Come sit down and join us. Spider and I are discussing the situation now."

After Arris had sat down, Spider told her, "Kent and Calais must have portaled from the moon on Bankos, but we don't have a clue where, as they left no notice that it was their plan. As far as Phoenix knew, they had planned to send a tracking device into the portal to find it source."

"How long has he been gone?" Arris almost stuttered the words.

"At least sixteen days, but that is a guess, because we don't know for sure when they portaled," Catella answered.

Arris was stunned. Kent had disappeared without a trace, and he had been gone long enough to have contacted NAHQ.

Before she could ask another question, Spider glanced down at his communicator and said, "Phoenix has just received a signal at base camp. He is trying to determine its origin. He asked if I could come in case we need to send a rescue team."

"I'm coming too," Arris said.

Spider glanced at Catella, who nodded his head, before saying, "Go get your pack, and I'll meet you at portal in one hour."

Arris stood up, told Catella thanks, and hurried to her room.

After Arris and Spider exited the portal on Bankos, Spider told her, "Phoenix has been trying to establish what happened on the moon. There was no portal activity, but an area was fenced off, and the two had set up a small campsite. The shuttle they used is still docked on the moon. Phoenix has set up a portable device that can open a portal once he has the coordinates. He is hoping that Kent will send a signal so that he can set up a connection." Spider pointed to a small ship that had just landed. "Here is our ride to the moon."

When Arris and Spider exited the transport, Phoenix rushed to meet them. "I've been able to determine the coordinates, but they don't make sense. Come look."

Phoenix, always the calm leader, was as excited as Arris had ever seen him.

Kent couldn't hide his excitement as he followed Calais into the large dining room. He wanted to discuss with Calais how to let whoever had answered his signal know of their dangerous situation. Kent felt sure it was Phoenix who had received his signal. Phoenix was aware of what he and Calais had planned on doing and of the pulsating portal activity on the moon of Bankos.

The tracker was out of power, and the Umbries' devices only had one click of energy left. Would it be enough power to stabilize a portal to get them back to the moon? As Kent tried to talk to him, however, Calais seemed to ignore the fact that they had been found and continued to walk ahead.

Kent called out, "Calais. Stop. We need to talk."

Calais stopped and turned around. From the look on his face, Kent could see that hearing of their signal being received had not brought Calais the gladness Kent had expected. In fact, the opposite expression was on Calais's face. Before Calais could say a word, Sonna hurried over.

Kent was surprised at the tears that ran down her face; he had never seen emotion from any of the Umbries. Calais put his arm around Sonna to comfort her.

"Sonna, what is wrong?" he asked.

Sonna had trouble forming the words, and her voice shook as she said, "Thale is gone. He went this morning after the meal." Sonna leaned into Calais's shoulder and sobbed.

Kent was shocked and saddened as the loss of his friend. He had become very close to the elder Thale from all the time they'd spent sharing knowledge. Thale was the last of the learned. Thanks to all his years of writing down their history, Thale would never be forgotten. The worth of what he had had left the others was beyond measure to Kent. In time, he was sure, Thale's efforts would be appreciated.

It was then that Kent noticed how quiet the huge room was. It was normally filled with varied sounds of talking, movement, and meals being prepared. But no one was talking, and most everyone sat quietly in groups after learning of Thale's passing.

"After meal tonight, we will remember him," Sonna said as she wiped the tears from her face, bringing Kent back from his thoughts.

Calais spent the rest of the day with Sonna, and Kent didn't have a chance to speak with him about opening the portal. Kent spent most of the time in his room going over the two portal coordinates, but there was no way he could determine the distance between them, the time it would take to travel, or the power that would be required to keep the portal stable while he and Calais returned to the moon of Bankos.

The evening meal was a somber event, as no one was talking; their thoughts were on Thale's ceremony of remembrance. Even Nerie was quiet as he ate his meal. After the cleanup duties were completed, everyone left by the same tunnel, one that Kent had not been down before.

Sonna walked with Calais, their arms entwined. Nerie held to Calais's other arm, leaving Kent to walk behind them. They waited in line for their turn to enter the crowded room that had been carved out of the mountain. Everyone was standing and watching two men carving something into a section of the wall.

Kent tried to read what was carved into the stone walls but was having trouble seeing the writing with everyone crowded around.

Sonna placed her arm on his and said, "Those are the names of the ones who are gone. We remember them by placing their names on the walls. We come in here to remember them and to honor them."

Kent pointed to words carved at the top and tried to translate them. The closest translation was "Fallen Heroes." He turned to Sonna and repeated the words.

Sonna smiled, nodded, and said, "Everyone is a hero in a different way."

When the men finished etching Thale's name into the wall, someone in the room began to sing, and one by one, everyone joined in the soulful song. The voices were low toned and melodious as they sang the song to honor the ones who had passed. Kent closed his eyes to listen to the peaceful song. It was the first time he had heard any singing since he and Calais had arrived on the planet. Once the song was finished, many of the Umbries stepped to the walls and touched a name to remember the one who was gone. Quietly, the room emptied, leaving Calais and Kent and Sonna by themselves.

"That was beautiful," Kent told Sonna, still in awe of the Umbries' tribute to their fallen heroes.

Sonna nodded and said, "I will come here often to remember Thale." Then she turned and walked from the room.

Calais and Kent followed.

That evening in their room, Kent broached the subject that Calais had been trying to avoid.

"I need your help to review the data to open the portal. I'm sure it was Phoenix who returned my signal. He must be at our campsite on the moon. I depleted the power on the tracker to send the signal, and the Umbries' two machines only have one measure of power left before they are depleted too. I really need your help to determine if there is enough power left to stabilize the portal on this end so we can get home."

Calais mumbled his response, and Kent wasn't sure he heard correctly.

"What?" he exclaimed.

"I'm not going back," Calais said, and he sat on the side of his bed and looked over at Kent.

Kent was shocked and stuttered, "Y-y-you can't be serious. We have responsibilities and others who are probably worried sick about us."

Calais smiled. "My responsibility as reader for the Riddan Galaxy? I can be replaced, and I'm surprised that I haven't been by now. Other than you, I don't have anyone worried sick about me."

Kent started to argue with Calais but stopped when Calais held up his hand.

"You have people who are worried sick, and your responsibilities at NAHQ can't be taken over by someone else. You have a special talent, and Catella depends on you. You need to go back, but I'm staying here."

Calais stopped talking, letting Kent adjust to what he said. Eventually, he continued, "Since we came here, I've found a purpose that I've been longing for. Living in a cave and helping these people to have a better life means more to me than all the technology and resources in Riddan. I belong here; you don't. Tomorrow, I'll help you with the portal. There should be enough power to stabilize the portal for one return. It's been a long day, and we have a lot to do tomorrow, so let's get some sleep."

Kent stared at Calais, knowing that he would be wasting his breath trying to argue with him. From the set of Calais's face, Kent knew his friend was determined to stay on this planet and help the Umbries.

"I think we have everything set up, so when you're ready, we can open the portal," Calais said, looking up from the equipment.

Now that it was time to test their theory, Kent was hesitant. He turned to Calais and wasn't sure what to say.

"You know the rocks the Umbries use for light?" he finally said. "I tested one, and it also puts out energy. If you harness enough of the energy, combine the more powerful stones, you would be able to power generators, but first you will need to build the generators." Kent laughed at his ramblings.

Calais stood up and wiped his hands. "I understand. This is hard for me too. But to leave Sonna and Nerie would be unbearable for me. I'm home here."

"I need to go and tell them and the others good-bye. I don't think having anyone else in here in the cave when we test our theory is a good idea," Kent said.

Nerie insisted that Kent stay for late meal and wouldn't budge. It was difficult to say good-bye to the Umbries. Kent received many thanks for all he did. As everyone left the large room after meal, Kent gave Nerie and Sonna one last hug, and then he and Calais returned to the cave.

"I can enter all the data on my wrist comm into Nebula's database and maybe identify where this galaxy is located. I have the coordinates and will continue to try to contact you. You just need to find a way to power the tracker and the Umbries' machines." Kent was torn at leaving his friend behind.

Calais laughed. "Watch the galaxies. When I can, I'll send a message; you'll have to find it, just like old times. There is so much to do here and so much to teach the Umbries, and they are willing to learn. Trying to stay alive over the years has taken the place of education. I'll make sure to keep this cave empty in case you can get a message through without an active portal. Ready?"

Kent nodded, and he and Calais clasped arms in a brothers' salute. Calais went to the Umbries' devices and powered them on for the last time. A portal began to lighten in the cave as Calais monitored the devices.

"We have a stable connection. Get ready. Safe trip brother."

With that, Kent stepped into the portal.

The End

ABOUT THE AUTHOR

sb white continues to entertain readers with her fifth book in the fantasy genre, The Nebula Chronicles Volume II. Visit the sbwhite.org website for a complete list of books and free stories for the beginning reader.